THE PURSUED

THE PURSUED

C. S. Forester

PENGUIN CLASSICS

an imprint of

PENGUIN BOOKS

PENGUIN CLASSICS

Published by the Penguin Group
Penguin Books Ltd, 80 Strand, London WC2R ORL, England
Penguin Group (USA) Inc., 375 Hudson Street, New York, New York 10014, USA
Penguin Group (Canada), 90 Eglinton Avenue East, Suite 700, Toronto, Ontario, Canada M4P 2Y3
(a division of Pearson Penguin Canada Inc.)
Penguin Ireland, 25 St Stephen's Green, Dublin 2, Ireland (a division of Penguin Books Ltd)
Penguin Group (Australia), 250 Camberwell Road, Camberwell, Victoria 3124, Australia
(a division of Pearson Australia Group Pty Ltd)
Penguin Books India Pvt Ltd, 11 Community Centre, Panchsheel Park, New Delhi – 110 017, India
Penguin Group (NZ), 67 Apollo Drive, Rosedale, Auckland 0632, New Zealand
(a division of Pearson New Zealand Ltd)
Penguin Books (South Africa) (Pty) Ltd, 24 Sturdee Avenue, Rosebank, Johannesburg 2196, South Africa

Penguin Books Ltd, Registered Offices: 80 Strand, London WC2R ORL, England

www.penguin.com

First published in Penguin Classics 2011

1

Copyright © Cassette Productions, 2011

Set in 11.25/14 pt Dante MT Std
Typeset by Palimpsest Book Production Limited, Falkirk, Stirlingshire
Printed in Great Britain by Clays Ltd, St Ives plc

978-0-141-19807-1

www.greenpenguin.co.uk

MIX
Paper from
responsible sources
FSC™ C018179

Penguin Books is committed to a sustainable
future for our business, our readers and our
planet. This book is made from paper certified
by the Forest Stewardship Council.

I

Marjorie had no feeling of impending disaster as she walked down Harrison Way from the railway station. It was a tranquil summer evening, there was a gentle breath of wind blowing which cooled without chilling, and set rustling the leaves of the little copper beeches which lined the edge of the pavement. The stars overhead were bright and friendly. Marjorie had no apprehensions.

She was sufficiently accustomed to being away from her children for the evening to have no worries about them at all. Since Anne had reached the age of seven she could be relied on to sleep soundly from the moment of going to bed, and Derrick, who was not yet four, did not cause trouble once in six weeks, and as both the children were fond of Dot they would have gone to bed without demur. Dot would have had a dull evening just sitting in the house doing nothing, but perhaps Ted had already got back from the billiard hall and set her free to go home to Mother – and in any event Dot seemed to like dull evenings, because she had often said she did not mind coming to so sit in the house while the children were in bed, and she never wanted Mother to come round too and share her loneliness.

Marjorie had enjoyed her jaunt tonight. She had been to town to visit Millicent Dunne. They had dined together in an Italian restaurant, with a waiter to attend to them, and a small flask of Chianti to drink, and after that they had gone back to Millicent's one-roomed flat at Victoria and had sat and talked for hours and hours, in fact until Marjorie had to hurry to catch a late train home. Marjorie contrasted, without envy, but with some curiosity, her quiet suburban life with Millicent's as a bachelor girl in town, her duties as a mother and wife with Millicent's interesting job as a welfare supervisor at a factory. Millicent was a polished and tactful woman of the world now, but – she would be an old maid one day. Marjorie felt that Derrick and Anne compensated her for any possible loss of a professional career; and in any case she thought she had never had enough brains for one. Millicent had always been far cleverer at school.

The hall light was alight, as Marjorie could see through the glass over the door when she reached the gate, but the sitting room was in darkness. Perhaps Dot was in the kitchen making herself a cup of cocoa; it was hardly possible that Ted should have been home so much before as to have had time to see her off and go to bed. Marjorie opened the door with her key and said 'Coo-ee' gently, as was her way. There was no reply, and then, as she passed the threshold, Marjorie smelt gas. The hall reeked with it; when she hesitated at the foot of the stairs she distinctly heard the hissing of escaping gas.

Marjorie sprang to the kitchen door, dropping her handbag. The kitchen was in darkness, and when Marjorie opened the door the stench of gas seemed to strike her in the face. She reached for the switch. Her head was sufficiently clear for her to wonder for a second whether it was dangerous to turn on a light in that atmosphere, and then to reassure herself that it was only matches or candles which would cause an explosion. The light revealed the kitchen with its blue and white paper; and it revealed, too, Dot in her pretty summer frock lying on the floor with her head inside the open gas oven.

Marjorie gave a little scream, and as she did so her lungs revolted at the rush of gas into them. She forced herself to recover, holding her breath. Rushing across to the oven, she turned off the tap; still holding her breath, she flung open the kitchen window and then stooped to lift Dot. But she could hold her breath no longer. A sudden gasp brought more gas into her lungs, and she felt her head swim. She could not lift Dot yet. It called for all her strength to totter out into the hall where the reek of gas was not too strong to breathe. Gasping, she pulled open the front door and stood on the front step. The cool night air was like water when she was thirsty. The little wind blew past her; she told herself that, blowing in through the front door and out of the kitchen window, it would soon clear the kitchen of the gas. She breathed deeply again, about to go back to the kitchen, when she heard the sound of steps coming down the quiet street, and someone singing in a subdued tone. It was Ted. She saw him in the lamplight, jaunty as ever in his waisted coat, his bowler hat tilted at its usual angle a little back over his ears.

'Ted!' she said. 'Oh, Ted!'

He gave a start of surprise at the sound of her voice, and hurried up the little path.

'What's wrong?' he asked.

'It's Dot – in the kitchen –'

He pushed past her, and pulled up short on the kitchen threshold.

'Is she dead?' he demanded.

'I don't know. I didn't have time to look –'

There was only a faint smell of gas in the room now. A sudden stronger puff of wind slammed the front door and made the little house shake. Ted took a step forward and then drew back.

'Nobody must touch her,' he said. 'Go and fetch help. Go next door. There's a 'phone there.'

Up to this moment Marjorie had thought clearly and rapidly, but now the succeeding events of the night began to grow unreal and nightmarish; and in Marjorie's memory subsequently there remained a series of pictures which, although vivid, were blurred at the edges. There was a picture of Mrs Taylor next door, in her nightdress and with her hair in two plaits, looking round her front door at her in bewilderment after Marjorie had banged loudly on her knocker two or three times. Mr Taylor had flannellette pyjamas with a brown stripe in them; Marjorie saw a tear under his armpit as he dialled for the police. There was a picture of Dot's face, strangely pink, as they lifted her from the floor with her head hanging. It was not that her cheeks were coloured artificially, for Marjorie knew that Dot only used powder. You could not imagine her dead, except that her skin was so cold that to touch it was repellent. There was a police sergeant there now and a policeman.

'Do dead people always look like that?' whispered Marjorie – she had never seen anyone dead before.

'Mostly they do when they've used gas, madam,' said the sergeant. 'I've seen a lot of them.'

The policeman was asking all sorts of questions about letters. She knew of none, but in the end she let the policeman poke about and look for them himself.

Now there was a doctor in a black coat, asking short cold questions of Ted, who was answering them bluffly and concisely. She admired Ted at that moment for being so unshaken and clearheaded. She could not have answered those questions – the doctor had indeed addressed one to her and she had not heard what he said although she had seen his lips move. Mother had come now, too, in her black coat and hat, neat and brisk and trim as she always was, with the quickness of movement natural to a tiny person like her. She was clear headed, too, and seemingly unshaken at her favourite child's suicide, or so Marjorie thought until she saw that Mother had tears on her cheeks and more tears in her grey eyes.

Then all the crowd has passed away, and she and Ted were alone together again, after a great deal had been written down in black notebooks. The children were still fast asleep, having slept through all the noise and bustle downstairs – at the sergeant's suggestion she had already gone up once and tiptoed into each room, to find each child quite quiet and no smell of gas noticeable, thanks to their closed doors and wide open windows. Marjorie listened outside each door again, automatically, as she always did before going to bed, while Ted was downstairs turning out the lights and locking the back door.

She had taken off her frock and was standing before the mirror letting down her hair when Ted came in. It was only then that a flood of realization broke upon her, that it was borne in fully upon her that Dot was dead, had killed herself, and she would never see her again, while here they were going callously to bed as though nothing had happened. She turned away from the mirror to her husband.

'Oh Ted!' she said. 'Ted, isn't it dreadful?'

She went towards him, and put her hands on his shoulders and rested her cheek on his chest. Her whole body jerked with the violence of her sobs, and she wept passionately, the first tears she had shed that evening.

'Don't let it upset you, old girl,' said Ted. He patted first her shoulder, and then lower down her back, where she sat down. During all their nine married years and before that, too, Ted had always patted her there as a gesture of affection; she would probably have missed it if he omitted to do so. By now she had attained indifference to it, but tonight she found herself wishing that he would not do it with Dot dead and in the police mortuary. And though her love for him was by now long dead, although there had been times when she hated him, or feared him, or despised him, although she was now as indifferent to him as she was to the front door knocker or her nightdress-case, he was all she had at the moment to turn to for companionship in her trouble. She clung to him, holding the lapels of his coat, still shaking as her sobs tore at her.

'Don't worry, lovey,' said Ted. 'Lovey' was one of the vulgar endearments he used when he was feeling affectionate. He put his hand under her chin and lifted her face to his, and kissed her mouth with thick, half-open lips. There was the smell of drink on his breath – she was used to that. But she realized with cold horror as she felt his hands on her body that Ted was proposing tonight to be 'troublesome' – that was her word for it to herself – tonight of all nights, when Dot had just killed herself in misery downstairs. She looked up at him. Apparently the rush and bustle of the last hour had excited him as rush and bustle often did. His eyes were very bright, and his forehead was twitching and furrowing spasmodically – a sure sign; it was nearly ten years since she had first noticed it.

'Kiss me, lovey,' he said, and she closed her eyes and kissed him. That was less trouble than refusing – once or twice she had refused herself to him, both with and without reasonable excuse, and it had always meant an unpleasant scene, and a sulky brute of a husband glowering at her next day until she yielded to him. His hands were searching her body as his tongue was searching her lips. He pressed himself against her, heated and excited; it was more than sexual excitement. She knew, in a clairvoyant moment, that the events of the evening had stimulated him to this pitch, and that to possess her would give him relief. Just as some men transmuted their sexual urgings to something loftier and nobler, so Ted in the opposite way translated all his stimuli into the plane of sex. There could be no denying him. She was engulfed in misery, but at least it was misery demanding some action from her, and not the black passive misery she had felt when she had turned to Ted from the mirror.

'Buck up, old girl,' said Ted. Instead of patting and pressing her to him he now gave her a little push away from him, and obediently she turned and went away into the bathroom. She was fortunately not revolted by the details of birth control methods, but merely and coldly indifferent to them. She dealt with herself meticulously, for now that she had two children she had no wish to become pregnant again. Ted was waiting for her naked when she came back. She had forgotten the time when it had given her a strange thrill of passionate daring to discover that he had thick black hair over his breastbone.

'Come on, lovey,' he said eagerly, as she came in.

Marjorie had known all along that there would be no sleep for her that night – she always lay wakeful nowadays, restless and jangled, after Ted had been 'troublesome', and tonight it was far, far worse. She supposed it must have been two o'clock when Ted went to sleep, hot and heavy beside her and with his breathing a tiny trifle louder than when he was awake. She lay on her back at the edge of the bed, with the pillow drawn under the nape of her neck, too weary now for tears, and with her emotions too tangled for her misery to be acute. She was only conscious of black, sleepless depression, of a more deep-rooted unhappiness than ever she had known before.

2

A suburban electric railway line ran at the end of the garden of the little semi-detached house. When the service was running the house shook at ten-minute intervals to the passage of the trains, for there was a twenty minute service in each direction, but the last train of the day went by at a quarter past one in the morning, and at first while Marjorie lay wakeful the house was wrapped in the tense quiet of a suburban night. It was midsummer, and the room never grew wholly dark. There was always the twin pale squares of the windows to be seen, and later she noticed that they were growing brighter. And then she noticed the sparrows and starlings beginning to twitter, and then, ever so far away, the trotting hoofs of a horse. That was a milkcart on its way to begin its round – now that the milkcarts had begun to use motorcar wheels you could only hear the horse and never the cart. While the horse was still within earshot she heard a distant rhythmical clanking.

It was an electric train running down the steep incline of the railway behind the house – up trains and down trains sounded quite different, to the practised ear, because of the slope. If the train were running down, it was ten or thirty or fifty minutes past the hour; if it were running up, then it was exactly the hour or twenty or forty minutes past. This was the first up train, and the time was therefore twenty minutes to six. Its clanking rose in a mild crescendo, the house trembled faintly as it went by, and then the sound continued in a steady diminuendo until it was suddenly cut short by a squeal of brakes as the train stopped at the distant station. Only when everything was quite quiet could one hear that last sound in Harrison Way; as it was the morning was so still that Marjorie heard the compartment doors slamming and the grinding sound of the train getting under way again.

When everything was quiet once more Ted suddenly stirred beside her. He grunted, and kicked out in very much the same way as little Derrick would kick in his cot when he was not fully asleep, and then he grunted again and turned over on his other side, towards her. This was a little surprising, because Ted usually slept as still as a log, especially after a night during which he had been tiresome. Furtively, and with infinite precaution not to disturb him, Marjorie worked down the bottom of her nightdress until it was over her feet. It may have been that movement which disturbed him, although Marjorie did not think so. Whether it was so or not, Ted grunted once more, and stiffened into wakefulness, and turned onto his back. He cleared his throat with his cigarette-smoker's cough, as he always did on awaking, while Marjorie pretended to be asleep.

More unusual than ever, he was muttering to himself under his breath, and then checked himself suddenly. He reached out a cautious hand and laid it on Marjorie's body, but Marjorie lay quite still pretending sleep; she was so unhappy and she did not want him to be tiresome again, even though she had never known him to mutter to himself as a preliminary to tiresomeness. Satisfied that she was asleep, Ted withdrew his hand. He lay rigid and still – Marjorie had the impression of an unwonted tenseness about him – and once or twice Marjorie heard him muttering again.

It was all odd, this early wakefulness, this tenseness, this muttering. For a moment Marjorie was at a loss to explain it to herself, until it dawned upon her that he must be seriously upset – far more upset than she had suspected or anticipated – by Dot's death. There was actual comfort in that for Marjorie; the knowledge that she was not alone in her misery in that house diminished her unhappiness to quite a large degree. Her heart warmed a little to her husband; she might even have reached across and touched him had she not been afraid lest he should misconstrue her action. As it was, she lay still, noting his sleeplessness and sensing the tension.

The other morning noises began now. Marjorie heard their own milkman's cart come up the road, and the sharp chink as he put the milk bottle on the step. Other trains went by with their rhythmical clanking and their accompaniment of a faint trembling of the fabric of the house. There was the snap of the letter box as the newspaper was put through. Then she heard Derrick beginning to sing – Derrick when he awoke always piped just like the awakening starlings, but he was a good little boy and stayed in his cot until he was told he might get up. Anne slept later and more heavily.

Marjorie felt she must make an early start today to be ready to face all the troubles that must soon begin. The police sergeant had spoken about an inquest. She knew nothing about inquests and the thought troubled her. She might have a great deal to explain to the children, too; and Mother would be sure to be round quite early, and she expected that the news would bring everyone else hot foot as soon as it spread. Mrs Posket, for instance, would be sure to come in when she heard about it. Mrs Taylor, of course, would want to talk about it again to her. The sooner she got up the better.

Marjorie slipped back the bed clothes and swung herself out of bed. Safely out, she looked back at her husband, who lay gazing up at the ceiling – or rather through the ceiling, clean out to the blue sky above, it seemed to Marjorie. She was touched at the sight of his distress, so much so that, as very rarely happened, she stooped and kissed him without an invitation. The kiss was not returned – Ted was unaware of her proximity until she touched him, and she appeared to startle him, for he jumped at the contact. He made no other sign of having noticed the kiss, and Marjorie, a little hurt, turned away and, picking up her clothes ran across to the bathroom in her nightdress.

Dressing was sufficiently an automatic process to leave her with the power to feel her unhappiness acutely, although not as acutely as it might have been because she was also a little puzzled over Ted's most unexpected distress and thought about that as well. Then, once she was dressed, a mother's routine engulfed her and she had no time to feel unhappy for a space. There was breakfast to be prepared, and she had to supervise Derrick's dressing – Derrick did his best to dress himself, but he always put his socks on with the heel to the front and this morning he contrived most ingeniously to put on his trousers upside down. Marjorie had to fry the bacon and lay the table and make some sort of replies to Derrick's insistent chatter and see that Anne washed behind the ears and have hot water ready for Ted to shave with. It was always an exacting, if not a very strenuous, three quarters of an hour before she got them safely seated at the table in the kitchen with their food before them.

There was comfort to be found in the fact that neither of the children asked questions about Auntie Dot – they had slept through all the noises of the night and took it for granted that, as often before, she had gone home after their bedtime when relived by the arrival of one of their parents. Yet on the other hand, even in the midst of the rush and bustle Marjorie found herself thinking with horror that she was giving the children food in the room where Dot had killed herself only twelve hours before, food cooked, moreover, on the very oven with which she had killed herself. She allowed Derrick's milk to boil over at that thought, and the gas flame beneath the saucepan was extinguished, and before Marjorie could turn off the tap she caught a whiff of gas which made her turn sick and faint, so that she sat down suddenly at the table just as Ted came in with his shoes in his hand.

He was pale, too. Marjorie thought they must look like a pair of ghosts; she was glad neither of the children noticed it.

'I'd better go to the office until they want me,' said Ted.

'Yes,' said Marjorie.

'Who wants you, Daddy?' asked Anne – all her life it had been impressed upon her that nothing in the world equalled in importance Daddy's punctual arrival at the office. Ted ignored the question.

'And what about Anne going to school?' asked Ted.

'Oh, of course she must go,' said Marjorie. She could not bear the thought of having Anne tagging after her all the morning.

'What are you talking about, Daddy?' asked Anne. 'Why shouldn't I go to school? Daddy! Mummy! What's happened?'

'Be quiet, Anne!' snapped Marjorie – and Marjorie was generally inclined to be specially gentle with Anne since she had realized that it was Derrick who had won her heart. Anne sat abashed, her lips trembling. It was sufficiently rare for her adored mother to speak sharply to her for the event to bring tears. She was just gong to cry when a sharp rat-tat-tat on the side door distracted her attention, Grannie came in from the side entrance, and Anne could never remember before Grannie arriving at breakfast time. Marjorie cried out gladly at the sight of her.

'Come and have a cup of tea, Mother,' she said, and rose automatically and began to prepare a place for her.

'Thank you, dear,' said Mrs Clair. She was the same trim, quiet, efficient little woman she always was, and spoke in the same soft voice. Marjorie felt a great wave of relief at her coming.

'Good morning, Ted,' said Mrs Clair.

'Morning, Mother,' said Ted. He did not look at her.

'Nothing happened yet?' asked Mrs Clair.

'No,' said Marjorie.

'What is going to happen?' asked Anne.

'Hold your row,' growled Ted, and the two women exchanged glances which Ted did not see because his eyes were on the floor.

Ted scraped back his chair.

'Well, I'm off,' he said. 'Ring me up at the office if you want me.'

He still did not meet their eyes as he went off.

'What will you want Daddy for Mummy?,' asked Anne. She remembered an incident two years old, when Mummy had been severely lectured by Daddy for daring to telephone him at his office.

'I don't expect Mummy will want him at all,' interposed Mrs Clair. 'And I like that pretty frock of yours more every time I see it.'

That was quite sufficient to satisfy Anne. She put on her hat and allowed herself to be seen off to school without another question.

It was only then that the two women could settle themselves to fresh cups of tea and, turning deaf ears to Derrick's chatter, could talk about the events of last night.

'Ted's upset properly, Mother,' said Marjorie.

'Anyone can see that. What about you, my dear? Did you sleep last night?'

'Not a single minute. Did you, Mother?'

'No, of course not. I was thinking too much. Marjorie, what made her do it?'

'I don't know, Mother. She'd always seemed so jolly to me. She didn't have a care in the world, I used to think.'

'She's been quieter than usual the last month or two, I thought,' said Mrs Clair.

But it was impossible to have a continuous conversation.

Interruptions began immediately. Mrs Taylor from next door, having seen off her husband to work, came knocking at the side door to hear the latest development. Mrs Posket from five doors down, with whom Marjorie had only the barest nodding acquaintance, but who was the notorious gossip of Harrison Way, came five minutes later, just as Marjorie had anticipated. She had awakened too late last night, by bad luck, only arousing herself just in time to see the ambulance drive off. She listened with envy to Mrs Taylor's breathless account of how Mrs Grainger's knocking had brought her down from bed, and of how she had come into the house, into this very kitchen, and had actually seen the dead girl lying with her head in the oven.

'Ooh!' said Mrs Posket. It was heartrending to think of what she had missed.

'Dreadful, it was,' said Mrs Taylor. 'I shan't forget it to my dying day.'

'All twisted up, was she?' asked Mrs Posket.

'No,' said Mrs Taylor reluctantly. 'Just lying as if she was asleep with her face on her arm.'

'I should have thought if she'd been suffocated she'd have all been twisted up,' said Mrs Posket, suspiciously. 'What did she do it for?'

'Nobody knows,' said Mrs Taylor. 'I was just asking Mrs Grainger when you came.'

'P'raps the inquest'll tell us,' said Mrs Posket. She exchanged significant glances with Mrs Taylor. Not until that very moment had it occurred to the dead woman's mother and sister that she might possibly have been pregnant – it took Mrs Posket's presence to wake that suspicion. Mrs Clair caught sight of Marjorie's white face.

'Here, Marjorie,' she said, briskly. 'Inquest or no inquest, the housework's got to be done. If you go upstairs and do the beds, I'll get these crocks washed up and answer the door.'

But even then there were certain interruptions which demanded Marjorie's personal attention. A policeman came with a thunderous rat-tat, and he had a letter for Mrs Grainger which he had to give into her hands – Mrs Clair would not do.

'I've got one here for your husband, Mrs Grainger,' said the constable.

'He's at his office,' replied Marjorie.

'The Gas Company's showrooms in the High Street?' asked the constable, studying his papers.

'Yes.'

'Then I'll deliver it to him there. Let me see. I've given your mother hers. That will be all, then. Thank you, madam.'

The envelope contained a command, backed up by hints of the severe consequences which would follow disobedience, to attend upon the inquest of Dorothy Evelyn Clair to be held at the coroner's court at eleven o'clock a.m. on the twentieth of June – tomorrow. In her dazed state of mind Marjorie only guessed at the meaning of the summons by intuition – its slightly archaic wording made but a small impression on her.

She had hardly returned upstairs to continue the weekly turning out of the big bedroom when there came another interruption. Derrick had managed to cut his finger, and he would not trust even his beloved Grannie to tie it up for him; no one would do except Mummy. Marjorie found a strip of rag and bandaged the nasty cut.

'How did you do this, sonny?' asked Marjorie.

Derrick only hung his head in silence, his howls suddenly stilled – a sure sign that he had been doing something he should not. His grandmother answered for him.

'That's what happens when naughty little boys open the dustbin,' she said, and continued, explanatorily. 'He'd been in the garden as good as gold for the last twenty minutes. He must have got to the dustbin the minute I was out of the kitchen. It was those broken bottles which cut him.'

'Broken bottles?' echoed Marjorie. As the only person who ever put anything in the dustbin she ought to know what was there, and she had no recollection at all of putting bottles, broken or unbroken, in the dustbin for months back.

'You look and see,' said Mrs Clair.

In the dustbin were the black fragments of two wine bottles – she could see there had been two because the necks and bottoms were still distinguishable. Marjorie guessed what they had contained; the highly alcoholic coarse red wine which had recently made its appearance in the local shops. Ted had brought a bottle home a few weeks back. Fermented and fortified in England, it saved the consumer a few pence in duty on every bottle, and was now, as Ted had pointed out, the cheapest drink (if speedy intoxication were the drinker's sole aim) obtainable. A man could get drunk on it for at least a shilling less than he could do on whisky. But what two bottles – broken ones at that – were doing in her dustbin she could not guess at all. Ted could not have put them there, because he did not come home last night after leaving the showrooms and going to his billiards match. It was one of those mysteries which her brain was too weary to deal with.

And then, a few minutes after twelve o'clock, Anne came running in from school.

'Mummy! Mummy! It isn't true about Auntie Dot, is it?'

Marjorie felt that she ought to have guessed that the news of a suicide would in twelve hours have penetrated even among the children at school.

'I don't know what you've heard, Anne,' she said 'but I expect it's true.'

Anne's face distorted itself ready to cry while at the same moment her mouth opened to say what she head heard, but with a quick gesture Mrs Clair called her attention to Derrick's presence, and with a shake of her head and a finger to her lip impressed upon her the need for silence so as not to upset the child. Anne was pleased with having in this fashion her immense superiority in age over Derrick acknowledged, at joining in a conspiracy of silence composed of three women.

Derrick, of course, had heard the words he ought not to have heard.

'Auntie Dot!' he said. 'Auntie Dot! I like Auntie Dot. I hope she comes again soon.'

The silence with which his remarks were received he took as indicating what a profound impression they were making. He started again.

'Auntie Dot! Auntie Dot!'

Ted had come in by now, and sat at the table waiting for his dinner.

'Shut up!' he blazed out suddenly at Derrick, and naturally Derrick howled again, and Anne cried in sympathy, and the meal was disordered and muddled. In the middle of the confusion Ted rose from the table and hurried out again – his lunch time interval was only three quarters of an hour, and he had in that time to walk up from the High Street and back – and left to the women the task of pacifying the children. When that was done Mrs Clair turned to her daughter.

'You're done up,' she said. 'You go straight upstairs and lie down. I'll see Anne off to school and then I'll take Derrick out in the park.'

Not more than once a month did Marjorie lie down in the afternoon, but today, a soon as her attention was called to her weariness, she found that she was yearning inexpressibly for rest. She hesitated a moment.

'What about you, Mother?' she asked. 'You're as tired as I am.'

'Oh no I'm not,' retorted Mrs Clair. 'We don't feel tired at my age. Off you go.'

Marjorie dragged herself upstairs, to the bedroom where the

hot afternoon sun was beginning to find its way through the windows. She found she was too tired even to take off her dress; she sank onto the bed, turned on her side, and slept almost at once. Yet in her heavy sleep she dreamed tumultuously. Some of the dreams were disturbing, although silly – dreams about black fragments of wine bottles lying in a dustbin.

3

On Friday morning as Marjorie, with Derrick holding her hand, was walking along the High Street to do her shopping, the poster of the *Weekly Advertiser* caught her eye.

'City Typist's Rash Act', she read, 'Inquest full report.'

The city typist was Dot, she knew, and her rash act was her suicide. Marjorie rarely spent twopence upon the local paper, but she did so today. More extravagant still, she went into Mountain's, the High Street café, where the rich women went, and she bought Derrick's silence for a space by a fourpenny ice cream and a moment's peace for herself in which to read the paper by her order for a fourpenny cup of coffee.

She found the column she was looking for quickly enough – a good juicy local suicide was bound to have prominent position in the local paper.

'Mr Harley Brown, the Deputy Coroner, sitting without a jury, found a verdict of "Suicide while Temporarily Insane", after inquiring into the death of Dorothy Evelyn Clair, shorthand typist, aged twenty-eight, of 16, Dewsbury Road, on the 18th of June last. Doctor Aloysius Montgomery, in his evidence, said that the cause of death was carbon monoxide poisoning as the result of inhaling coal gas. Deceased had eaten a meal and had drunk a perceptible amount of alcohol shortly before death. It was not unusual for persons contemplating suicide to drink freely in order to stimulate their courage. It was rarer for them to eat food, but he could not say that it was remarkable. He had known many cases. Deceased was three months pregnant.

'Sergeant Hale, of the Metropolitan Police, gave evidence that he came to 77, Harrison Way, in reply to a telephone call, and found the girl there dead on the floor with her head inside the gas oven. He found no letters or any other indication of any motive for the act.

'Marjorie Grainger, married, sister of the deceased, described how her sister came to look after the house at 77, Harrison Way during the evening while her husband and she were out. On returning home shortly before midnight she had smelt gas and on entering the kitchen had found the deceased as described. The kitchen was full of gas from the oven tap, and after turning out the gas and opening the window she telephoned for the police. She knew of no reason why her sister would be unhappy; she had always been bright and cheerful. She knew of one or two little flirtations on her sister's part, but of no serious affair, certainly none in the last two years. Edward Grainger, her husband, corroborated.

'Martha Clair, widow, mother of the deceased, said that her daughter had lived with her all her life at 16, Dewsbury Road. She was always a bright and cheerful girl, although she thought she had noticed a change in her during the last few weeks. Deceased had known very few men, and if there had been a serious affair she was sure she would have known about it.

'Mabel Somerset, charity organizer, said the deceased had been in her employ as shorthand typist for the last four years. She had always found her diligent, cheerful and active. The course of her employment would bring her into contact with very few men. She knew of no reason why the girl should take her life. Her affairs were all in order.

'Mr Harley Brown, in returning the verdict as above, said there was no doubt that this unfortunate girl had been betrayed by an unscrupulous man who did not have the courage to come forward and confess. He wished he knew who he was, although the publicity would not be sufficient punishment for him.'

Marjorie dropped the newspaper on her lap when she had finished the column. The short, bald sentences, mangled by the reporter's painful rendering of them into *oratio obliqua*, gave no clear impression of the scene in the court. Certainly it gave a wrong impression of the way she had given her evidence – of her stupid tears, and of the kindly questioning by the bald-headed Deputy Coroner which had coaxed her evidence from her; just as it gave no real picture of the Deputy Coroner's righteous indignation, which had made him go all pink in the face, when he spoke of Dot's betrayal – just as that cold, wicked word 'deceased' summoned up no picture of Dot, pretty and lighthearted and gay.

But there were two little passages in that report which stood out as though written in letters of fire. 'Deceased was three months pregnant.' Marjorie had known nothing of it – she had not even known while she was giving her evidence, as they had kept her out of court while the doctor was testifying. She had thought that the coroner's kindly questions were directed to finding out if Dot had had an unfortunate love affair. Marjorie could not guess at all who was responsible, who it was who had been blessed with the free gift of Dot's sweetness and virginity. There was no one she knew who was worthy of it. And surely if Dot had loved anyone dearly enough to do that, she would have told her about it. There had never been secrets between Dot and her.

'Deceased had drunk a perceptible amount of alcohol.' That was unlike Dot, too. Wine at weddings and a glass of Invalid Port on Christmas Day was all she had ever known Dot drink. It was hard to imagine Dot sitting down to drink herself drunk, even if she were so desperate as to be going to kill herself. A vision danced before her eyes suddenly – a vision of black fragments of broken wine bottles lying in the dustbin. But she could not picture Dot smashing wine bottles. It was puzzling, and made her head swim.

'Mummy!' Derrick was saying. 'Mummy! Look at *me!*'

The shrill persistence of his voice had penetrated at length through her abstraction. Derrick, having long finished his ice, had sought distraction by balancing a spoon on the top of his head. Marjorie suddenly became conscious of the amusement of the two well-dressed women at the next table, and of the hostile polite smile of the manageress. She snatched the spoon and checked Derrick's protests with a shake, smiled apologetically at the manageress and passed out of the restaurant to pay her bill.

The street was hot and full of blinding sunshine, and of course, as she saw by Tomlin's clock, it was ever so late. She grasped Derrick's hand and began to hurry home, up the High Street, past the Gas Company's showrooms – answering a patient 'Yes, dear,' to Derrick's shrill announcement that that was where Daddy worked – up Simon Street with its steep slope until she reached the last turning, which was Harrison Way. The very name of that road revealed the fact that it was of post-war construction and built by a speculative builder for sale, not for rent – a long road of pairs of semi-detached houses, stucco built and with tiled roofs, two little rooms and a kitchen downstairs, two little rooms and one still smaller and a bathroom upstairs. Yet in the glowing sunshine it was quite a pretty road with its copper beeches and red tiles.

Marjorie wondered if she could bear to live there any longer, to go on working in the kitchen where Dot had died. And now everyone in the road knew that her sister had killed herself because she was going to have a baby and was unmarried. It was horrid for herself and would be beastly for the children – but with Ted's office in the High Street it would be silly of them to move far away even if they had the money to do so. Ted's small salary was worth far more to them than some men's because Ted had no fares to pay and could get home to dinner every day.

And there was the question of Mother. They had talked about that last night. Mother was an officer's widow, as Marjorie was always proud to remind herself. The father whom she hardly remembered had been a bank clerk and a temporary officer who had been killed in the War. The little house in Dewsbury Road had been his own, and with that and the pension and the insurance money and the handsome gratuity from the Bank, Mrs Clair had been able to bring up her daughters satisfactorily enough – in fact after Marjorie had married and Dot had begun to earn she had been really comfortable. But Mother was alone now. Marjorie, daring the certainty of Ted's wrath, had asked last night if Mother would come to live with them, and he had refused, saying very sensibly that it never did for a mother-in-law to live with her son-in-law (and Marjorie knew in her heart of hearts that there was no love lost between Ted and Mother).

Marjorie turned in at No. 77, opened the door with her key and persuaded Derrick to go out into the garden, all automatically, so that her train of thought was hardly interrupted. But still, Marjorie did not like the idea of Mother being alone. Ted had made the really sensible suggestion that perhaps Mother would like to have a young man lodger, more for the sake of the company he would give than the money he would pay.

'Yes,' Mother had said, 'that's a good idea. But young men lodgers are hard to get nowadays.'

'Young George Ely would come if I told him to. You said you liked him, and he'd come all right. You bet he would.'

There had been the hard businessman's look on Ted's face when he said that. George Ely was Ted's assistant at the showrooms.

'But I wouldn't like Mr Ely to come against his will,' said Mother.

'He was saying only last week how rotten his digs were,' countered Ted. 'I'll mention it to him.'

Marjorie hoped George Ely would accept. She liked him. He was slender and fair and quiet and even-tempered; just the opposite of Ted in every way. He would be sure to get on all right with Mother.

It was nicer to think of that than about Dot's death, but she could not keep the latter out of her mind, either, as she moved about the kitchen getting the dinner ready. Marjorie remembered now that some weeks ago Ted had brought home with him a printed report issued by the Association of Gas Producers dealing with the question of suicide by gas poisoning. She had not read it herself, but she knew that Dot had done so. Perhaps it was that which had put the idea into poor Dot's head. Ted had studied it very carefully, but of course it was his job to do so, as down at the showrooms where he had to persuade people to use as much gas as possible he had to be able to argue about every single thing to do with gas.

But what – the old picture danced up into her mind's eye quite irrelevantly, as she started to lay the cloth, as it always did – what in the world were those smashed wine bottles doing in the dustbin?

'Mummy!' said Derrick, tapping on the kitchen door. 'Mummy!'

It was too good to expect Derrick to stay in the garden, even on a fine morning like this, for more than half an hour without attention. And Ted and Anne would be in soon, expecting their dinner. And Ted's temper had been very uncertain lately, ever since Dot died.

'That's a clever boy,' said Marjorie, as Derrick managed to unbutton his garden shoes all by himself.

It was a little surprising that Ted should be so upset. Perhaps it was because it would not do him any good at the office to have his sister-in-law kill herself in his house, and for that reason, too.

'Hullo, Mummy,' said Anne, coming in by the kitchen door. She was a grave, quiet little woman, although she was a light on her feet as a fairy.

'Hullo, dear,' said Marjorie. 'Dinner's nearly ready. Get your hands washed.'

Anne had been very good and sensible about it all, asking no questions even on the day of the funeral.

Who was the lover Dot must have had, about whom she had not even told her sister?

4

Marjorie had taken Derrick round to Dewsbury Road to have tea at Grannie's, and Anne was to come and join them as soon as school was over. Derrick was playing happily on the floor of the dining room with Grannie's solitaire board and bag of glass marbles, so that Marjorie was able to go into the kitchen and potter about with Mother while preparing the tea tray.

Marjorie admired her mother all the more nowadays. She had not been weak and weepy about Dot's death, the way Marjorie had, although Marjorie knew perfectly well that she had felt it just as much. Mother had remained calm and still and grave. She was such a capable woman, too, thought Marjorie admiringly, and conscious of her own inadequacies. She was so tiny and frail, and yet Marjorie knew she was very strong, never ill, never even occasionally indisposed. Although her hair was grey her complexion was pink and white like a young girl's, and there was a peaceful placidity about her expression – not like Marjorie's, for Marjorie knew she had a deep line between her eyebrows which worried her, although actually it indicated only petulance and not the bad temper which she feared.

Mrs Clair set the tea tray, her expression peaceful and placid, like a nun's.

'I met Mr Lang today,' she said. She was paying close attention to her work and did not look up as she spoke.

'Yes?' said Marjorie. Mr Lang was one of Ted's boon companions, and Marjorie was not very fond of him.

'He spoke very nicely to me about Dot,' said Mrs Clair, opening a milk bottle with elaborate care. 'I thought it was very kind of him.'

'Yes?' said Marjorie. She knew there was something more to be said, and something important, too.

'I'm trying to remember just what else he said,' went on Mrs Clair, quietly. 'I want to tell it to you exactly as he told it to me.'

'I'm listening, Mother,' said Marjorie.

'He said that Ted was so lively and excited on that Wednesday night when – when it happened. He said that Ted came in very late for his snooker match, all puffed and out of breath from hurrying from the office, and although Mr Lang (it was Mr Lang that he had to play) wanted to wait and give him a chance to get steady, he insisted on playing at once, and he beat Mr Lang. Mr Lang says he never saw Ted play such a good game.'

'I'm afraid I don't quite understand,' said Marjorie.

'I went on talking to Mr Lang,' said Mrs Clair, 'and I got him to say what time it was when Ted came in. Mr Lang didn't notice what I was doing. He said it was after nine o'clock.'

Mrs Clair lifted her gaze from the tea tray and met Marjorie's eyes. Yet her face was still mild and expressionless.

'Mother!' said Marjorie.

Ted usually left the office at six o'clock, and during the summer time when things were slack he was never known to be delayed.

'Mr Lang said that Ted was ever so funny about it. Ted said that it was hard luck on him that while he could only enter for snooker tournaments in the summer when he could be sure of being free it would go and happen that the only enquiry to keep him late for months should come on the night of the semi-final.'

Marjorie had heard nothing of Ted being kept late at the office that night. The arrangement made in the morning was that he should go straight to the billiard hall from the office and make his supper of sandwiches there. If he had not really been detained by an enquiry, there was a period of three hours of his time unaccounted for.

'Of course,' said Mrs Clair, quite evenly, 'it may not mean anything at all. He may have been at the office, after all. But in that case it's odd that he didn't tell us, or the Coroner. And he may have been with some other woman.'

'Yes,' said Marjorie, 'Y-yes.'

There was a sudden flood of revelation in her mind. There was only man in all the world about whom Dot could have told her nothing if he had been her lover. And now that her attention had been called to it, she could remember one or two isolated, vague incidents in the past. There was that time when she had come suddenly into the sitting room where Dot and Ted were talking, and the conversation had been broken off abruptly. She could remember twice intercepting an exchange of smiles between them. Nothing had made any impression on her at that time. Not Dot and Ted! She could not suspect them. And yet she knew – none better – what a wheedling clever way Ted had with women when he wanted to. And Dot was passionate and wayward. Oh, it was possible – just possible.

'The kettle's boiling,' said Mrs Clair. 'And Anne won't be a minute now. We can make the tea and see what that young Turk has been up to in the dining room.'

But Derrick had managed to be quite good during the few minutes he had been left alone. He was always pleased and excited at visiting his grandmother's, and the solitaire board and the marbles, with which he could only play on these visits, were very favourite toys of his. He was talkative as Marjorie lifted him and swung him into his chair, and he talked, as children do, with no reference to anything he had been talking about before.

'Auntie Dot was funny yesterday,' he said. 'Ever so funny.'

Marjorie's nerves almost gave way.

'You didn't see Auntie Dot yesterday,' she said, very sharply. She would have shouted it, shrilly, if it had not been for the habitual self-control she practised with her children.

'Yesterday a long time ago,' said Derrick, reproachfully. Yesterday was still the same as a week ago or a month ago to Derrick's mind. And Derrick did not know that Auntie Dot was dead. He looked up at the two women, and was surprised and delighted at the impression his words were making.

'She was funny yesterday a long time ago,' he continued. 'I heard her singing downstairs when I was in bed after she said goodnight to me, and I ran downstairs. Auntie Dot was funny and Daddy was funny. Can I have some brem butter please?'

'With jam on it?' asked Mrs Clair.

'Yes please,' said Derrick.

Mrs Clair bent her head to spread the jam, and with lowered head, in her still calm voice which won every child's confidence, asked the question which would set Derrick talking again. She showed none of the excitement which would confuse him.

'How was Auntie Dot funny a long time ago?' she asked.

'She was singing,' said Derrick 'an' she was dancing round. She an' Daddy had red stuff in their glasses. That pretty red stuff, and I wanted some. Auntie said she'd smack my botty-bot for me, and when she ran after me she fell down on the stairs. But she didn't hurt herself, Grannie, because she laughed. She laughed ever such a lot. Then Daddy came and put me back into bed.'

'That *was* funny,' said Grannie.

It was marvellous how calm and natural she was, while Marjorie sat sick and dizzy, feeling her skin flushed hot, and the sunlit room seemingly dark and misty. Through the dark and the mist she was most conscious of Mother's steady glance – a Sphinx-like glance full of a meaning which she could not read.

'Here's Anne!' said Mrs Clair, looking out through the window into the street; and Anne's arrival naturally broke the thread of Derrick's discourse. Marjorie shook off her weakness and greeted her daughter. She was reaping the benefit now of seven years' self-control. When Anne was born she had resolved never to allow her own particular mood to affect her behaviour towards her children, never, for example to be cross with them because some extraneous influence made her cross. By now it had grown into a second nature with her, so that the reverse reaction was possible – contact with her children steadied her where previously she had steadied herself in preparation for contact with them.

But later, when Anne had settled herself at the table, and was spreading bread and jam for herself, and had entered gaily into conversation with her grandmother and Derrick, Marjorie found herself with leisure to think once more. There were terrible, dreadful pictures floating before her eyes, pictures tinged red as if with blood. She could visualise it all so clearly. Dot lurching drunkenly about the room, with Ted at hand finding always some new excuse for filling up her glass – Ted had always been good at finding reasons and excuses. Probably he had made that rendez-vous with her that night on the specious excuse of discussing what they were going to do now that Dot found for certain that she was going to have a child. For a second Marjorie could visu-alise that earlier meeting too, with Dot saying 'But what are we going to *do*?' and Ted saying in that convincing way of his 'Don't you worry, old girl. I'll make it all right. Tell you what, Madge is going out next Tuesday. I'll say I'm going to be out, too, and then you come to mind the kids. Then we can talk it over and get it settled.'

Then in the house Ted would arrive with the wine. It was a hot stuffy evening and Ted would coax and cajole her, first one glass and then another – so easy for Ted to do with his glib tongue. Ted knew all about that wine, because he had told Marjorie about it three months ago – just as he knew all about the number of people who killed themselves with gas, and whether or not they had drunk anything before doing it. There would be the momentary interruption when Derrick came padding downstairs barefooted and in his pyjamas, and then— One more glass, two more glasses, perhaps, with Dot saying 'No, really, I'll be squiffy if I have any more,' and Ted saying 'Don't be silly, old girl. This won't hurt you. We've got to finish the bottle,' and pouring it out firmly. Dot would be dazed and stupefied. Unconscious, perhaps, and Ted's arms were strong, well able to lead her or carry her out to the kitchen. Only a second or two for further preparation needed now – to smash the bottles in the dustbin, rinse out the glasses, close the kitchen window, perhaps with Dot murmuring, stupidly, 'What's all the trouble, Ted?' Then – turn on the gas, and close the door, and hurry away, quickly, to the billiard hall where Mr Lang is waiting and looking at the time. Ted would be excited, keyed up, right at the top of his form – oh, she knew him so well! – able to win his match with ease, able to come home and face the police, keyed up to a higher tension still by that excitement so that he would become tiresome to his wife that night. And then, after that, the reaction, depression, jumpiness, raw nerves. Everything fitted in, everything.

'Marjorie!' Grannie was saying, 'Mummy! Would you like another cup of tea?'

'Yes please,' said Marjorie, passing her cup. So vivid had been the scenes she had been visualising that her present surroundings were dreamlike and unnatural. The familiar room and furniture – she had done her homework on this very table every evening for years – her mother's kindly smile, the very faces of her children, were unreal and surprising.

'Mummy's daydreaming,' said Anne, displaying an unexpected capacity for observation and bringing an unexpected word out of her vocabulary, in the manner of seven-year-olds. Anne had begun to lose her teeth, and her gap-toothed grin was inexpressibly charming. Love for the children tore at Marjorie's heart strings, deepening her misery. She drank her tea thirstily, avoiding meeting anyone's eyes. She must not have the children noticing anything. All their lives she had done her best to protect them from beastliness.

'How are you getting on with Mr Ely, Mother?' she asked.

'Splendid,' said Mother. 'Really, he's no trouble at all. He's so quiet you'd hardly know he was in the house. He gets up when he's called, and he comes in early, and he'll eat anything without a word sooner than say he doesn't like it.'

Mother sighed a little, and Marjorie knew why. Happy-go-lucky Dot, the last person Mother had to look after, had been quite the opposite – falling out of bed at the last moment, clattering about the house, unrestrained in her speech, with holes in her stockings for Mother to mend always at the last minute. Marjorie struggled to maintain the conversation at an ordinary level.

'And it's nice to have a real man to look after, isn't it, Mother?' she asked.

'Yes,' said Mother, simply.

'Please may I say grace?' said Derrick.

'Yes, dear,' answered Marjorie.

Derrick clasped his hands and shut his eyes and gabbled through his grace; Anne's eyes were closed and her hands were clasped, too, devoutly, and Marjorie smiled maternally as she looked as their serious faces. She had dropped out of the habit of church-going, and she sidestepped the question of religious instruction for her children. She had had them baptised, and she saw that they said grace after every meal and nightly prayers. More than that she felt she could not do. But they looked sweet while saying their grace.

'Please may I get down?' went on Derrick.

Marjorie looked at her mother, who nodded agreement, and Marjorie gave permission.

'Come and look at *this*, Anne,' said Derrick, squatting down beside the solitaire board. Mrs Claire and Marjorie, alone now at the table, had leisure and opportunity for an exchange of glances.

'He'll forget all about it soon,' said Mrs Clair. Her gesture indicated that she was referring to Derrick, conversing clamourously on the carpet with Anne.

Marjorie nodded.

'I don't expect he'll ever speak about it again,' went on Mrs Clair. 'And you know what children are like. No one will ever be able to *get* him to talk about it.'

So Mother had drawn the same conclusions from what Derrick had said as Marjorie had. And she had gone farther than that, too, as far as to wonder whether Derrick might have to give evidence. Marjorie clenched her hands. No one would ever, if she could prevent it, drag her Derrick into a police court and stand him up and allow lawyers to ask him questions.

With a sudden revulsion of feeling it dawned upon her that her thoughts and imaginings had brought her up against terrible realities. It was a shock to realize all the implications, that Ted was a murderer; that he was in some danger of being arrested, hanged; that Derrick and Anne might have to go through life bearing the stigma of being the children of a murderer. It was too horrible, too fantastic, too dreadful to be true. Her mind refused to tolerate the thought any longer. She could not bring herself to face it; her mind shied away from it like a restive horse from a gate. She was suddenly conscious of the fluttering of her heart in her breast, and she knew she had changed colour. She stared at her mother across the table, and her mother was as placid and as immobile as before.

'Are you feeling all right, dear?' asked her mother, gently.

'Yes, thank you,' gasped Marjorie.

In search of any avenue of escape from reality her eyes sought out the clock on the mantelpiece.

'It's time to go home now,' she said. 'It's nearly Derrick's bedtime.'

It was like relief from the startling agony of childbirth to allow herself to forget the grim horrors which had loomed up before her and to lapse into the little ordinary things of life again. To coax Derrick into replacing the marbles tidily in the bag, to tilt Anne's hat to the correct angle on the back of her head, to start for home along the ordinary streets facing the problem of what to cook for Ted's supper; all this was bliss, a soft bed after a couch of flints. An hour before, the grimmest realities she had had to face had been Ted's tiresomeness and Derrick's tendency to tell lies. She could not believe now that they had ever worried her; she clung to them, fondled them in her mind, would not let them go lest the other things should come back into her thoughts.

It never occurred to her at all that she was doing something at which an unsympathetic world might look askance, walking back home quietly to rejoin there a husband whom she had just discovered to be an adulterer and the murderer of her sister. To her mind she was going back home, back to the ordinary things for a space. There was a definitive dissociation at present between the Ted with whom she had lived for ten years, the Ted with a tendency to be tiresome, the Ted for whom she was going to cook supper, between him and the Ted whose guilt had just been made plain to her. Some time must necessarily elapse before the two figures should merge together.

A puritan or a moralist might maintain that Marjorie had no business to go back to Ted that afternoon, that she should have cut herself off from him, drastically, on the instant, and never set eyes on him again. Such an argument makes no allowance for the human factor; it would have been impossible for Marjorie to have done that, unaccustomed as she was to making quick decisions on matters of supreme importance, and unfitted by nature as she was for dealing with crises. Perhaps – certainly – it was weak of her, and the weakness was of the quality which leads to tragedy, but it was a weakness that calls for no apology and small explanation. There is no need to stress the next argument, which actually only occurred to Marjorie some time later, that to separate from Ted would be to start gossip, to direct suspicion upon him, and to involve them all in his ruin.

5

In the warm evening Sergeant Hale was wheeling his bicycle up the steep slope of Simon Street when he met Mrs Clair walking down – in fact Mrs Clair crossed the road just before the encounter so that they passed on the same side of the road instead of on opposite ones. Sergeant Hale knew her at once; he had that royal gift of memory for names and faces without which no constable can hope to rise to sergeant's rank.

'Good evening, madam,' said Sergeant Hale.

'Good evening,' said Mrs Clair, and the sergeant was a little surprised when she lingered, as if to enter into conversation with him. Most people connected with a tragedy, even remotely, were inclined to shun those members of the police force with whom the tragedy had brought them into contact, presumably because the sombre blue uniform recalled to their memory too forcibly what they desired to forget. Sergeant Hale halted on the kerb, his hands resting on the handlebars; Mrs Clair as he looked at her was a charming old lady, so neat and cool that even her mourning did not look greatly out of place in the summer streets.

'I'm afraid,' said Mrs Clair, 'that I never thanked you properly for the kind way in which you carried out your duties at my daughter's house. You treated her very nicely, and it's thanks to you that she was not more upset. I am very grateful to you, sergeant.'

'Don't mention it, madam,' said the sergeant, stroking his

black moustache. 'We all have our duty to do, and it's up to us to do it properly. That was a very sad business, though, madam.'

'Yes,' sighed Mrs Clair. 'And yet, thinking about it now, it might have been worse. Suppose the children had been involved!'

'Yes, that would have been nasty,' said the sergeant.

'If they had seen anything, it would have been dreadful. They might even have had to come and give evidence!'

'Well, I don't know about that, madam. How old are they?'

'One's seven and one's four.'

'The law says that a child has to know the nature of an oath before it can give evidence. When they're seven it's possible – I've known it once. But not at four, madam. Not even in a coroner's court, and certainly not in a police court.'

Sergeant Hale smiled with amused tolerance at recollections of the easygoing procedure of a coroner's court, so oddly in contrast with the strict rules of evidence laid down by English law.

'Well, it's a relief to know that, even if it didn't happen,' said Mrs Clair. 'But I'm glad the children knew nothing about it. It would have been a shock that they wouldn't have forgotten all their lives.'

'That's so, madam.'

'Well, thank you again, sergeant,' said Mrs Clair, smiling prettily upon him. 'Good evening.'

'Good evening, madam.'

Sergeant Hale emptied his mind of the incident as he went on pushing his bicycle up Simon Street, but Mrs Clair dwelt upon it as she went on walking down. She had spent all her spare time for the last three days walking about the streets in the hope of just that encounter. Now she had the information she needed, confirming what she had believed all along. There was no possibility of Derrick being called upon to give evidence against his father. As far as her clear-thinking but inexperienced mind could decide, Ted was in no danger at all of being hanged for the murder of her daughter. There was no evidence whatever which could bring that about. He had been clever enough, cunning enough, to arrange it so.

Mrs Clair's shoe-heels tapped to a brisk rhythm as she walked quickly along to Dewsbury Road. Nobody would turn and look at her as she went by; she was just a little elderly widow, neat and trim but nothing striking, walking along a suburban road. Her unwrinkled face and her pink and white complexion gave no sign of the volcano of deadly hatred that seemed to her to be tearing her heart in two. There were words and phrases coming up into her mind which she would never have dreamed of using before – she had hardly thought of them twenty years ago in connection with the Kaiser when the telegram came telling her that her husband had been killed in France.

She would have liked to have the filthy villain hanged, the dirty beast who had defiled both her daughters, who had killed Dot, dear, sweet little Dot. She would have liked him to suffer the three weeks' torment of the condemned cell, to be dragged out, fainting with fright, by hard-faced warders to the scaffold where the hangman awaited him. That would serve the devil right. But there was no chance of it, and in another way she was glad. It would never do for Marjorie to be known to the world as a murderer's widow, and Derrick and Anne as a murderer's children.

Yet come what might, the beast must be punished, must be made to suffer, must be killed so that he died in agony, so long as Marjorie and Derrick and Anne did not suffer. She could imagine quite easily the sort of death she would like him to die, and as she thought about it her step quickened and she clenched her little hands tighter and tighter until with a little 'pop' the black kid glove on her right hand split over the knuckle.

She clucked her tongue with annoyance as she looked at the damage done. But it was a warning to her. She had been hurrying carelessly along the street, up to that moment, at a speed which would call attention to herself. She had burst her glove through sheer thoughtlessness. She must be very much more careful than that in future, if she were going to lay plans to destroy beastly Ted. She must remain unobtrusive, unnoticed. She must walk along quietly – so; she must keep her expression calm and neutral – so; she must carry her hands and her sunshade without calling attention to herself – so. People seeing Mrs Clair arrive at the gate of 16, Dewsbury Road, and walk up to her front door would have thought that she had just returned from a quiet evening service at St Jude's.

In her bedroom she took off her hat and gloves, and saw that her grey hair was as neat as ever; she washed her hands and face in the bathroom (she neither powdered nor needed to) and went quietly downstairs in time to greet George Ely, flannelled and with tennis racket in hand, as he returned from the club.

'Did you have a good game, Mr Ely?' she asked.

'Fine, thanks.'

'I'll put your glass of milk and some bread and butter in the dining-room, ready for when you've washed your hands. Now please don't forget it tonight. I think I'd better see that you have it.'

George Ely was blonde and good looking, twenty-four years old, and with a hint of good-natured weakness about his mouth and chin. He came down obediently to drink his milk and eat his bread and butter while Mrs Clair fluttered about him, brushing aside his polite protests.

'It was only a little supper that you had before you went out,' she said. 'You need something after playing tennis all the evening. And milk is so good for you. Wouldn't you like another glass? I've got some more in the kitchen.'

All the hatred in the world might afflict Mrs Clair's bosom, but she was still capable of kindliness towards someone inoffensive and young; she was still able to feel a secret pleasure at having to look after a man after twenty years of exclusively feminine society. And Dot used to drink milk in the evening, too, while her mother fluttered about her – George Ely was some sort of substitute for Dot.

In the drawing room George looked listlessly through his evening paper again for half an hour while the evening wireless programme continued and while Mrs Clair, sitting primly in a stiff armchair, knitted away industriously at Derrick's new jersey. Then he yawned a little and got to his feet.

'Good night, Mrs Clair.'

'Goodnight, Mr Ely. I hope you sleep well. You're looking tired.'

When the sound of his footsteps overhead had ceased, Mrs Clair put her knitting tidily away in its bag, went out and shut the drawing-room door, saw that everything was well in the kitchen and the back door locked, and slowly climbed the stairs to her bedroom. She drew the blinds and made her simple preparations for bed. That grey hair of hers was a tiny bit sparser than its tidy appearance would have led one to suspect – the thin plait reached hardly to her shoulders. The corset which she laid neatly on a chair was old-fashioned, with bones in it; Mrs Clair always thought that it was lucky that Tomlin's in the High Street continued to stock that type of corset, for she would have disliked to be forced into wearing one of the new-fangled rubber ones. The white underclothes were of good artificial silk – a concession to modern fashion – but severely plain. When Mrs Clair was newly married it was only for gala occasions that a woman threaded coloured ribbons through slots in her underclothing. She slipped her plain nightdress over her head as soon as she had taken off her corset, and contrived the rest of the undressing beneath it, before putting her arms out through the armholes. Then she knelt with her face in her hands and her hands on the edge of the bed.

'Our father,' she prayed. 'Bless Marjorie and Anne and Derrick.'

She had to be a little careful with that list now, lest other names which she had grown habituated to including should slip in again. Dot's name had to be omitted, for she had heard vaguely that it was sinful and impious to pray for the dead. And Ted's name had to be omitted, of course. She continued –

'And Mr Ely. And please see that Ted is punished, Father. Damn him, Father. Kill him, Father. Make him pay for what he did to Dot.'

Mrs Clair stopped for a moment while a tumult of anger and indignation eddied within her. Then at last she was able to finish her prayer, with the words she had used every night for nearly sixty years.

'And make me a good girl. Amen.'

She turned out the light and slipped into bed, curled like a child on her side with one hand under her pillow, the thin grey pigtail peeping over the sheet. She was still unsophisticated enough to be surprised that her tangled feelings did not allow her to go to sleep at once as she had been accustomed to do before the tragedy occurred. Later she turned restlessly on her back, with the warm night around her, looking up into the darkness, thinking.

Ted must not be tried for murder; that was definite. Yet he must be punished. She and Marjorie must do it, then. But Marjorie was so weak, and after what she had been through that was nothing to wonder at. No, that was not true. Mrs Clair spurned herself for having tried to find excuses for Marjorie. Marjorie would never make up her mind to take any decisive action unless some superior force compelled her to. Of course, she was hampered by having young children, and she had no money, but besides that she was a creature of habit, and ready to go on treading the daily round simply because it was the daily round. It would not be easy to screw Marjorie into action, but she must try.

And just what was it she was going to do to Ted? Kill him! That was absolutely sure. Rat poison which would burn out his bowels, the way the advertisements said, would be what he deserved. Mrs Clair dallied pleasurably with the notion for a space, before she put it regretfully aside and chided herself for being foolish. Good though it might be to poison Ted, it was far too dangerous. Mrs Clair's mind ran back through vague memories of newspaper readings about Crippen and Armstrong and Seddon. Poisoners were always discovered, and she must not risk discovery – not for any fear of what the law might do to her, but because of the affect on the children's lives. Yet it was nice to think of Ted being poisoned, thought Mrs Clair, harking back regretfully again, and then shaking off the insidious temptation angrily, cross with herself for being so weak.

It must happen some other way. Ted had thought of a good way, the devil that he was. He was absolutely safe except from his mother-in-law's vengeance. That idea of making it look as if Dot had killed herself was a good one. She must think of something as good as that, or better. If a stupid man like Ted could make a plan like that, surely she could think of a better one. She must.

Mrs Clair pressed her lips together in the darkness and tried to compel herself to solve the problem. But inspiration would not come just for the asking. She was too conscious of her handicaps, of the weakness of her position, of her lack of strength. Whichever way her mind turned she found herself up against hard practical difficulties. She wanted help, an instrument, a tool – she could, and would, make one out of Marjorie, if that would suffice, but she doubted if it would. Somewhere, surely, she could find something more effective.

Then she broke off this train of thought again, as being too vague and theoretical at a time when she had to be definite and practical. Instantly the thought of poisoning leapt up again into her thoughts, to be welcomed while she was off her guard and then to be stamped fiercely down once more. Oh, she must think, think, think.

The night went on, with dull misery alternating with a strange elation. Sometimes she slept, in little ten-minute snatches, only to awaken again and go on thinking – a night typical of many more to come. Yet she did not feel unduly weary when morning came. When the clock hands had crept round to half-past seven she stripped back the bedclothes from the bed and knelt to say the morning prayer which dated from a year or two later then the evening one.

'Almighty God, direct my footsteps aright during this new day, and make me a good girl. For Christ's sake – Amen.'

Then she dressed ready to go downstairs to prepare Mr Ely's breakfast tea and bacon.

6

There were nearly enough ordinary domestic matters to keep Marjorie from brooding over the present situation. The butcher, baker and greengrocer demanded nearly as much of her attention as could be spared from the clamourous needs of Derrick and the equally urgent but not so vocal demands of Anne. It was only with difficulty that Marjorie could find time and strength enough to think about her husband, and to wonder, with despairing ineffectiveness, about what she should do. And a new domestic crisis of any magnitude could be sufficient to occupy her thoughts to the exclusion of the strange and terrible business which she did not want to think about. This letter from the seaside, for instance.

Every year for the past four years they had rented The Guardhouse, furnished, for three weeks in July and August. Marjorie remembered with regret the happy holidays they had spent there; The Guardhouse (its name was reminiscent of the old days when the South Coast was garrisoned for fear of a Napoleonic invasion) was a little stone house half a mile from the shingle beach, still lonely enough although year by year the bungalows crept nearer and nearer to it. They had been able to afford its four-and-a-half guineas a week rent by all clubbing together, Ted and Mother and Dot – although Marjorie strongly suspected that Ted usually owed some of his share to his mother-in-law for most of the year following, and knew positively that Dot did.

Happy holidays, those had been, with Mother and Dot to talk

44

to and share the domestic work, and Ted carefree and vigorous, even consenting to play with the children on the beach. Marjorie had come to love The Guardhouse, and it was with the utmost regret that she had written, soon after Dot's death, to cancel their booking of it. But there was no thought of their being able to afford it now; Dot was dead, and Mother would not be able to leave her new lodger. Only later had Marjorie come to console herself with the thought that even if they had gone the holiday would not be nearly as nice as before, alone with Ted and without Mother and Dot.

And now came this letter from the owner of The Guardhouse. He could not agree, he said, to the cancellation of the booking so late in the season, and he must accordingly request the payment of the agreed rent – thirteen and a half guineas, less one pound deposit, balance thirteen pounds three and sixpence. Marjorie had read this letter at breakfast time in the intervals of preparation, but at that time of day she had not dared mention it to Ted. And at lunch time he had been both surly and hurried, too. She would have to bring up the subject this evening, all the same. The matter was urgent. Even if Mother bore her share of the loss (and Marjorie did not want that to happen) Ted would have to find six pounds ten – and Marjorie knew her husband's way with money too well to think that he had six pounds ten to spare. It would be all their holiday savings, if he had it.

On the other hand, Marjorie remembered vaguely that Ted had said something about the auditors wanting to come and go over the books of the branch about that time. If that had been agreed upon now, Ted would have given up hope of a holiday this year and would have lavished away the holiday money already. They would not be able to go way, and yet they would have to meet this demand for rent. Marjorie could see no way out of the tangle at all as she walked with Derrick to her mother's to discuss it.

Happily, Mother was not nearly as discomposed by the news as Marjorie had feared. She was not cast down in the way one might have expected at the prospect of having to find so vast as sum as thirteen pounds three and sixpence. Yet her behaviour was a little strange – Marjorie, watching her anxiously, noted the play of expression on her face.

'I don't think he'd write like that,' said Marjorie, 'if he wasn't sure we'd have to pay. And what are we going to do?'

True, Mother had looked blank at first, as well she might, in the face of that demand. And then, suddenly, her expression changed, as if she had thought of something. There was a calculating look on her face, something almost cunning, and then the cunning had faded out, to be replaced by a far-away look, an appearance of lofty exaltation, with an obviously quickened pulse and a hint of new colour in the cheeks; and then the exaltation had died away and the cunning look had come back. Marjorie could not have found words to describe this play of expression at all; she was merely sensitive to it without being able to draw any deductions from it.

'You needn't worry about the money, at any rate,' said Mother, calmly. 'I can see about that, if Ted can't.'

Mother was marvellous in that way; she always had money in the bank ready for emergencies.

'But it's a shame that we should have to pay and not have any holiday at all,' said Marjorie.

'I suppose Master Ted's just as hard up as usual,' remarked Mother, casually.

'I don't know,' replied Marjorie, embarrassed. 'I suppose so, He hasn't said so. But you know what he's like.'

'I should just think I did,' said Mother. She looked sharply at Marjorie with her innocent eyes, and Marjorie was more hotly embarrassed than ever. There were so many aspects of her relations with Ted which she had never discussed with her mother, although she had an uneasy feeling that Mother, for all her innocence, knew all about them.

'They don't pay him nearly enough,' said Marjorie – the habits of ten years of married life still led her, despite herself, to defend her husband instinctively. 'As manager of the branch he ought to have a big salary, instead of the little bit he gets. And he has to pay all sorts of things out of his own pocket because he's manager, too.'

'Yes, dear,' said Mother, soothingly. 'I know. Well, I'll see what I can think of. I'll come round this evening when I've given Mr Ely his supper and we can talk it over then. But you see what Ted has to say about it, first, before I come.'

Ted was cross and sullen about it, naturally. To begin with, he never could reconcile himself to the fact that if he came home at his earliest, round about the children's bedtime, he had to boil his own kettle and make his own tea while Marjorie was engaged in seeing the children into bed – the alternative of waiting until Marjorie was free to do it for him was equally distasteful to him. Tonight, of course, he was home early, and, manlike, he made as much fuss about making a pot of tea as a woman would do about a day's washing. He was sitting grouchily listening to the wireless programme when Marjorie at last was able to come and open the subject to him. He had taken off his shoes – during this hot weather he always experienced trouble with his tender feet – and was gloomily contemplating his socks.

'Ted, dear,' began Marjorie, despairingly. 'It's about our holiday this summer.'

'Holiday? We aren't having any holiday this year,' said Ted, and then, looking up at his wife, 'I told you a week ago I'd settled with head office to have the auditors come in this August, seeing there was no chance of our getting away. Did you write and cancel our booking for The Guardhouse, the way your mother and me told you to?'

'Yes, dear,' said Marjorie 'but –'

She had not yet noticed that she only called her husband 'dear' nowadays when there was a state of stress between them. Nor had Ted; but it is possible that, without actually hearing the word, he had come to be warned by it of an approaching argument. He read with growing irritation the letter from the owner of The Guardhouse.

'This is all rubbish,' he said explosively. 'The man must be mad. Of course we haven't got to pay.'

'He seems quite sure of it,' said Marjorie.

'He can be as sure of it as he likes for all I care,' said Ted. 'He can whistle for the money. Thirteen three and six! I haven't got thirteen bob to spare, let alone thirteen quid.'

'But aren't we going to have a holiday at all this year, dear?' said Marjorie.

She had dared to hope, just before Ted came home, that perhaps they might have made the best of their compulsory tenancy of The Guardhouse by her going there with the children while Ted remained in London – under her mother's care, possibly. That ideal had seemed far more desirable than attainable.

'No, we're not going to have a holiday this year,' snapped Ted. 'I'm not. And you're not. What do you want a holiday for? Sheer waste of money. What are the parks for, I should like to know? What do you think I pay rates for? What – '

In a few minutes Ted had passed from a state of mere irritation to one of frantic rage. He was shouting now, and beating the air with his fists. His face was darkly flushed.

'Ted!' said Marjorie, horrified. That was the moment when she was first able to see the husband that she lived with (as opposed to the husband she thought about) as a murderer. The ungovernable passion in the face, the working of the thick lips, the distortion of the forehead; all this gave her some insight into the hitherto inconceivable mentality of a man who would now allow a human life to come between him and his convenience. It was a horrible moment. Perhaps enough of the horror was apparent in Marjorie's face for Ted to notice it even during his transports of irritation. He appeared to check himself, to bring himself deliberately under control. Marjorie, in a flash of insight, could realize at that moment that since Dot's death the fear of detection had made him more readily irritable while at the same time he was acutely aware of the necessity for being always on his guard.

He looked at her suspiciously from the depths of his chair. She tried, wavering, to meet his glance from the edge of hers. He mastered his expression, his voice, everything, and spoke naturally.

'You'll have to write again,' he said. 'Tell him I won't pay. Tell him – '

Tat-tat-tat sounded at the front door.

'That'll be Mother,' said Marjorie; she, too, was trying to speak naturally and to keep the relief out of her voice. She went out of the room to let in her mother. Mother was so calm and cool, so natural and simple and self-possessed, like a draught of water after hours spent in overheated rooms.

'Good evening, Ted,' said Mrs Clair. She had taken off her gloves, and hung her little coat on the hallstand. The little hat, which might have looked almost saucy on anyone else, was exactly right and yet perfectly decorous on her grey hairs. She looked round the room, smiling.

'Well, children,' she said, 'I don't expect you'd ever guess what I've been talking about to Mr Ely this evening?'

They looked at her blankly. No thought of George Ely had crossed their minds.

'Holidays,' said Mrs Clair.

Even then they were hardly enlightened. Mrs Clair had to explain. She talked brightly. No one would ever guess at the ingenuity with which she had sounded George Ely regarding his proposed arrangements, nor at the feverish rapidity with which she had formed her plan – nor at the dexterous tact with which she was now putting it forward.

'It's Ted who's the one who's got nothing to be pleased about with this,' she said. 'He comes off worst, the way husbands always do.'

She beamed across at Ted in a way which might have softened the hardest heart.

'Let's have it,' said Ted, stirring uneasily. Yet anyone could see that this little preliminary speech had made him far more receptive than he had been a moment before.

'Mr Ely said that he thought you'd let him have his holiday for this time you'd arranged to have yours before you'd heard about the auditors,' said Mrs Clair. 'Do you think you could, Ted?'

'I suppose so,' said Ted, warily. 'It wouldn't matter much, anyway. He's no more use round the office than a sick blasted headache.'

'That's fine,' said Mrs Clair, resolutely ignoring the indelicate adjective. 'You see, if he has his holiday then, he can come and board at The Guardhouse. He won't be any trouble there – he never is. Then we can manage easily – there'll be the money for his keep and I shall have a holiday and will pay my share, and then Marjorie and the children can have their holiday too.'

'And what about *me*?' said Ted.

'I said you'd come off worst,' said Mrs Clair, sympathetically. 'You'll have to stay at home and look after yourself.'

'Oh, I will, will I,' said Ted – but it was easy to see that he was not irrevocably decided against the scheme. There seemed a glimmer of hope that he might be persuaded.

'You see, we've got to pay the rent of The Guardhouse, anyway,' said Mother. 'But Mr Ely's money will pay some, and I'll pay some, and what you haven't got you can owe me for, Ted.

Then Marjorie won't need any more money that what she usually has for housekeeping.'

'Oh, won't she? What about fares? What about spades and pails, and ice creams on the beach, and all the rest of it?'

'Ah,' said Mother. She looked round at them again; she obviously had another surprise to spring. 'Marjorie won't want any extra money, will you, dear? You can manage on your housekeeping for the extras, can't you?'

'I suppose I could, Mother, but what about the fares? I couldn't pay those.'

The prospect of a holiday without Ted, a holiday where she might have time to think, seemed inexpressibly, unattainably wonderful to her.

'There won't be any fares to pay,' said Mrs Clair, beaming.

'And how's that?'

'Mr Ely's going to buy a little car for his holidays, and he'll take us all down.'

The secret was out now, and they could all look at each other, wordless for a moment. They did not belong to that stratum of society which owned motorcars as a matter of course – Marjorie could count on the fingers of one hand the privately owned motor cars in which she had travelled.

'He's going to sell it again afterwards, of course,' explained Mrs Clair. 'So it won't cost him much. As a matter of fact, that's what he was going to do anyway. He didn't know where he was going to stay, though. He thought perhaps he'd stay at home and just go for runs each day. So of course he likes this idea much better.'

"So I should think,' said Ted. 'These bachelors with their cars have a hell of a fine life.'

Ted's mind rushed off into a sudden digression. If he had not plunged so recklessly into marriage, he could have had a motor car by now, too. He would be a carefree bachelor – and – and – .

His mind baulked there. Something else would not have happened, but his mind refused to admit to itself what that something else was. A sudden sense of insecurity made itself apparent, and not for the first time in these last few days. He felt slightly sick, friendless and lonely, with the whole world against him. He looked round the room for friends; he saw his mother-in-law's face, placid yet hopeful, and his wife tensely, breathlessly expectant. If he were to deny these women what they were so hopeful of having they would be bitterly hurt. For a moment he saw with his mind's eye, as plainly as if it had happened, the change in their expressions if he were to say they were not to go. Madge would be disappointed – as likely as not she would cry about it. Mrs Clair would not merely be disappointed; she would be hurt and offended – striving hard not to show it, and yet feeling it all the more because of that. It would be the quickest way of making an enemy of her, and Ted flinched from that. Perhaps some premonition, some prophetic instinct, warned him that his mother-in-law was a person to be feared, or perhaps plain common sense told him that while his wife was so susceptible to her mother's influence his comfort and happiness depended in large part on not offending his mother-in-law.

'Well, don't you think it's a good idea, Ted?' asked Mrs Clair brightly. 'Don't you think we could do it?'

'I suppose so,' said Ted, and then, anxious to make a good job of it, and conceal his reluctance, he went on hastily, 'I think it's grand. You're a champion, Mother. I'll tell Ely tomorrow at the office that he can have my dates for his holiday.'

'Oo-ooh!" said Marjorie, ecstatically.

She loved The Guardhouse, and the flat green meadows where it stood, and the shingle and the sea beyond, and the green Downs behind; she felt she even loved the horrible little bungalows which littered the landscape now. She would have Mother there to help her with the children – even with the smallest help from Mother for three weeks she would have a freedom incomparably greater than any freedom she knew during the other forty-nine weeks of the year. Ted would not be there, and she knew now that she was frantically, madly desirous of being free from Ted for a space.

And yet, like the old comparison between sixpence and the moon, immediate trifles seemed as large as the vital questions with which she had to deal. The prospect of sharing a holiday with someone who owned his own motor car was dazzling. There would be none of those earlier struggles of taking children and luggage in a bus up to Victoria, no tedious journey, no toilsome carriage of baggage from the station to The Guardhouse. Instead she would just step into the car outside her door and sail easily down to the seaside, through the green fields and past the celebrated road houses she had heard of. Mr Ely would be generous with his car, she felt sure. Some days he would take her and the children down to the beach in it, along the rough road, before setting out on his own expedition, and so save her the trouble-some mile-long walk with the buckets and spades and towels. It was even possible – almost probable, although she hardly dared admit the probability – that once or twice he might even ask her to come with him. Mother would look after the children, and she would sail in the car to Hastings and Eastbourne, perhaps even to Brighton or Folkestone, where there would be fashionable crowds on the promenade, and a pier and a band, and smart hotels and unimaginable delights. Marjorie could think of no source of pleasure as perfect as a motor car.

For a space this train of thought made her quite oblivious of her urgent troubles. She could forget that the husband with whom she lived, whose bed she was going to share in an hour's time, had seduced and killed her sister.

'Oo-ooh,' she said.

'That's ever so sweet of you, Ted,' said Mrs Clair. 'Ever so nice. I did so hope you would, but I was afraid it would be asking too much of you. Do you think you'll be all right here by yourself all that time?'

Mrs Clair was speaking very clearly and incisively. Marjorie came to herself with a start, and realized that her mother was directing her voice at her just as much as at her husband. It would be bad tactics, bad policy, to dwell with too obvious an enthusiasm on the imminent delights of the holiday without displaying a proper appreciation of the sacrifice he was making and a proper concern at his approaching discomforts. He could quite possibly change his mind if he were not considerately handled. Marjorie did her best to respond to the call her mother was making on her.

'I'll leave you some nice cooked food, dear,' she said, hurriedly. 'That'll last you for a day or two and will be better than nothing. That chocolate blancmange that you like. And you can have a good dinner every day at Mountain's Café. Ted's great at frying bacon and eggs, you know, Mother.'

'Of course,' said Mother. 'We can trust Ted not to starve. He's much too sensible, not like some men. Don't worry yourself about that, dear. What I was worrying about, though, Ted, was in case you might be too lonely.'

'Lonely?' said Ted.

He had not thought of the possibility of being lonely or rather, he had not thought that loneliness would trouble him. He was anticipating, vaguely, three weeks of freedom. Three weeks when he would not have to account for his movements to the small but irritating extent that prevailed normally; when he could come home when he liked, and go to bed when he liked – and bring a girl home with him too, that was a notion – and generally revel in the bachelor freedom whose delights he had almost forgotten.

"Oh, if I'm lonely I'll just have to put up with it, I suppose,' he said, resignedly.

'You *are* a good soul,' said Mrs Clair, with appreciation. 'We're ever so grateful to you, aren't we, Marjorie?'

'Yes,' said Marjorie, 'ever so.'

Ted basked comfortably in their admiring gratitude. The friendless, imperilled feeling had disappeared altogether. He had not been in the least anxious to spend a dreary three weeks at the seaside with Madge and the kids, with the nearest pub two miles away. There was always a cold wind down there, and the women were all mothers of packs of yelling kids, nothing in a bathing costume worth looking at. He would far rather be at home here, even if it did mean making his own bed and cooking his own breakfast – the rest of the housework could go hang, of course. It was lucky that he'd thought of cancelling the holiday. Ted came, in the expansive moment, almost to believe that the whole new situation was the result of his own planning, and he felt pleased with himself in consequence. But he did his best not to show it, because it would never do for the women to guess that he was not making any special sacrifice. He was more pleased with himself, less jumpy and nervous, than he had been since the day after Dot's death.

'It's Saturday week we'll be going,' said Mrs Clair. 'Only ten days now. You haven't got much time to see that all Ted's things are mended up to date, Marjorie. We must leave him as comfortable as we possibly can. I'll come round tomorrow and see if I can help.'

The old exhilaration was creeping over Ted now; when his mother-in-law stood up to go he made no effort to detain her. Rather on the contrary he displayed by his whole attitude that he was not in the least unwilling to see the last of her that night. When Marjorie came back into the sitting room from the front door he clapped her on the haunches with the old gesture she had come to hate.

'Bed time now, old girl,' he said.

She looked up at him, and then round the room, at the familiar two armchairs and settee which were beginning to show the results of nine years' wear, the two pictures of woodland scenes which had been presented to them by the company from which they had bought their furniture, the little bookcase with seven books in it, the little table with the fern, the flowered hearth-rug, the radio set on the table against the wall, the curtains at the French windows. This was the home of which she had once been so intensely proud, and with which she had been so inordinately pleased. The mood of happy anticipation fell away from her like an unbuttoned cloak. The room was shabby, and so was life – dreary, ugly, impossible.

'What's the matter, lovey?' asked Ted. Even he, and in his present mood, could see that something was amiss.

The question opened Marjorie's eyes to the bottomless gulf at her feet. This was the first time Ted had felt like this since the night of Dot's death nearly three weeks ago – and Marjorie, shuddering, realized that the length of this interval was one more proof of his disquietude and his guilt – one more proof which would have no weight in a court of law. Weakly, she had not given a thought to the question of what she would do when this situation arose. That other question, the matter of leaving Ted altogether, could be fenced with, set aside, shelved, with the reassuring thought that she would deal with it later. When she had time to think. But this – this was urgent, imminent, frightening.

'Come on, lovey, what are you mooning about?' said Ted. 'Give us a kiss, old girl.'

A woman of colder or more cynical temperament might have told herself that as she had been weak enough to postpone the other decision she must of necessity give way in this matter; submitting to life with Ted meant submitting to everything else, so that all that was left to her was to make the best of a bad job and go through with it with resignation carefully concealed. But there was hot passion in Marjorie, the same hot passion which had led Dot to her death – a passion which Ted could no longer rouse. The imminent future was abhorrent to her. In the briefest interval of time a whole stream of thoughts poured through her mind. There had been a sort of edge to Ted's last words, a veiled command, possibly. The holiday was by no means yet a settled and certain thing. A word from Ted and there would be no holiday, and she would never, never get away from him, but be doomed to drag on this existence with him always. That thought roused panic. At all costs she must get away for that holiday, so that in the placid seclusion of The Guardhouse she would have that period of peace for which she longed. At all costs. Only ten days till then, she told herself, as a salve to her conscience for this present weakness – the weakness which makes tragedy possible. She forced herself to turn her face and kiss him, forced herself to simulate passion, parting her lips for him as he seized upon her.

She heard, that night, sleepless, the last train coming running down the gradient from the station past the house, and the first train grinding up it in the early morning.

7

Mrs Taylor, who lived at 79 Harrison Way, next door to Marjorie's house, and Mrs Posket, who lived at No. 69, four doors down, were old friends. Childless both of them, and in their early thirties, with husbands who went to the City every morning and stayed there all day, they spent a good deal of time in each other's company, went shopping together and to the cinema, and in the winter played bridge at each other's houses alternately, one married couple against the other. Today they were coming back together from the summer sales, a little weary, and yet triumphant, with parcels under their arms. As they reached the gate of No. 79, they both of them looked up at the house of No. 77. Although it was three weeks now since Mrs Grainger's sister's suicide, and although the summer sales had begun, that event was still fresh enough in their memory to be recalled to them by the sight of the house.

Little Mrs Taylor, blonde and vivacious, had acquired a story there which she had already told many times over, and would tell, interminably, to the day of her death – it was by no means everybody who had actually seen a suicide lying dead in the very attitude in which she had died. Mrs Posket, thinner and taller and darker, had missed that, and had to be content with the very minor distinction of having actually been in the house, talking to the dead girl's married sister, the day after it happened. Mrs Posket was known as a gossip. Romance had passed her by – the husband who went to the City every day failed to supply that. Nor was the cinema a satisfactory substitute, nor were the summer sales, nor was the little house which provided her with an hour or two's daily work.

Perhaps somewhere within Mrs Posket there were the instincts of a pioneer, the unsatisfied curiosity of an explorer, the logical faculty of a scientist, or the constructive urge of a novelist. The creative ability was alone wanting; it may never have existed, or it may not have survived the childhood among drab people, the faulty education at a bad school, the married life of bridge and shopping and concealed economies. So that Mrs Posket had become an observer, rather than an actor. The latent urges made her an enthusiastic, a fanatical, observer. It was to her a supreme example of the world's irony that such a dramatic event should have been seen through the blind blue eyes of Mrs Taylor rather than through the dark farseeing eyes of Mrs Posket – it must be added in parenthesis that she loathed the name of Mrs Posket and always tried to think of herself by her maiden name. It was Mrs Posket's ambition, which she had never progressed so far as to express in words even to herself, of which in fact she was quite unconscious, to see or hear something some day of vital and dramatic importance. This was the reason why Mrs Posket drew the milkman and the baker's delivery man into conversation, and peered out through her bedroom window, and noted what her neighbours were buying when she met them in the shops.

Derrick came running up the road in the opposite direction in advance of his mother, and stopped short at the gate at sight of the two women.

'Good afternoon, Derrick,' said Mrs Posket. Derrick smiled shyly at her and turned away to rattle the latch of the gate.

Shy one moment and bold the next, in childlike fashion, he turned back to her.

'I can't open this old gate,' he piped. 'Silly old gate.'

'Shall I do it?' asked Mrs Posket helpfully, coming forward. 'There! What do you say?'

''Hank you,' said Derrick.

'That's a good boy. And are you going to have a nice holiday this year, Derrick?'

'We're going to the seaside,' said Derrick, breathlessly.

'Which seaside, now?'

'The Guardhouse, of course,' said Derrick. The only seaside he knew was that which lay near The Guardhouse. He condescended to explain further to this stupid adult. 'We're going in a moty car, in Mr Reely's moty car, and Daddy's going to stop at home!'

'Oh!' said Mrs Posket. This was a marvellous piece of advance information. That just showed, as Mrs Posket expressed it to herself, that you never knew – in other words no stone was too insignificant to leave unturned when information was being sought. She would have asked Derrick further questions if Marjorie had not come hurrying up the street. Marjorie was a little out of breath, for she had walked as fast as she could directly she had seen who was talking to Derrick – as fast as she could while making desperate efforts not to appear to be hurrying. Marjorie was a little pale as well as breathless, for an awful fear had come upon her when she had seen Derrick and Mrs Posket in conversation. With a little boy like that one never knew what fantastic or illogical thing he might blurt out. He might – there was undoubtedly the chance of it, small though the chance might be – even say something to Mrs Posket about what he had seen that night, about Auntie Dot and Daddy.

She caught Derrick's hand and held him to her side and a little behind her, half concealed by her dress, as she said good afternoon to Mrs Taylor and Mrs Posket.

'Derrick was just telling us what a nice holiday you were going to have, Mrs Grainger,' said Mrs Posket, smiling.

Marjorie's apprehension died away; truth to tell, she was nearly as excited as Derrick about this approaching holiday.

'Yes,' she said, ecstatically, and then she forced herself to speak calmly, so that her audience would not guess that there was any connection between her ecstasy and what she was going to say next – it was better to come out with the latter boldly than to leave it to be discovered, as it inevitably would be. 'My poor husband can't get away from his office after all, and he's having to stay at home. Isn't it bad luck on him?'

'Derrick told us that, too,' said Mrs Taylor, rather to Mrs Posket's annoyance – a source of information loses half its future value if it disclosed.

'He's a chatter box,' smiled Marjorie.

'Who's going to look after Mr Grainger?' asked Mrs Posket.

'Oh, he's going to look after himself. He says he can.'

'My goodness!' said Mrs Taylor. 'I expect you'll have to start your spring cleaning when you get back. You know what men are like alone in a house.'

'I daresay,' said Marjorie, still smiling.

The secret knowledge that her husband was a murderer and an incestuous seducer compelled her to act the part of an indulgent wife far more vigorously than would have been otherwise the case.

'Well,' said Mrs Posket 'as long as you have good weather on your holiday I don't expect you'll mind.'

'No,' said Marjorie. 'I shan't mind *anything* in that case.'

When Marjorie had gone in with Derrick the two other women lingered for a moment longer outside Mrs Taylor's gate.

'H'm,' said Mrs Posket. 'Holidays apart, eh? D'you suppose it's true that Mr Grainger can't get way from his office? I don't expect he's as important as all that.'

'Oh, I should think it was,' said Mrs Taylor.

'She didn't want Derrick to talk to us,' said Mrs Posket. 'Did you see how she snatched him away from us?'

'Yes, I thought she did, too.'

A memory nearly thirty years old came up into Mrs Posket's mind. As a child scarcely able to read she had had a coloured picture book which included a vivid jungle picture entitled 'Tigress defending her Young.' At this moment she could recall that picture with extraordinary clarity, the black and yellow markings, the bared white teeth, the cub thrust behind and to the side.

'Like a tigress,' she said, vaguely. 'I wonder – '

'You're always wondering, Grace,' said Mrs Taylor with a laugh.

'Well, I wouldn't have to wonder about what my Dick would say if I wanted to leave him for a fortnight or three weeks or however long it is. I know already.'

Indoors Marjorie was worrying about the problem of how to hint to Derrick not to speak about domestic affairs to anyone outside the family, and at the same time how not to destroy his charming trustfulness with strangers. It was the same old problem of how to eat her cake and have it, and yet she did not consider that she was being weak about it.

'I don't think,' she began cautiously, as she cut the bread and butter for tea, 'that Mrs Posket was interested in our holiday. You needn't have told her about it.'

'She asked me, mummy,' countered Derrick.

'Oh yes, but I don't expect she really wanted to hear.'

'But she asked you, too,' said Derrick, with the exasperating logic of a four-year-old.

'I expect she did, but you don't have to tell Mrs Posket things.'

'What things, mummy?'

'Oh, you know what I mean. Things about us.'

'What things about us, mummy?'

It was just like a child to be so sharp one minute and so exasperatingly stupid the next, and the discussion ended as one might have expected – as even Derrick, with his brief experience, had philosophically come to expect discussions to end.

'Oh, don't bother me now. Why don't you run out into the garden and play until tea's ready?'

Soon after the children were in bed there was a knock at the front door. That puzzled Marjorie for a moment, because it was not Mother's knock. When she opened the door she was surprised to find herself regarding Mr Ely's shy good looks.

'Good evening, Mrs Grainger,' said Mr Ely, quite pink with excitement. 'I've brought the car!'

'Really!' said Marjorie. 'Is it outside? Can I see it?'

Mr Ely proudly led the way down the garden path to where the little car stood at the kerbside. It was only a tiny seven-horse-power saloon, long past its first youth, but it meant far more to Mr Ely than any Rolls-Royce did to its millionaire owner, and to Marjorie it was like Cinderella's fairy coach.

'It's lovely!' she said, and meant it. Loveliness in a vehicle to her mind began with the possession of four wheels, the ability to move under its own power, and the retention of sufficient roof to keep most of the rain out.

'I wanted to show it to you,' said Mr Ely, 'so that you could see how much luggage space there'll be. There won't be much, you see, with five of us in the car.'

'Derrick can sit on my knee, or Mother's knee,' said Marjorie. 'And Anne's not so very big.'

'It's not only that, though, I'm afraid. We mustn't have too much weight for the old bus to take along.'

'Oh, I see. I'll be ever so careful then. We'll only have a little.'

Marjorie's mind started working busily on the problem of how to cut down weight. There was a good deal she could manage without, she decided.

'I suppose,' said Ely, shyly again, 'you wouldn't care to come for a run in her tonight?'

'Oh!' said Marjorie, and then, her disappointment evident, 'I'm sorry, I can't. Ted's out tonight, and won't be back till late. I can't leave the children alone.'

Ely was disappointed too, and looked it. This was his first day of possession, and he longed to go out, driving about. To a man condemned to subordination there was a delicious thrill of mastery in putting down one's foot and feeling the car surge forward obediently; in swinging accurately round corners; in leaving behind the buses and trams in which one had so often before crawled tediously along, subject to driver and conductor, and even subject to people on the pavement who could stop one with a single uplift of the hand. But at the same time he was chary of driving alone through the traffic of the suburban roads. He wanted someone beside him to tell him of vehicles on his near side, and to look behind for him when he had to make a right-hand turn. The tennis club girls were all too superior. They might laugh at his gear changing. Ely believed them to have all been familiar with motor cars since childhood.

Ely did not think Mrs Grainger was superior. He did not stop to think whether or not she was familiar with motor cars. He admired Mrs Grainger and her dark beauty; and he felt more at his ease with her than with any other young woman; without ever going to the length of analysing it he had when he was with her a feeling of friendliness, of companionship, which was absolutely wanting when he was with other women. That was the main reason why he had jumped at Mrs Clair's holiday suggestion. He would be at the seaside at no more expense than in his lodgings – that was important, with all his savings locked up in his car – but the main thing was that he would be at the seaside with friends; Ely had spent lonely holidays at the seaside and had been unhappy all the time. The loud-voiced girls on promenade and pier had no attraction for him.

Marjorie was surprised to see that Ely's disappointment

equalled hers. She was a little thrilled and a little touched by it, too.

'Mother would come in and sit in the house, I expect, if we asked her,' she said, thinking rapidly. 'It isn't her evening for church, is it?'

'No. She was at home when I left. Shall I go and fetch her?'

'Yes, do.'

It was marvellous that with a motor car you could send a message to Mother and bring her back again, all in less than ten minutes. In Marjorie's experience that would have taken at least three quarters of an hour on foot, although Mother could still walk quite fast. A motor car meant freedom in all sorts of ways.

Mother seemed quite pleased to come around. She beamed upon Marjorie and Mr Ely, and waved to them as they set off down the road with a crashing of gears. Mrs Clair walked back from the gate and settled herself in the shabby sitting-room – with the door open so that she could hear the children if they cried – still smiling, but now it was a smile without any hint of kindness behind it. It was a hard, tight-lipped smile, and although her eyes had a faraway look there was no softness in them, either. Mrs Clair sat, straight backed, her hands in her lap, gazing out into space. She was seeing visions, wherein her son-in-law should receive the punishment he deserved. Her plans were bearing fruit already. Even her daughter's chastity would not be too high a price to pay. At least, if Marjorie were unfaithful to him, that would be one injury done to that devil, one instalment of the repayment.

Her quick ears caught the sound of the car drawing up at the gate when they returned, and she went out to meet them. Ely was helping Marjorie out of her seat; they were both pleasantly flushed and excited.

'Shall we both stay to supper with you, dear, as you're all alone?' asked Mrs Clair.

'Oh yes,' said Marjorie. 'You will stay, won't you, Mr Ely?'

'Thank you,' said Ely.

The long summer evening was only just ending with the fall of night. He had enjoyed himself so much, despite the tension of driving through traffic, that he did not want to have to admit to himself that the day was over, nor return lonely to Dewsbury Road.

They had a jolly little supper party all together in the kitchen with scrambled eggs on toast, and the remains of a trifle, and several cups each of the strong tea which Mrs Clair was inclined to drink to excess – her only weakness. Mrs Clair showed herself as properly impressed when Marjorie described the route over which they had driven – they had covered twenty miles of main road in the country at the cost of ten miles of suburban streets.

'When we're at The Guardhouse,' said Ely – he had fallen into the habit, along with the others, of alluding to the Sussex coast as The Guardhouse – 'we'll be right in the country to start with. We won't have to go through miles of traffic every time we want a run in the old bus.'

'Won't that be good!' said Marjorie.

What Ely had just said was an enormous relief to her. It assured her that Ely had no intention, during the imminent holiday, of standing on his rights as a board-paying lodger and going off to enjoy himself by himself every day. He was going to consider himself as one of the party, and she would be asked to accompany him sometimes at least. The worldly pleasures of Hastings and Eastbourne would be open to her, and all the fabled inland to which char-à-bancs penetrated, Bodiam and Herstmonceux and Chanctonbury Ring. Mother would be glad to take charge of the children on those occasions. She glanced across at her mother, and was surprised to detect a glint of pleased triumph in her eye – Mother was evidently glad, too, that her daughter was going to have a good holiday this year. She looked rather like a matchmaking mother whose daughter had just brought home an eligible suitor – Mother was a perfectly sweet old thing.

8

On Saturday morning the children awoke early, full of excitement at the fact that their holiday was due to begin today. Even Anne, who was generally so self-possessed, was infected by Derrick's excitement. Before seven o'clock they were running through the house in their night clothes, and came pattering into their parents' bedroom, which meant a bad start to Ted's day – to lose half an hour's sleep and to have to deal with children before breakfast were both of them maddening things to have happen. Marjorie precipitated herself out of bed and shooed the children from the room. She took her clothes with her so as to dress with the children and disturb Ted as little further as possible.

'This is like Christmas,' said Anne, pulling down her vest over her wriggling body – getting up early, and visiting her parents in her night clothes, while full of a feeling of delightful things about to happen, had been the start of the odd association of ideas.

'Thank goodness it isn't as cold as Christmas,' said Marjorie, fastening her suspenders, and looking sideways out of the window where the blessed sun was already promising another hot day.

It had been very hot during the night – Ted had snored and tossed and disturbed her. Partly, too, that was because he had wanted her again last night. He had put hot hands on her at bedtime, and sent her into a sudden panic, because she had been dreaming flimsy dreams that the morrow's separation was going to be permanent, and this crude reminder of her present entanglement had come as a shock to her. Panic stricken, she had told him hurriedly the only lie she could think of at the moment – one she hardly ever dared to employ, because Ted was so sharp. But even in face of a good excuse Ted had always shown resentment and annoyance.

'That's a nice thing to happen,' he grumbled. 'The last night we're going to have for three weeks.'

Because of his annoyance, Marjorie verily believed, he had snored and tossed during the night and kept her from sleeping. She had loathed his hot coarse hairy body last night.

'Christmas!' Derrick was shrieking. He had found the big drum-shaped toffee tin which was one of his chief treasures and was beating on it with a stick, making a noise which would disturb Mrs Taylor, let alone Ted.

'Be quiet, children,' said Marjorie, and then, desperately, 'Go out into the garden, both of you. You can go into the lane, if you like, if you're very careful and don't climb on the fence.'

That was a sufficient inducement to make the children go quietly. The lane was a little footpath which ran between the back gardens of that side of Harrison Way and the electric railway. Generally speaking, Marjorie forbade the children to set foot there, because with only one low line of railing between them and the rails she was afraid lest they should climb over. So it had all the fascination of forbidden ground to the children, with the added attraction that from the lane they could see – what was hidden from their view in the garden – the roofs of the trains passing up and down along the shallow cutting.

But breakfast, after she had prepared the meal and called the children in, was an unpleasant affair. Ted was gloomier and surlier even than usual, partly perhaps because of last night, and partly because no man with the prospect of three weeks' hard work with the auditors during a heat wave could be expected to listen with patience to prolonged chatter about a holiday which other people were going to enjoy. And Derrick made matters ever so much worse. His vague memories of other holidays were flooding back to him, mingled with distorted mental pictures of this motor car which had loomed so large in Mummy's and Grannie's conversations of late.

'Is Auntie Dot going to be in the moty car?' he asked.

'Be quiet, Derrick,' said Marjorie, too late.

Ted had dropped his knife and was glaring across the table at him.

'Silly little fool,' he said.

No one yet had told Derrick that Auntie Dot was dead – Marjorie had been trying to shield him from the knowledge of death, and was hoping that he would just forget about her. But (as she told herself now with bitter self-reproach) no one could ever rely upon a child either forgetting or remembering anything. Derrick was frightened now, and yet sturdily set upon asserting his individuality.

'Not a little fool,' he said, and Ted reached across the table and clouted the side of his head. That sufficed to change Derrick from an upstanding child into a howling baby. Marjorie ran round behind him. The habits of years were just strong enough to hold her back from imperilling discipline by picking him up and comforting him and taking his side against his father. She was on the verge of casting aside discretion, all the same; nor was she mollified by the sight of Anne's white face on the other side of the table – Anne, who, without being told, had guessed at Auntie Dot's death, and hated to hear her name mentioned, and hated her father's violence even more.

'Why don't you ever teach the kids sense, Madge?' demanded Ted. 'Silly bloody fools the whole lot of you. Too much of this holiday business, that's what it is. For two pins I'd say you weren't to go.'

He saw a flash of fear pass over Marjorie's face, and exulted in it. He wanted to hurt someone.

'It'd do you all a world of good,' he said 'to find there's something you can't have. That silly blitherer Ely and his motor car! Motor car! Ten years junior to me in the office, and buys a car!'

That was a fortunate digression. Ted's grievances had tumbled out so fast that he had been led into a mention of George Ely when actually it was Marjorie and the children he had been wanting to attack. When he had finished his sneer at Ely he had to stop and collect himself before resuming his tirade, and once having stopped it was not so easy to start again. He gulped and swallowed, and Derrick's howls put up a sturdy opposition and hindered the clear thinking necessary for the resumption of a really damaging offensive.

'I can't even finish my breakfast in peace,' he said, casting about for a fresh grievance, and that recalled him to the habits of ten years. He looked at the kitchen clock. 'God! I'll be late at the office.'

His violence was directed now into a hurried pulling on of his shoes. He grasped his hat and fled, with one last malediction on a household where there was never time for a second cup of tea at breakfast time, and the only comment on his behaviour was supplied by Derrick, who, tears forgotten, announced solemnly:

'I think Daddy's silly.'

'Sh! You mustn't speak about Daddy like that,' said Marjorie, instinctively again. She had tried for years now to maintain, for the sake of discipline, a loyal attitude towards her husband, and she could not abandon it now.

Upstairs beds had to be stripped, and windows closed, and blinds pulled down, and yesterday's packing completed. Downstairs there was a joint and vegetables to be cooked, so that Ted could have a last good meal before they left him, and so that there would be enough cold meat to carry him over the weekend. Anne was able to master her excitement sufficiently to dry up the breakfast things for her mother, and lay the dinner table, but for all her help Marjorie had enough to do that morning (thanks also to the necessity for seeing that Derrick did not get into mischief) to keep her in a whirl all the time. There were a thousand things to remember about the milkman and the baker and so on; Marjorie hoped she had remembered them all. It was so hot in the little house – Marjorie ran up and down the stairs twenty times that morning, flushed, and with her hair untidy.

Not until Ted had come back from the office and dinner was actually on the table did she have any time to feel excited. She would have said that she did not feel excited at all, not even when she saw, from her seat at the table, that the clock said a quarter past one and she recalled to herself that Mr Ely was coming for them at two-thirty. Yet she could hardly eat a mouthful of the dinner she had cooked – roast beef and baked potatoes and peas and Yorkshire pudding, and apple pie and custard, a real Sunday dinner, in fact, on a Saturday.

Ted did not notice her lack of appetite – he never had eyes for things like that – but he ate with relish, the morning's bad temper dormant. Ted liked a good dinner, especially beef and Yorkshire. After dinner he went into the sitting room, much to Marjorie's relief, and turned on the wireless, so that Marjorie could fly round again, washing up, putting everything ready, and then run upstairs to take off her overall and put on her summer frock (with a coat over it) and carry downstairs the bags and parcels which were waiting. There were half a dozen last-minute domestic matters about which she wanted to remind Ted, but she would not risk it now. She might write to him about them when she reached The Guardhouse.

For so long in her life had her primary duty been to run her house well that even now she acted automatically as if that duty was to continue. She even averted her attention, uneasily, from the thought that it might not be the case now. She did not think she was being weak. She thought she was being driven by irresistible circumstances. With a little shudder she shook herself free from all this nightmare. She was going to escape from it for three weeks, and she need worry about nothing for that time.

She resettled her hair, which had been disarranged by putting on her frock, and looked at herself in the glass. Her experiences of the morning, she decided, had left hardly any trace. The summer frock made her look fresh and cool, she was discreetly powdered, and – exceptionally for her – she had reddened her lips so that they were not quite so pale as they had become of late. However foreign to her nature it might be to pose as something she was not, there was nevertheless somewhere at the back of her mind a mental picture of herself, cool and leisurely and *soignée*, walking gracefully out to the motor car to be borne away to her three weeks at the seaside.

She heard the squeak of a motor horn at the gate, and then loud squeals from Anne and Derrick.

'Mummy, Mummy, the motor's come! Mummy, Mr Reely's here! Is Grannie there, Mummy? Is the luggage ready, Mummy? Mummy, have you got my boat?'

The picture she made in the sunshine, walking out to the gate, with the children capering beside her and a heavy bag in each hand, was really far more attractive than the one she had visualised, for the thought of the contrast made her show her white teeth in a friendly smile. Ted came grouchily after her with the remaining bundles, but he was sufficiently sensitive and flexible not to display bad temper in front of Ely and Mrs Clair. They packed themselves in with difficulty – there was only just room for everything and everybody – and it was only when the door was shut on them that Marjorie realized that she had not kissed her husband goodbye, and this was the first time she was leaving him since Derrick was born. She was glad it had happened that way. She waved her hand, and Ely let in the clutch and the car moved jerkily down the road. At the corner Marjorie looked back and wondered, before she resolved not to let unpleasant thoughts mar her holiday, how she would be feeling when she saw it again. Fifty yards further on was the corner where the little lane at the back of the houses emerged into Simon Street. Mrs Posket was there, walking up to the station to meet her husband – she often took the path along the railway, because the backs of houses are often so much more informative than the fronts. She waved to them, pleased at having seen such an important thing as Mrs Grainger going away for a holiday with young Mr Ely from the gas showrooms – not that she *meant* anything by that, mark you.

9

The holiday was not perfect right from the start, of course. George Ely took three hours to drive the seventy miles of crowded Saturday afternoon main road down to The Guardhouse, and by the time they reached it everyone was very cramped and tired, and hungry and thirsty. Derrick, in fact, had cried with fatigue before they had gone half way, and had not been comforted by the sharp words which his overwrought mother had flung at him over her shoulder. And at The Guardhouse when they arrived there were of course no provisions, no tea, nothing; even the beds would have to be made before they could rest. Marjorie contemplated with sick weariness the three-quarter mile walk to the shops.

Mrs Clair it was who rose to the occasion with a decision and energy which would have been creditable in a woman half her age – just as it had been Mrs Clair who had soothed Derrick into silence when he had cried in the car, and who had coaxed him into dozing for the rest of the way.

'Now, first we want some nice flowers,' she said, brightly. 'Anne, can I trust you and Derrick to pick me some nice ones in the field there?'

'Oh yes, Grannie,' said Anne; if a suggestion were presented to her in the right way she was an amenable child enough, and the responsibilities of the task given her were delightful. Her enthusiasm infected Derrick, and the two of them ran into the field with their fretfulness and hunger forgotten for the time at least, to set about the business of gathering dandelions and buttercups.

'There's the beds to do,' went on Mrs Clair briskly to her daughter, 'but we want tea first, I think, don't we? I'll go off to the shops. We'll want bread, and milk, and – '

Mrs Clair ticked off on her fingers the interminable list of items necessary for the weekend shopping and of a household devoid of every single necessity. Young Ely, having stretched his cramped legs in the garden, came up in time to listen. He was dizzy and tired with the strain of driving – the farthest he had ever driven as yet in one day, and amid traffic all of which had seemed to him to be hurtling along at dangerously high speeds. But he was a helpful soul, and oddly domesticated despite (or perhaps because of) the recent years he had spent in lodgings.

'Well, here's me and the car,' he said, 'what can we do towards it?'

The simple question took a load off Marjorie's mind at once. She had not really forgotten the existence of the car, but, acting on the assumption that Mr Ely was like Ted in domestic affairs, she had taken it for granted that she and her mother would be left unaided to make everything ready while Mr Ely want off to bread and cheese and beer in the local inn, only to return when all the work was done. She smiled gratefully at George.

'Thank you, Mr Ely,' said Mrs Clair, recasting her plans. 'I tell you what, you take Marjorie to the shops while I get tea laid and do what I can in the house.'

It was marvellous to have a car in which to go shopping. Three-quarters of a mile was nothing in a car, and when the things were bought there was the whole back seat on which to lay them, instead of having to drag them, with increasing backache, from shop to shop. All Marjorie's weariness and sudden disillusionment dropped away as she appreciated this joyous state of affairs. She smiled, and she threw back her head to smell the distant sea, and her lighthearted gaiety infected Ely as well so that he thoroughly enjoyed the fifteen minutes' brisk bustle through the three shops which the bungalow village possessed.

Back at The Guardhouse Mother had the table laid and the kettle boiling, and although the children had early tired of their flower gathering it took only a moment to set before them the bread and jam and milk-and-hot-water which dissipated their fretfulness like magic. From year to year Marjorie had forgotten the tragic misery of their first arrivals at The Guardhouse, only to remember it with renewed disillusionment and bitterness the next time. But this arrival was different already. It was barely six o'clock, and here they were having tea with half the work completed. In the old days even Dot, scatterbrained and light-hearted, had been snappy and morose by the time the children were in bed and the house in running order. Marjorie laughed and talked, and Mrs Clair smiled and held her tongue, and the children behaved like angels.

'Mr Reely! Mr Reely!' said Derrick, smiling just like a cherub despite a fleck of strawberry jam on his cheek. 'Mr Reely! Can I whisper?'

George Ely obediently bent his head. There was something oddly winning about the touch of Derrick's arms round his neck.

'Mr Reely,' said Derrick in a whisper as clearly audible as his normal tone of voice. 'We wanted you to take us to the sea after tea. Anne and me.'

'Can they go?' asked Ely, looking at Marjorie.

'You don't want to be bothered with them,' answered Marjorie.

'I should like to, honest I would,' protested Ely.

'We haven't seen the sea yet, not all day,' pleaded Anne.

'Very well then, if Mr Ely will take you,' agreed Marjorie, adding to Ely. 'Just for half an hour. It's nearly bed time already. Are you sure it's not too much trouble for you, Mr Ely?'

'No, really it's not, Mrs Grainger.'

While the children were hastily gathering buckets and spades, and Ely was gulping down his last up of tea, Mrs Clair interposed.

'All this "Mrs Grainger" and "Mr Ely" sounds out of place down here,' she said. 'Would you mind if we called you "George"? Then the children could you call you "Uncle" – that's better than "Mr Reely". Would you mind?'

'Not a bit, I should like it.'

'Then you'd better say "Marjorie" instead of "Mrs Grainger". I suppose I'll still be "Mrs Clair", though – I'm too old for Christian names.'

'Call her Grannie,' suggested Marjorie.

'Yes, I will,' said George.

After George had gone off with the prancing children Mrs Clair sat still for a moment at the table.

'He's a very nice boy,' she said thoughtfully, and as if to herself.

'Yes, Mother,' said Marjorie.

The success of that holiday – and right up to the end it was infinitely the most successful holiday Marjorie or George could ever remember – was largely due the unobtrusive tact and energy of Mrs Clair. It was she who started the success, and afterwards she remained at hand to give a discreet push or two when necessary to keep it moving, so that the success grew snowball-fashion, from day to day. She was helped in her designs, of course, by fortuitous circumstances – the blessed fine weather, for example, as well as Ely's decision to buy a car – but she contrived to wring the utmost possible advantage from them, without anyone noticing it sufficiently to attribute to her any other motives than general kindliness and a desire for efficiency.

Presumably it was the tumultuous bitterness in her heart driving her on which stimulated her into such a subtle awareness of human reactions and which gave her the strength to see the business through. On Sunday morning – the first morning – she could guess at George's temporary surfeit of driving the car and at his awkward wondering about what he should do instead, and she packed him off to the beach with Marjorie and the children while she stayed behind and cooked the dinner.

George enjoyed Sunday in consequence after all; it was pleasant to lie and roast in the sunshine, and to help Anne and Derrick while they excitedly built their first sand castles of the year. They swam, too – George had never been very partial to swimming before, because without knowing it he had felt more than usually lonely, somehow, in the cold water with no one to talk to. It was very different bathing with Marjorie, who had a laugh for every moment of the swim. Marjorie had a straight figure, only a tiny shade more pronounced than the current fashion demanded, and she swam well. George noticed how well she swam, although matters between them had not yet progressed nearly far enough for him to notice her figure. It did occur to him, however, that her white bathing cap, buttoned close under her chin, set off her dark beauty and made her seem younger and more girlish and approachable.

He was happy enough not to notice the discomfort of having to dress and undress with no more shelter from the eye of the public than that provided by an extremely inadequate depression in the shingle; George would have noticed it fast enough in less fortunate circumstances, for he was young enough and shy enough and badly enough brought up to feel embarrassed at having to change on an open beach even when everyone else bathing had to do the same.

The unwonted exercise and sunshine tired him a little, and he spent the afternoon idly turning the pages of the book of adventure he had brought with him for holiday reading. Marjorie, at her mother's instigation, went unashamedly to bed to recover from the strain of the last few days, while Mrs Clair kept the children amused in the convenient adjacent field. In the evening they all three sat together in the deep verandah of The Guard-house watching the sun slowly set behind the Downs. They put their feet up on the rail, and they smoked cigarettes, and chatted lightly and with a growing intimacy. Marjorie kept to herself the feeling of the difference it made to her to have a man with her who could contemplate with equanimity the passage of a whole evening without drinking beer. For years now all her relations with the one man she had anything to do with had been coloured and influenced by the fact that on each evening, no matter where they were or what they were doing, beer had to be drunk or at least violent grumbling indulged in instead. A sequence of three thousand days, each subject to this special condition, had formed so strong a habit of mental anxiety on the point that the relief from it was intense.

Nor was this the only, or by any means the main factor, which determined Marjorie's mental poise this evening. She was free for three weeks to come of the pressing need to decide upon what she should do in the matter of her husband. Three weeks of perma-nence to her, after the dreadful insecurity of the days preceding the holiday, seemed unendingly long. There was nothing to worry about. And she had enjoyed a long and satisfying rest that after-noon. No wonder that she was vivacious and lighthearted, chattering freely, and keeping the other two amused all the time.

George Ely was drawn irresistibly into the gaiety of it. He felt as if he had never lived before this holiday – he felt it although naturally the feeling would never be expressed like that in words, George being an inarticulate young man, and one who had never acquired, either at school or in the world, the ability to think in orderly fashion. Like so many of his breed, George directed his affairs under the guidance only of instinct and impulse. All he was conscious of at the present moment was a feeling of wellbe-ing and superiority, and he made not the smallest attempt to discover why.

That night, when they were going to bed – Marjorie was sharing with her mother the room which on previous holidays she had shared with Ted, while George had the room Dot had shared with Mrs Clair – Marjorie said, 'It's been a lovely day. I think I'm going to enjoy this holiday more than any holiday I've ever had.'

'I hope you will, dear,' said Mrs Clair. 'I'm sure I hope so!'

Mrs Clair wriggled out of her underclothes under cover of her nightdress, and pulled out from under her nightdress collar the pathetic little pigtail of grey hair. She knelt down beside the bed to say her prayers – but with Marjorie in the room she said them to herself, and not in the reverent whisper she usually adopted. When she got into bed she watched Marjorie cold creaming her face at the mirror. Marjorie's nightdress was of frivolous cut, and her bare arms were lovely in the subdued light. The long dark plait of her hair swayed to her movements, and the curve of her bosom as indicated by her nightdress was exquisite. Her mother thought of her as a beautiful caged bird, whom soon she was going to set free – just as she thought of her husband as some loathsome reptile, exuding venom, whom she was going to crush under her heel.

Marjorie finished her preparations, and walked round to her side of the bed. For a moment she hesitated – she had long abandoned the practice (which her mother had so strictly enjoined during her childhood) of saying her prayers nightly. But in deference to her mother's presence she went down on her knees and put her face in her hands. Tumultuous thoughts, but all of them vague and nebular, streamed instantly through her mind. Blurred pictures of George Ely in some of the attitudes in which she had seen him during the day, moved momentarily before her eyes. Then she turned out the light and climbed into the bed beside her mother.

10

There were days and days now of a happiness and a companionship which neither Marjorie nor Ely had known before. The motor
car was in frequent use; they ate ice creams on the promenades
of half a dozen seaside resorts, where they could watch with a
satisfying feeling of superiority the crowds of red-necked young
men and loud young women who did not live in a pleasant stone
house outside the noisy towns and who did not enjoy the proud
privilege of owning a motor car. They eyed, wonderingly, the grey
beauty of Bodiam, and its moat with its ducks and waterlilies, and
the thin thread of the Rother winding down through its valley.

The motor car nosed its way into the quiet lanes through the
woods about Hawkhurst – Marjorie, by anxious application,
learned quickly enough how to read a map so as to pilot Ely, who
was still far too engrossed in the business of changing gears and
rounding corners to carry any route in his head past the first
crossroads. Certainly it was the motor car which supplied their
earliest bond of union. When, labouring heavily, it managed to
crawl up some minor gradient in top gear, Marjorie was quick
to nod her appreciation – she was early infected with Ely's enthusiasm for this first motor car of his. The first puncture was an
event; they felt they had achieved something well out of the
ordinary when, with no expert help at all, they had jacked up the
little car and changed its wheel and found that the car went as
well as ever afterwards.

Marjorie thought Mother was perfectly adorable during this time; she was always ready to assume responsibility for the children so as to set them free, and she was avid of housework, so that domestic duties consumed little of Marjorie's time or energy. And it was the little friendly things that Mother said which helped to establish the friendly and carefree atmosphere of that holiday – other holidays had been tainted with bickerings with Ted, and even occasionally with Dot. This holiday was a period of quite unalloyed happiness.

Ely felt the same about it. He might be called almost an embittered young man in that experience had taught him always to expect disappointment. It was a delightful surprise to him to find that the long hoped for ownership of a motor car brought him all the pleasure he had wished for, doubtfully. It was still more of a surprise to him to discover that Mrs Grainger, the wife of his official superior, was so sympathetic and approachable, so readily infected with keen enthusiasm. No other women had ever found any use for or any merit in George Ely, and this was the most beautiful woman he had ever known, as well as the cleverest. Long hours of driving together imprinted indelibly on Ely's mental retina a picture of her profile (a composite picture acquired in many hasty glances when a clear road enabled him to relax for a second his concentration upon steering), alert and yet sympathetic and reposeful.

And besides those blissful drives there were happy hours spent upon the beach, warm in the sun, with the chatter of the children to keep him just awake – George Ely was not experienced enough to realize how Marjorie's tact and prompt interpositions prevented the children from ever annoying him, so that he had all the pleasure of their company and none of the annoyances or responsibilities. George was naturally fond of children, and he came to delight in the touch of Anne's soft hands and in Derrick's rogueish friendship. It was small wonder that for both Marjorie and George those weeks slipped by so fast.

At the end of one of those golden days Marjorie came out onto the verandah after having put to bed two weary and ecstatically happy children. George was washing his hands now that the bathroom was clear – one of the contrasts between George and Ted was the frequency with which the former washed his hands – but Mother was sitting knitting in her deck chair.

'Well, my dear?' she said, as Marjorie emerged.

'Derrick was asleep before I could get Anne into bed,' laughed Marjorie, sinking into her chair. Her head dropped back, and she thrust forward her bosom as though to meet the embrace of the evening sun which streamed in upon her.

'This holiday's done us all a world of good, I'm sure,' said Mother.

Perhaps there may have been something of finality in the tone of her voice, some implication of the ending of a chapter in the way she spoke. Marjorie stiffened a little, and the sunshine seemed to her to lose some of its mellowness, and the gold and green landscape assumed a tinge of grey. For the first time in those mad weeks Marjorie remembered that they must end, and soon.

'What's today?' asked Marjorie, hurriedly.

'Wednesday,' said Mother. 'We'll be going home on Saturday. I was just thinking when you came out that we'll have to start finishing off the food here, dear. And if I were you – I don't want to interfere, dear, but I thought I ought to remind you – I should start making out a list of the shopping you'll want when you get home. You'll need pretty nearly everything, and you'll only have Saturday night to get them in.'

Marjorie said nothing in reply to this homely speech – she only half heard it. There were only two full days left between her and Ted, or between her and the decision she must make. She was appalled at the realization, like a spendthrift staring at the newly arrived and unexpected notification from the bank that his account is overdrawn. Mother went on placidly with her knitting – of course there was no chance of her suspecting Marjorie's unhappiness, despite the sharp eyes which she lifted from the busy needles.

Marjorie set herself desperately to think, but time and again her mind swerved away from the problem. She was in a panic now; she even had to exert a little of her will to keep herself from actual physical flight.

'Ah, here you are, George,' said Mother, as Ely made his appearance. 'Are you going to sit down?'

George took the third deck chair, and Mother's needles went on clicking, and the sun sank lower in the west.

'You haven't been out in the car today at all,' said Mother, conversationally.

'No,' said George. 'I was too busy making a castle with Derrick and Anne.'

'It's a lovely evening,' said Mother. 'Why don't you go out now?'

It was a fine suggestion, in George's opinion. He looked at Marjorie.

'Oh, yes,' said Marjorie, and then, with a twinge of conscience 'What about you, Mother?'

'I shall be all right,' said Mother. 'I want to turn this heel before I have to put the light on.'

That physical panic which Marjorie had felt was still very noticeable. She wanted to get into the car and drive and drive and drive, as though that would carry her away from the crisis which she dreaded.

'Let's go,' she said, rising from her chair.

George coaxed the car out through the narrow gate with a facility painfully acquired, and Marjorie, who had been piloting him out, climbed in beside him.

'Where shall we go?' asked George.

'Oh, I don't know. Anywhere, I don't mind,' said Marjorie desperately.

'I shall go to bed if you're late,' called Mother from the verandah. 'But come back when you like.'

The car headed towards the golden sunset. It reached the main road, busy with the summer evening's traffic, swung off into a by-road which George remembered, swooped down into a wooded valley, and climbed a wooded hill, climbing and climbing round tricky turns. In the premature twilight cast by the trees rabbits skipped and scuttled across the lane. The car rattled gallantly up to the crest, where suddenly the trees fell away on either hand. Far off over the grassy sky line, they could see the blue sea, with a big red sun hovering over it.

'Ooh!' said Marjorie, and George instinctively stopped the car and switched off the noisy engine.

They watched the sun sinking down towards the sea. Everything was silent round them, except for the singing of the distant birds. George had never devoted much attention to the scenery before, but this evening was too lovely to escape his notice. There was agonising pain in Marjorie's breast as the sun sank lower. There was the sheer loveliness of the place, the sadness of the evening, the regret that this happy time was ending, all this was working on her while she battled with herself to try and reach some decision about Ted. Her head was whirling; she could not think consecutively.

George felt her stir beside him.

'Let's walk over that way,' said Marjorie. 'I want to watch the sun go right into the sea.'

A few steps took them to the edge of the woods again, and lifted the sea's horizon above the grassy crest. Here the stump of a tree seemed as if it had been grown there especially to provide a seat, and they sat together on it, close (of necessity), and watched the single straight bank of cloud above the sun change from orange to blood red, while the sun's disc was on the point of reaching the sea. On that perfect August evening, clear and still, it almost seemed as if one could hear a hiss as the fiery ball touched the water. Then it sank lower and lower, until for a second there was only a red spot on the horizon, a spot of warmer colour amid the red and gold which surrounded it. Then it disappeared, and the eye was suddenly conscious of a three-quarter moon which had been present, unnoticed, on the other side of the sky.

'Oh, it's gone, it's gone,' said Marjorie; with the setting of the sun her worries pressed in upon her harder than ever before, and the red sky and the silver moon were still there to torment her bosom with their beauty.

George, looking down at her, saw that her eyes were wet.

'Marjorie!' he said. 'What's the matter, Marjorie?'

And Marjorie turned to him and clung to him, like a child, and he held her, clumsily, and his brain was whirling now as well. For a space the mere contact satisfied them.

Then Marjorie moved in his arms as a whole torrent of reactions overwhelmed her. Fear of the future, horror at the thought of going back to Ted, fear of leaving this island of peace which she had found so unexpectedly in the middle of her life, all these assailed her on the one side; on the other was the thought that here might be a protector, someone sweet-tempered and gentle. There may have been a trace of her fatal weakness there, too – finding herself in Ely's arms meant a new problem to distract her from the one which demanded a solution, and gave her an excuse for postponement. Besides all this, there was the urge of her body. Three weeks of carefree holiday, of sunshine and leisure had had their effect on her. The masculine scent of George's tobacco was nicely blended with the delicate underlying odours of toothpaste and shaving soap. All the passion which Ted had so well known how to rouse was still there to be roused. George was something cleaner and finer. She moved in his arms, and, not knowing what she did, she lifted her face to him, and George kissed her, and she kissed him back, and clung to him. That was when passion carried them both away for a mad five minutes.

Those kisses were like strange mixed wine to Ely. The kisses he had known had been few and unsophisticated, and Marjorie kissed as Ted had taught her to – with her lips parted for him, hotly and eagerly, and her sweet bosom pressing against him. It was his first, his very first glimpse of adult passion. His head swam and his arms as they held the lovely thing within them trembled although he did not know it. The boy was drunk with love and desire. All the respect and affection and admiration he had felt towards Marjorie were transmuted by those kisses. He grew hot and eager; perhaps it was only his clumsiness and inexperience which prevented the consummation of the affair on the spot.

As he grew more pressing, Marjorie saved herself by a last effort of self-control. She stiffened a little in his arms, abandoned the lax self-surrender which had maddened him. She was hungry for him now, and her heart had gone out to this clean sweet boy who suddenly seemed so very much younger and more inexperienced than herself. But her experience warned her that here it was barely twilight, that other people might come at any moment – she told herself this, making excuses to herself for postponing the issue, and making no attempt to ascertain her real motives. She was maternal towards him, lingering in his arms, loath to leave them. With her hands she stroked his soft cheek, and neck – soft and smooth to her, accustomed as she was to Ted's tendency towards bristles and pimples. She smiled into his eyes, but her touch was soothing him now, and her maternal bearing and slightly unyielding attitude drained the urgency from him.

'George, dear,' she said, and kissed him, gently.

'Sweetheart,' he answered, charmingly – and he had never said any endearment to a woman before.

'We must be sensible,' said Marjorie, slipping from his hold and sitting upright again upon the tree stump. 'Look, we've lost all the sunset.'

George brought himself under control. He was shaken, and a little ashamed of himself. He had no business to kiss married women – especially the wife of his office superior. He was a little frightened now at the memory of the unsuspected abyss of passion he had found opening at his feet, for he had never dreamed of such a thing, just as he had never dreamed of the sort of kisses Marjorie knew how to give. For the moment, in reaction from the discovery, he was glad to sit quietly, gazing at sea and sky, with the moon brightening above them, with Marjorie chattering beside him, while they pretended that nothing had happened.

Then, after a little while, Marjorie shivered.

'It's turning quite cold,' she said.

'These clear nights do get cold,' agreed George.

'We'd better be getting home,' said Marjorie.

They got into the car again, without a kiss or even a handclasp, and George started the engine. He drove cautiously, for he was not yet accustomed to night driving, and as they proceeded along the wooded lanes the headlamps called up bizarre beauties of hedge and foliage. Rabbits skipped, amazingly, in front of them. Once they saw the green eyes of what Marjorie thought must be a fox, but which George suspected of being merely a prowling cat. They went down over the bridge, past the old cottages, into the high road ablaze with headlamps, along which the dazzled George could only crawl.

Still only good friends, and not lovers, they turned into the by-road to the sea, and coaxed the car through the gate into the garden of The Guardhouse. It was there, after they had put out the lights and were feeling their way to the door of the house, that the balance tilted once more, and this time irrevocably.

Their outstretched hands touched, just at the moment when Marjorie was suddenly realizing all her troubles again, that she had still reached no decision, that this was Wednesday night and on Saturday she would be in bed with Ted again, that Mother would be inside waiting for them as placid as ever.

The realization and the contact broke down again the frail barrier she had set up between herself and George – perhaps between herself and her inner self.

'Oh George!' she whispered, 'George!'

They came into each other's arms in the darkness, and they kissed again, and she strained to him, making him conscious of the precious flesh under his hands. It was madness, delirium, only to be dispelled when a chattering party of holiday makers went down the road close beside them. Then she tore herself free from him.

'Mother must have heard the car,' she said. 'She'll think it's funny if we don't come in. Kiss me darling! There! Oh, we must go in. Tomorrow –'

She turned to the door.

'I can't come in yet,' said Ely, thickly. 'You go in. I'll come in a minute.'

Mother had nearly finished that sock of Derrick's, though no one knows what hatred or hope she had knitted in with it.

'Had a good run, dear?' she asked.

'Lovely!' said Marjorie. 'We saw the sunset. Did you see it?'

'Yes, I saw it. Where's George?'

'Oh, he's just doing something or other to that old car of his,' laughed Marjorie. 'He takes more trouble over it than we do about Anne and Derrick.'

Marjorie passed through the room to take off her hat and coat. She thought her woman's talent for intrigue had prevented her mother from guessing what had happened. That is possible, but Mrs Clair was keen-eyed, and she probably guessed. Certainly she must have guessed later, when George came in, for the cigarette he had been frantically inhaling outside had not wholly calmed his nerves. He was pale, and his eyes were bright and yet vacant as if he had been drinking. He excused himself at once and went to bed.

II

It seems a plausible theory that it was that last change of mind of Marjorie's in the darkness of the garden which precipitated affairs and made disaster possible. The kisses she had given George at sunset – even those particular kisses – might have been forgotten, and George might have come to look back on the incident as an unaccountable lapse on Marjorie's part, never to be expected again. But she had changed her mind in the garden, and when she had changed her mind once she might be expected to do so again. And there was that fateful word 'tomorrow', which she had uttered. Marjorie had meant, if she had meant anything at all by it, merely that she wished to postpone all thought of the matter to some indefinite date, but to George's simple mind the word meant literally that on the morrow she would kiss him again; it was that thought which helped him through a restless night during which, like any young lover, he went over in his mind every unconsidered action of hers, and analysed every single word, reading meanings and drawing inferences which were as likely as not quite unwarranted.

Deep within him Marjorie had wakened into activity a volcano of passion which might perhaps have appeared unlikely in someone as insignificant and retiring as George Ely. He had reached his comparative maturity with little or no contact with women. Now that the spark had been fired he was as ardent as any boy. The last few weeks had piled up explosive ingredients within him at a rate far greater than had been the case during the preceding years, and Marjorie last night had touched them off. He was mad with a man's first love. He worshipped her dark beauty, and what he considered to be her poise and her tact and her ability. He tossed and turned through the night, conjuring up pictures of her before his mind's eye, and waiting expectantly for the morning – it would be hard to say exactly what he expected of the morning, but he expected something.

Needless to say, the morning brought him small comfort. His glance followed Marjorie round the room as he devoured her with his eyes, but she tried to avoid meeting it; she appeared to be a tiny bit more preoccupied than usual with attending to the children and serving the breakfast. She granted Derrick's petition (while they were all debating how they should spend the day) that she should accompany him and Anne to the beach that morning, and it was only in reply to a direct question from Anne that she agreed that 'Uncle' should come too, if he cared to. He cared to. He accepted the invitation eagerly.

Yet on the walk down to the beach Marjorie had Anne on one side of her and Derrick on the other, and when they had chosen their place for the day, on the leeside of a groyne, she was very busy suggesting to the children what game they might play. George was on the point of sulking before he was able to secure a moment of her attention when the children were not about. He caught her hand.

'Marjorie!' he said urgently, leaning towards her, compelling her to look at him. 'Marjorie! What's the matter this morning?'

The touch of him, and the anxiety in his face, broke down the indifference she had striven to assume.

'Oh don't,' she said pitifully. 'Wait. Wait till this evening.'

That was enough for George. It was all he wanted. He cursed himself for being a blind tactless fool – of course she would not want to risk word or gesture to him which might be observed by her children. That would of course be horrible, although (as George assumed quite for granted, without thinking for a moment of the cost) they would be looking on him as their father in a few months' time. As long as Marjorie still loved him he was content to spend all day on the beach, to play with the children, to go bathing with her and to pretend the heart-whole camaraderie he had felt towards her when this holiday had begun, to treat her in her mother's presence with what he intended to be respectful indifference and which did not deceive Mrs Clair for a single instant, neither when they came in to dinner nor when, with the children tired and sleepy, they finally left the beach and arrived for tea.

At tea time Mrs Clair made a surprising announcement.

'I want to go and see my young man tonight,' she said, archly.

'Your *what*, Mother?' asked Marjorie, a little startled.

'My young man. Gary Cooper. He's on at the Majestic in *Mr Deeds*. It's no good asking you to come, of course. You've seen it already with Ted. Besides, someone's got to stay at home and I think it's my turn to have an evening off. Don't you think, so, George?'

'Yes,' said George, fighting down the eagerness in his voice.

Mrs Clair was clever. It was perfectly true that someone had to stay in the house while the children slept. But it was equally true that Ely was a lodger and his own master; it was unthinkable that he should be asked to stay while the two women went out. He must be allowed to do whatever he chose.

'Is George going to take you in the car?' asked Marjorie. That might mean a postponement.

'Oh no. I wouldn't think of troubling him. The six-thirty bus will do for me quite well. I've travelled in it often enough. And there's the bus at ten-thirty to bring me back.'

'Oh,' said Marjorie, with no inflexion of tone in the monosyllable at all.

'I know you won't think I'm rude, George,' said Mrs Clair. 'I do want to see that picture. Everyone says it's so good, and I'm dreadfully fond of Gary Cooper. It's such a good chance for me now that it's on down here after I missed it in London. And tomorrow night we'll be too busy packing.'

'Of course,' said George.

'Will you barf me, Uncle?' said Derrick, hastily. He had remained out of the conversation for quite as long as a small boy could be expected to.

'Uncle doesn't want to be bothered with little boys,' put in Marjorie, more by instinct than by reason.

'He likes little boys,' said Anne. 'He told me so. But he likes little girls best.'

Derrick was a sociable little creature at bath time,, and it seemed as if the collector's instinct was early manifesting itself in his case, judging by the way he tried to add new names to the lengthy list of people who had bathed him. He had his way, and while Mrs Clair put on her hat and coat it was Ely who, a little nervously, soaped him and rinsed him and dried him, and buttoned up the blue and white pyjamas which Derrick had laboriously demonstrated, as he had proudly boasted, he could put on all by himself. Derrick rode triumphantly on Ely's shoulder to say goodnight to his mother, who with Anne's assistance had just completed washing up the tea things.

'Goodnight, Mummy,' he shrieked, wriggling on his lofty perch while Ely held him in an anxious grip. 'Goodnight, Anne.'

Ely took him away and lowered him into his bed. He lay there looking like an angel with his hair all newly brushed and his fresh-washed baby's complexion.

'Goodnight, Uncle,' he said. He was sleepy already, in his usual startling contrast with his high spirits of a moment ago. He snuggled down into his pillow.

'Goodnight, old man,' said Ely. Tenderness was welling up

within him. It was as unusual for him to be fond of a child as of a woman, but as he did not stay to analyse his feelings he was not surprised at himself.

His mind was in a turmoil as he sat down in the living room and listened to the splashings upstairs which told that Anne was in her bath under Marjorie's supervision. Yet nothing had come of the turmoil when Anne came scampering in in her nightgown to sit at his feet while she ate the two biscuits which constituted her supper.

'I want Uncle to put me into bed, too,' said Anne, with decision, when Marjorie appeared to fetch her away.

'You big silly,' said Marjorie. 'Uncle can't put little girls to bed.'

'Yes he can. You will, won't you, Uncle?'

'If it's all right,' replied Ely, looking up at Marjorie.

'If you don't mind, I don't,' said Marjorie.

Ely picked up the little skinny creature in his arms and bore her away. The touch of her arm round his neck was oddly pleasant – so was the sight of Derrick, already fast asleep in the other bed.

'Prayers first,' said Anne. She crouched beside the bed and whispered earnestly to herself. Then with a whisk of spider limbs she scrambled into bed and pulled up the clothes.

'Did you hear what I said?' she asked anxiously.

'No.'

'You weren't supposed to hear, because I said something nice about you to God,' said Anne. She snuggled down just like Derrick. 'Goodnight, Uncle.'

'Goodnight, dear,' said Ely.

He came out of the room and shut the door quietly behind him, his mind still in a turmoil. Marjorie would be downstairs.

At the head of the stairs he heard a slight noise through the door of the women's bedroom beside him – a faint 'ping' as a hairpin or a brooch was laid down in a glass pintray on the dressing table. Marjorie was not downstairs; she was in there. He was not properly conscious of what he was doing as he put out his hand to the handle and opened the door. Marjorie was standing at the mirror close beside him; she had taken off her frock and was in her petticoat, with her neck and arms bare, and her hair loose. She had fled to this sanctuary ostensibly to put right the disorder in her appearance consequent upon bathing Anne; actually because she had found the seconds of waiting while George was away too much to bear, and had come up here to occupy her mind on the only task she could think of at that moment. It would help to postpone the inevitable tête-à-tête with George, at which she did not know what she wanted to say nor what she ought to say.

Marjorie looked round as the door opened. It was as though her doom had descended upon her. She felt her knees go weak at the sight of George. There was something like tears in her voice.

'George!' was all she could say – she was not ready with any other speech. She put out one hand and moved towards him as though to drive him back, but it was only the feeblest of gestures.

'George! I – you – '

George had nothing to say at all. The last traces of any hesitancy on his part were erased by the sight of Marjorie on the verge of tears. He came forward to comfort her, and then the touch of her flesh put an end to the thought. Marjorie came into his arms; out of a desert of indecision into a sweet oasis of heedless submission. The bed was there beside them. For one second, like a lightning flash across a darkened sky, the thought came into Marjorie's mind that her husband was a murderer. When it had passed all that remained was a greater eagerness to anticipate this new lover's every wish. Ely was an inexperienced lover, gentle and yet clumsy, infinitely tender while passion tore at him. Marjorie felt her whole heart and soul go out to him in love.

'Darling,' she said. 'Darling. Darling.'

12

Mrs Clair was sure next morning that they were lovers. She had been nearly sure last night, when on her return from the cinema she had found Marjorie asleep in the tumbled bed, her hair disordered and her clothes abandoned with an untidiness she had never permitted in Marjorie as a child. Mrs Clair had crept into the room, forbearing to switch on the light, and making use of the shaded light of a candle on the dressing table. Marjorie slept peacefully and breathed regularly. Mrs Clair, peering at her, could mark the relaxation of her attitude and the flush on her cheeks. She smiled as she crept about the room making ready for bed.

And next morning those two had only eyes for each other and no attention for anyone else. The children's chatter was unheeded by them, although Ely had a pat on the shoulder for Anne and spared time to tickle Derrick's fat neck. Mrs Clair intercepted a brief meaning smile which passed between Ely and Marjorie, and she remembered how once she had intercepted just such a smile between Ted and Dot; in her innocence in those days she had attached no importance to it. She hugged the comparison to herself. It seemed almost a shame to blight their happiness, but Mrs Clair had other objects in view than just the cuckolding of Ted. There must be a worse punishment for him than that, and in the end they would be far, far happier than they would be merely as guilty lovers. She rapped on the breakfast table to command attention, and she looked round at them all with a magisterial air.

'Ladies and gentleman!' she said. 'No one seems to have remembered it except me. This is our last day. What does everybody want to do on our last day?'

Certainly no one seemed to have remembered it. Both George and Marjorie revealed by their faces with what a shock the reminder came to them. Anne was sorry, too. Only Derrick remained equable – the prospect of one more whole day at the seaside made tomorrow's return still very remote to him.

'Well, what does everyone want to do?' repeated Mrs Clair.

'Let's go on the beach,' said Anne.

'Let's go on the beach,' echoed Derrick.

'Some people seem to know what they want, at any rate,' commented Mrs Clair. Neither George or Marjorie had anything to say.

'There'll be packing to do later on,' said Mrs Clair. 'You'll be busy then, Marjorie. Suppose you and George take the children on the beach while I do the housework this morning?'

They agreed, eagerly.

It was different on the beach this morning from yesterday morning. Instead of dragging out the process of settling down beside the groyne Marjorie hastened it. Instead of lingering over starting the children at their play she cut the business short. She made the fantastic offer of an ice cream for each of them, to be eaten not out of a packet, but sitting up at a table in a real café, if they managed to build this morning a sandcastle worthy of such a stupendous reward. That set the children to work at once – Derrick labouring with his wooden spade to raise a mound big enough for the genius of his sister to work on, Anne with her chin in her hand walking round him, dreaming architectural dreams. Then Marjorie was able to come to George as he sat beside the groyne. She could press his hand and smile at him, and he could smile back at her, and for a space they forgot the world about them.

Not for long. There suddenly welled up in Marjorie's mind a fountain of ugly thoughts – her mother's reminder that this was their last day had been cunning indeed. Tomorrow she must go back, to where Ted awaited her. There would be the house in Harrison Way, of which she had once been so proud. It was a digression, but a very relevant one, to think how dirty and untidy the house would be after Ted had lived in it alone for three weeks, and what a mountain of washing there would be to do on Monday. There would be the shabby sitting-room, the thought of which Marjorie could hardly endure, and the bathroom and the bedroom, and Ted with his beastly lips and hands. Hands which had one pawed Dot about; hands which were red with her blood. Marjorie shuddered convulsively.

'Sweetheart,' said George. 'What's the matter? What's the trouble, dear?'

'What are we to *do*?' asked Marjorie. She tore at his hands with her fingers as fresh realizations broke upon her; she spoke like a madwoman. 'What are we to *do*? What are we to *do*?'

'Do?' said George sturdily. He was not perturbed as yet. Vaguely in his mind he had felt that there would be a way out of the obvious difficulties before them; his present happiness had been too intense for him to think about details. 'Oh, we'll be all right, dear. It's not so bad nowadays. We can get a – '

'Divorce,' had been the word he was gong to say, but it remained unspoken. As soon as he came as near as that to reality, he saw far more plainly the objections to that course. Marjorie voiced them for him.

'A divorce? What, me from Ted? George darling, we can't. Just think – . What about your job?'

For three weeks George had given no thought to his job. He was Grainger's subordinate in the branch showrooms. His future was practically at Grainger's mercy. Not merely that, but there was the managing director of the vast company, higher far than Grainger, who was notorious for being straitlaced, and for dismissing without hesitation any member of the staff who strayed in the least from what he considered the path of rectitude. George's dismay showed in his face, and involuntarily he uttered the managing director's name.

'And there's Mr Hill – !'

'Yes,' said Marjorie. 'I've thought of him, too.'

She knew of Hill's reputation – and yet it was not until that morning that she had realized suddenly that it was that reputation of Mr Hill's which had done most to frighten Ted last June into doing what he had done – just another piece of evidence only of weight with those few people intimately acquainted with all the circumstances.

Suddenly Marjorie became aware of George's unhappy expression, and was all anxiety and contrition.

'George, darling,' she said, putting out her hand to him. 'Don't worry so. It'll be all right.'

She smiled bravely at him. She was far more deeply and passionately in love with him now than she had been before she gave herself to him – that was quite typical of her. But her troubles were so many. They surged up again despite herself.

'There's the children,' she said, miserably. 'You know what Ted's like. He hates children, but if I tried to leave him he'd keep Derrick and Anne just to spite me. And he'd be horrid to them, too. I know he would. I couldn't, I *wouldn't* leave them with him.'

Her lips were trembling, but George had no word of comfort for her in that moment.

'That's so,' he said grimly. He knew enough about the law to be sure that any wife who left her husband voluntarily would be compelled to hand over the children to the husband who ostensibly had a home open to her. And he hated the thought of

Derrick and Anne at Grainger's mercy, too. He set his jaw and tried to think clearly about the future. The idea of a divorce grew more unattractive the more he thought of it. Grainger was bad tempered and vindictive, as well he knew. George could foresee that not only would he lose his job but he would be faced with heavy legal costs; and he had a vague idea that an injured husband could recover not merely costs but damages from a co-respondent. If it were possible, Grainger could be trusted to do it. He would not rest until Ely had been utterly ruined, until he was begging in the streets, and Marjorie too, and both of them tormented with the thought of what was happening to the children.

'We've only got until tomorrow,' said Marjorie at his side. 'I shall have to go back to him tomorrow. Oh, I can't, I don't want to!'

The bare thought of that drove him half mad.

'I don't want you to, either,' he said, desperately. 'I don't want you to.'

It was Marjorie who was being the practical one of the two of them now, for a space. Her mind quested about for a solution of their difficulties.

'Darling,' she said – there was a faint chance that there might be a helpful answer. 'Have you got any money?'

'No,' said George, bitterly. 'I drew out all I'd got to pay for the car. I'll get twenty quid for that, though, when I sell it again.'

'Twenty quid's not much,' said Marjorie. 'And I haven't any. The housekeeping's nearly all gone. I'll have to let the bills run for a week after I get back.'

It was strange how those last few words slipped out unexpectedly. To most minds – not to George's – they would have constituted proof that Marjorie was reconciling herself to the thought of returning home. Actually the explanation lay in that to leave her husband was such a tremendous step that

Marjorie could not really think except in terms of not having done so.

They sat side by side on the sunlit beach, the groyne at their backs. All round them were holiday makers, the nearest party not more than five yards away. Children ran and laughed and shouted. Far out, where the distant sea, at the lowest point of the ebb, broke feebly in the shallows, there were shrieking groups of bathers. A seagull wheeled overhead, magnificently white against the blue sky. To a casual observer George, open shirted and grey flannelled, and Marjorie, in her summer frock, would appear no different from the hundreds of other holiday-making couples, presumably discussing the seaside price of food, or last night's film. Life and death hung on their words.

Marjorie sat with her hand at her heart; to her the blue and gold of their surroundings were all drab and tinged with grey. The first of her troubles was returning to her consciousness now with renewed force – for a space she had almost forgotten it in the excitement of having a lover. Her husband was a murderer, the murderer and seducer of her own sister. That appalling fact was more appalling still, now. It loomed up before her like an iceberg before a liner. Sheer terror took hold of her. She cringed before circumstances far too powerful for her to contend against for a moment, like Gulliver in the grip of the giants. Terror – and self-pity – broke her down. The tears welled up into her eyes and poured down her cheeks. She was shaken with sobs, as she sat there with her back against the groyne. The casual observer might guess that now he was witnessing a lovers' quarrel.

The sobs recalled Ely to consciousness as he sat staring grimly along the beach.

'Sweetheart!' he said as he turned to her. 'Don't cry, darling. Oh don't. Everything'll be all right in the end. Really it will. I swear it will. Oh darling, I can't bear it when you cry.'

He put his hands out to her, and she sank towards him, and

he kissed her quickly and furtively, on her lips and her wet cheeks. Her tears tasted salt to him – even at that moment he noticed it.

'Tell me you love me, darling,' moaned Marjorie.

'Oh, I love you, dear. More than anything else in the world.'

'Whatever happens, you'll still love me?'

'Of course, of course. Whatever happens.'

They kissed again, hurriedly, and then tore themselves apart as they remembered how public was the place in which they sat. The casual observer could guess now that the lovers were reconciled again; but if that had been the hypothesis upon which he had been working he would have been puzzled to account for Derrick and his relationship to them, when the little boy came running up to them.

'Mummy! Uncle! Come and see what me and Anne have made! Come and see! Can we have our ice cream *now*?'

They followed him down the beach while he gambolled and galloped ahead. Anne was putting the finishing touches to a vast rococco palace, elaborate in its battlements and ramps and wings. Seaweed, shells, and pebbles had all been called in to help in its decoration. There was even a paper flag streaming stiffly from a flagstaff on the tower. Anne was brooding over the whole effect with a faraway look – the look of a creative artist just emerging from dreams – in her eyes.

'Lovely!' said Marjorie. It was second nature to her now, after eight years of motherhood, to put on that bright tone when speaking to her children, no matter what she was suffering herself. 'Did you do it all by yourselves?'

'Yes!' shrieked Derrick.

'Of course we did,' said Anne. 'At least, Derrick didn't do much of it.'

'I made the pile!' expostulated Derrick.

'I think it's perfectly wonderful,' interposed Marjorie. 'Don't those shells look nice on the sides.'

'Derrick found those,' said Anne, honestly.

'Can we have our ice cream now?' clamoured Derrick, capering wildly and waving his spade.

'Can we, Mummy?' asked Anne.

The earnestness of her tone was due to her yearning for this solid proof of appreciation of her talent, rather than to any gluttony.

'I suppose so,' said Marjorie, helplessly, with a side glance at George.

'Oh yes, of course,' said George. He was not as practised as Marjorie at mastering his emotions in the presence of the children, but he did it for her sake, and with a nice appreciation of her motives. 'Come on, kids. Which café shall we go to – the Beach or the Willow Pattern?'

They made their way up the crowded beach again, threading a path through the seated groups. Marjorie looked at the children as they ran ahead, Derrick plump and sturdy in his bathing costume, Anne – ethereal, not skinny in that golden sunlight – graceful in her scanty frock, her arms and legs tanned golden brown. For a moment Marjorie reverted to the discussion which Derrick's coming had interrupted.

'I couldn't leave them, could I?' she said, pleadingly, and she lifted her eyes to George's face and put her hand on his arm.

George shook his head.

'No,' he said. 'You can't leave them, dear. I can see that. We'll think of something soon, dear.'

Yet during the rest of that nightmare day the question 'What are we going to *do*?' arose time and again. Marjorie asked it again wildly, in the afternoon. She had found herself, somehow, alone in the kitchen with Ely, and they had kissed, madly, half swooning, but when the insane seconds had passed Marjorie held back at the full stretch of Ely's arms and said 'What are we going to *do*?' There was panic in her eyes and voice. She was as conscious now of the passing hours as a condemned criminal. Tomorrow she would have to go back to Ted; the hands of the clock seemed to be travelling faster than usual.

Later that afternoon another idea came to her.

'Take the children out down the road,' she whispered urgently to Ely. 'Buy them some sweets – anything. Please dear.'

Then when she was alone with her mother she asked her help – she was like an animal trapped in a shed, running to each corner in turn in a vain search for a chance of escape.

'Mother,' she said, breathless, 'I don't want to go home tomorrow.'

Mother had chosen the shady corner of the verandah and was taking her knitting out of her work bag. Her face was necessarily averted while she was doing this; it was some seconds before she sat upright again, and she adjusted her needles with what was to Marjorie maddening slowness before she spoke.

'I'm not surprised,' she said, placidly. 'This is the best holiday we've ever had, I think. But everybody has their own work to do as well, you know, dear. Life can't be one long holiday.'

It was exasperating to be misunderstood like this.

'I don't mean that,' said Marjorie. 'I don't care a hoot about the holiday. I mean that I don't want to go back and live with Ted. Not ever.'

The face which Mrs Clair raised from her knitting wore convincingly the expression of blank surprise which she had been getting ready to exhibit ever since George took the children out.

'My dear!' she said. 'Whatever do you mean?'

'What I say, Mother. I can't go back to Ted. I can't. Oh, do help me, Mother.'

Mrs Clair was ready for this. The solitary days and evenings she had spent this holiday had given her ample time to make up her mind as to what she wanted. Merely to deprive Ted of Marjorie, to leave him in possession of the children, would not be nearly enough.

'Marjorie, dear,' she said. 'I'm surprised at you. Leave your husband? Whatever for? I don't see how I can help you to do that.'

'Because of Dot, Mother. And you know all the other things. But you can't expect me to go back to him after what he did to Dot.'

'Really, my dear, I don't understand what you are talking about. What has poor little Dot got to do with it? And what are all the "other things"?'

Marjorie was conscious of a profound shock at that; she had misunderstood Mother, then, that day when Derrick said what he did. Mother had not guessed about Ted and Dot, after all. It was not specially surprising, now that she came to think about it. Little innocent Mother, sheltered from the world, of course would not be able to guess at the wickedness around her. Marjorie felt that she could not enlighten her – that indeed it would be a hopeless task to attempt to do so. She was the only one who had penetrated the secret. In that case it would be equally hopeless to seek Mother's aid in leaving Ted – Mother would be the last person on earth to encourage a wife to separate from her husband. Marjorie's head was swimming. She was exhausted by the emotional strain.

'Oh, Mother,' she said, in growing despair. 'You don't understand.'

'I'm sure I don't understand,' said Mother, primly. 'I try not to be very old-fashioned in my ideas, but I do think that a woman's place is by her husband's side unless there is some very good reason against it. My dear, I hope you haven't been letting your thoughts run away with you about Mr Ely? He's such a very nice young man. You haven't done anything wicked, or foolish?'

'Oh no, Mother,' said Marjorie, in utter panic now. To admit anything of the sort, she saw now, would be to forfeit all hope of Mother's help. She ought to have guessed that earlier – and yet, hoping against her better judgement, she had cherished the thought that Mother might have been sympathetic towards herself and George. 'As if I'd do anything like that!'

'I never thought you would, dear,' said Mother. 'But when you spoke so wildly I was half afraid in case – . But we needn't talk about that. I hope I won't hear any more of this nonsense about not going back to Ted. I expect it's just because you don't want this holiday to end. As soon as you get home and settle down again into running your home you'll be much happier. Just try it, dear, and you'll see.'

'Yes, Mother,' said Marjorie.

'All men are a little trying sometimes,' said Mother, as if this observation came from the profoundest depths of her wisdom. 'Even your dear father was, once or twice.'

'Yes, Mother,' said Marjorie.

Another of these few, fleeting hours left to her and gone now. She looked incredulously at the clock, and her mother followed her gaze.

'Time's getting on,' said Mother. 'I think we'd better start the packing before the children come back.'

Circumstances seemed to be edging Marjorie forward, as a criminal is edged towards the scaffold from the condemned cell by the warders round him. Packing, making tea, washing up, bathing the children – another huge section of the day whirled by, to Marjorie's dismay.

'Are you two going out for a last run this evening?' asked Mother. 'I should if I were you.'

They drove out to the woods where they had first kissed, but when they reached the place they did not linger in the car, nor sit on the stump whence they had watched the sunset. Without any discussion they plunged together farther into the woods, out of sight of the lane, and there Marjorie turned and flung herself, half weeping, into Ely's arms, and he clasped her hungrily.

Ely, as might be guessed from the hopeful way in which he

had spoken of the divorce, was not the sort of young man to grasp at the favours of a married woman thankful for this solution of the eternal problem of how to avoid both celibacy and marriage. He was besotted with love for her. It had never occurred to him that he might hope to conduct a convenient intrigue with Marjorie in the future. He had thought of nothing, save his mad passion for her. He had been with her all day long with nothing more granted him than a hand clasp. The memory of last night was driving him frantic; he was sick and faint with desire, and the woods seemed to spin round him as he held her to him, hotly. All the plans Marjorie had made while sitting at his side in the car, to the effect that now they really would discuss the future with sanity, went by the board. They kissed and whispered until twilight had nearly given place to night before Marjorie was able to bring herself to ask the question again which she already asked once that day –

'Darling, what are we going to *do*?'

The question pricked the bubble of Ely's ecstasy, already stretched to breaking point by what had just happened.

'I don't know,' he said, gloomily. The intertwining branches overhead were black against a pale sky.

'Tell me you love me, darling,' said Marjorie, urgently – the gloom in his voice has roused a new fear within her.

'Oh, I love you, I love you, sweetheart,' said Ely.

'I was afraid you didn't. I thought you might be – you might be disgusted with me,' wailed Marjorie.

'Of course not!' said Ely, aghast. 'How could I be, darling?'

'Oh – '

Then came a fresh fear.

'Promise me, darling,' said Marjorie, 'if ever you find you don't love me any more you will tell me, won't you, dear? Don't pretend, will you?'

'Sweetheart,' said Ely. 'I'll always love you.'

It was two or three minutes more before the question arose again –

'What are we going to *do*?'

'I don't see what we can do at present,' said Ely.

'Mother seems to take it quite for granted I'm going back home tomorrow. And – and – there's nowhere else I can go, at all.'

'That's so,' said Ely, simply.

'Do *you* want me to go back to Ted?' asked Marjorie.

It was the first time, to Ely in his simplicity, that this aspect of the question had presented itself with any clarity. It had not occurred to him before to think about tomorrow night, but now he was horror stricken. Years of close contact in the office with Grainger had given him plenty of insight into the latter's nature. There could be no doubt at all about what would happen tomorrow, when Grainger welcomed his wife home after three weeks' absence. He felt jealousy envelope him like a flame.

'He'll want me to sleep with him,' said Marjorie, struggling desperately now to say everything that had to be said.

Ely clasped her until it hurt, as if by mere physical strength he could keep her out of Grainger's embraces.

'You can't,' he stammered. 'You mustn't!'

Marjorie could see the anguish on his face in the faint light. Even in the intensity of that moment she felt a little thrill of pleasure. Ted had never been like that. Ted had been dominating, possessive, masterful. Years ago she had loved him – although she would not admit the fact to herself now – but even while she had loved him she had been conscious that she had meant less to him than he had meant to her. She might have been able to annoy him, but never to hurt him, not like this poor boy with the tortured look on his face who was shuddering in her arms.

It hurt her, too, unbearably, to see him like that. She felt she would do anything, promise anything, to comfort him. Her love and her tenderness redoubled; it was in her nature to return love for love.

'Darling,' she said 'don't worry like that, please, darling.'

But Ely's overstimulated imagination was still set on picturing Marjorie in Grainger's arms. There was no relaxation in the bleak misery of his expression.

'Darling!' wailed Marjorie again. 'Don't, please don't worry. It'll be all right. I'll see that it's all right, dear.'

To end the tension she would promise anything. And in Ely's arms, and in that comforting dark, with the trees whispering solemnly overhead, it was easy to make promises, reckless of whether she would be able to fulfil them.

'I won't sleep with him. I won't let him,' she said.

To her at that moment it seemed easy enough, too. She would be able to head Ted off for a space. It would be easily within her power to do so for a few days at least. After that she might be able to induce Ted to listen to reason. At any rate she would have a few days in hand, and in the urgency of this crisis the gain of a few days meant much to her. 'Tomorrow' was imminent. 'Next week' was not. She was gratified by the way George's expression cleared.

'Really?' he said. 'Do you think that will be all right?'

'Yes, of course it will,' she said, determinedly.

'I don't want him to make you unhappy, darling.'

'He won't do that. Not as long as you love me.'

If Ely reflected at all, it was to the effect that Marjorie and her husband had been married for the best part of ten years, and had in consequence reached a stage in their mutual relationship mostly incomprehensible to him, who had but lost his virginity twenty-four hours ago. He was prepared to believe anything Marjorie told him in that connection. He caught her to him again, and kissed her again and she poured out silly, exalted vows to him.

She would never allow Ted to lay a finger on her. As far as she was concerned Ted must be celibate from now on, although she wouldn't care what he did outside the house – the more affairs he had the better she would be pleased. She was going to keep herself pure for George. She was all his, and only his. It all seemed to her not merely possible but easy in that wild moment.

And on Marjorie was thrust the initiative, the direction of the affair – if it could be said to have any direction. She had been meaning to tell George about her suspicions regarding Ted and Dot, but she shrank from doing so now. It would do no good, for they had agreed that there was nothing they could do, and to tell George would not alter that. And it might do harm; George would be terribly worried at the thought of her living with a murderer. She could not bear to have him worried; rather than that she would continue to bear the burden of her knowledge unshared. More than that – George might not believe her, might think her mad, might conceivably cease to love her, and not for worlds would she risk that. There were the four or five days which she had in hand. She could at least put off telling him until then, and as she could, she did.

They went back through the dark lanes to The Guardhouse calmer and happier than they had been all day. Mrs Clair, looking sharply at them as they entered, blinking in the light, was puzzled by the look on their faces. She could not guess what decision they had reached, if any. But she could afford to wait, and see what would be the outcome of the matter.

13

In every respect except the continued good weather Saturday was a terrible day. In the earliest morning Marjorie and Mrs Clair had to be up and about, completing the packing and then putting the house into ideal order. Another family would be moving in that afternoon, and the result of their efforts would be under the close inspection of another housewife, who would be able to criticize unhampered by their presence. Even though they could never hear what the newcomers would think, they could not bear the thought of being considered slovenly. Everything had to be cleaned and dusted and polished; and there were arrangements to be made about the trifling bit of laundry work to be done; and the milkman had to be waylaid and paid; and the inventory gone through with the caretaker, and agreement reached regarding breakages; and the keys had to be handed over; and the luggage – which seemed incomprehensibly to have doubled in bulk since their arrival – had to be packed into the car.

By the time Marjorie took her seat beside George she was already tired; nor was the journey to London any rest to her, because Derrick, with complete lack of consideration, chose this day of all days to develop car sickness. He nearly succeeded in making Marjorie sick as well. Ted was standing at the gate in the hot midday sunshine when at last the car drew up outside No. 77 Harrison Way. Marjorie climbed stiffly out of the car and put Derrick (who had sat on her knee for the last half of the journey) on his legs on the pavement. She tried to greet Ted in a way which would satisfy him and not rouse George's jealousy.

The sun was hot overhead, the road was dusty, the little front garden with its few unambitious plants looked neglected and forlorn. The house looked somehow derelict and shabby, and the paint was peeling from the gate upon which Ted was leaning.

'Hullo, old son,' said Ted to Derrick.

It seemed to Marjorie as if she was hearing his voice for the first time; it sounded strange and unmusical. Derrick hung back shyly – it was three weeks since he had seen his father, and no one had taken any pains to keep him familiar with his memory. The others struggled out of the car, and approached the gate, laden with parcels. Marjorie saw the upper front curtain twitch at No. 69, and knew that Mrs Posket was watching their arrival.

'Good morning, Mr Grainger,' said Ely. He did his best to speak naturally, but he was conscious of awkwardness.

'Good afternoon,' said Ted.

That told Marjorie that Ted was expecting to be given dinner today, and that he was hungry, and that he considered their arrival over-late.

'Is there anything in the house to eat, Ted?' she asked hurriedly.

'A bit of bread three days old,' said Ted. 'Nothing much else.'

'I'll have to run down to the shops and buy something, then,' said Marjorie.

'I think you will,' said Ted.

'I'll run you down in the car, Marjorie,' interposed Ely, returning from having piled the luggage on the doorstep. 'Mrs Clair won't mind.'

'Perhaps not, but I do,' said Ted. '*Mrs Grainger* is quite capable of going by herself. I'd rather she wasn't seen by the shop keepers driving round in a car with a young man.'

The stress on the words 'Mrs Grainger' showed that Ted had noticed and resented Ely's use of the Christian name.

'Oh, I'll walk, I don't mind,' said Marjorie. 'It won't take a minute. You'd better get on home with Mother, Mr Ely.'

She was trying to appear cheerful despite the gloom that was descending on her, unconcerned despite the evident tension, trying to convey to George that he must not take offence at what Ted said, to tell him by her tone that she still loved him although prudence dictated that she should call him 'Mr Ely', and yet to make Ted think George meant no more to her now that at the beginning of the holiday. George still hesitated, but Marjorie held out her hand and ended the situation.

'Goodbye, Mr Ely,' she said. 'Thank you very much for all you've done for us. I can't think how we should have got along without you. I hope you've enjoyed your holiday, too.'

'Goodbye,' said George, and, getting into the car, he slammed the door a little too hard.

'Goodbye, Mother. See you soon,' said Marjorie, trying to appear gay.

The car rolled off, gears clashing as usual. Marjorie had no time to look after it with regret.

'You children had better come down with me to the shops,' she went on. 'It'll do you both good after sitting in the car.'

'Don't want to,' whined Derrick.

'You'll come at once,' snapped Marjorie. She took Derrick's hand and Anne's, and hurried them off. Both of them were hungry and cross, and Marjorie's hasty shopping in Simon Street was a tiresome ordeal. When they reached home again the luggage was still piled on the doorstep – apparently Ted had gone inside without carrying it in. Marjorie hurriedly opened the door with her key, and set the children to work dragging the packages into the hall while she hastened into the kitchen to prepare dinner. From the sitting room came the music of the loudspeaker – Ted was listening to Radio Normandie as his habit was on Saturdays.

The kitchen was a scene of horror; the little scullery was even worse. There was dirt and muddle everywhere, dirty crockery, dirty saucepans. Marjorie glanced at the dresser, which she had left so orderly three weeks before. Now it was stripped bare – every single piece of crockery in the house was dirty and littering up the sink or the kitchen table. There were cigarette ends on the floor; the sink stank, and a quick investigation revealed that its drainpipe was stopped up.

Marjorie nearly wept. Then with a determined effort she pulled herself together and faced the task before her. She remembered her bold promise to George. She was not going to allow this return to her old life to upset her at all.

The little kettle was dirty – apparently something had actually been cooked in it – but the big one was clean. She filled it and lit the gas under it – the oven was encrusted with black stickiness, but that could wait – and then she fled round the kitchen, clearing away the mess. On the table was a cloth; it had once been white but now bore black rings where saucepans and frying pans had been stood on it, and a yellow lake of spilt egg. She whisked it away, found a clean one, washed up sufficient crockery for dinner, laid the table. It was only twenty minutes before the kitchen was respectable enough on the surface and dinner was laid and ready.

'Eggies!' said Derrick with satisfaction. At the present time he preferred a boiled egg to any other sort of food, consuming it by the process of dipping into it 'fingers' of bread and butter.

'Boiled eggs?' said Ted in utter discontent. 'And God damn it, Madge, I'll swear this brawn came from Marshall's. Haven't you got the sense to guess I've been living on Marshall's brawn and eggs for the last three weeks?'

'I didn't have time for anything else,' said Marjorie. 'It's half past two now.'

'A fine dinner to give a man on a Saturday, I must say,' said Ted.

Marjorie maintained a dangerous calm. She glanced at Ted,

who was battering disgustedly at his egg with the convex surface of his teaspoon, and experienced a wave of pure satisfaction when she thought of George's kisses last night. That was a pleasant revenge; nothing Ted could do or say could distress her when she had those thoughts to comfort her.

The moment dinner was finished and Ted had retired with his last and strongest cup of tea into the sitting room to continue to listen to the wireless, Marjorie's activities began again. She had to start by scrubbing out the kitchen – she could not bear to leave that a moment longer – and then to complete the washing up, and to scour the saucepans (at least two were spoilt beyond remedy) before she could start on the rest of the house. She worked like a slave in the tiring heat. Hall, dining room, bedroom, all were in a state of filth and neglect. She did not look into the sitting room where Ted was; she could guess that to be in a worse condition than anywhere else, and she had neither time to spare for it nor the desire to risk trouble by upheaving Ted from his armchair.

In order to keep the children quiet and out of the way she had to make the concession she always hesitated over – to give them permission to play in the lane that ran between the end of the garden and the railway, from which they could see the trains running by in the shallow cutting. Fortunately the children were no trouble; they were happy and occupied in the inspection of their old haunts and in ascertaining what changes had occurred during their absence. And Anne was really helpful in laying tea when the time came and in getting nearly everything ready for the meal.

At six-thirty Marjorie was almost satisfied. She had the bedroom fit to sleep in again, beds fit to lie in. She called the children in to put them to bed, and in the hall she encountered Ted in the act of reaching down his hat from its peg.

'Oh, you're not going out, Ted, are you?' she ventured to ask.

'Of course. It's Saturday night. I'm late now.'

Saturday evenings he always spent in a bar with a band of his friends.

'But I've got to go out,' said Marjorie, blankly. 'There's all the weekend shopping to do. There's nothing in the house to eat. Not a thing.'

'I can't help that,' said Ted. 'I'm not staying in on a Saturday night, not for anyone. You ought to have done your shopping this afternoon.'

'Oh, Ted.'

'Pottering round the house all day, leaving everything to the last minute like this. Just like a woman. I can't stand here arguing all the evening.'

With that he was gone, leaving Marjorie contemplating with dismay the prospect of toiling round the crowded Saturday night shops with two cross children, long after their bedtime. She was reprieved by a gentle knocking at the door.

'Mother!' she said, with unfeigned delight as she opened it.

'I thought I'd just slip round and see if you were all right,' said Mother.

She made her way through into the sitting room, and halted abruptly at the sense of disorder there.

'I haven't had time to do this room,' said Marjorie hastily.

'I don't expect you have. What about your shopping?'

'I haven't done that either.'

Marjorie's lips were trembling.

'Well, pop on your hat and run and get it done. I'll see the children into bed.'

That was a great help. When Marjorie returned, just as it was growing dark, laden down with the innumerable parcels necessary to re-equip the house with all its necessary stores, she found that Mother had done better still. Not only had she put the children to bed, but she had set about the sitting room. The place was cleaned and dusted, the carpet had been taken out and beaten; the pleasant smell of furniture polish lingered upon the air.

'I thought I'd just do it,' said Mother apologetically. 'I hadn't anything else to do after the children were in bed.'

Marjorie tried to stammer her thanks, but it was not easy. She was too tired.

'Well,' said Mother. 'I'm going to run off home again now. Mr Ely said he didn't know whether he'd be in for supper or not.'

Those last words discomposed Marjorie. She wondered what George was doing. With a little pang of jealousy she found herself running through in her mind the list of possible places where George might be having supper. It unsettled her. She was abrupt in her goodnight to her mother – and was conscious of it, and regretted it at the same time – and when she came back into the sitting room and sank down into a chair it was not to experience the delicious rest she had been anticipating, but to sit, stiff and jangled, and on the verge of tears. Then something penetrated part way into her consciousness, like a sound heard while dozing. She sat tensely for a space, until she heard it again. Someone was whistling, there was no doubt about it, in the lane at the end of the garden. It was a three-note call which she had heard George whistle on the beach when trying to attract Anne's attention. Her fatigue and unhappiness were forgotten now. She put out the sitting-room light, opened the French window, and stole down the garden to the wooden gate. It was George, sure enough. She fumbled open the gate and fell into his arms.

Later she had a moment of prudence.

'Come into the garden,' she whispered. 'Someone might come along.'

They kissed again in the garden, in the darkness by the elderberry tree.

'Darling,' she whispered. 'I never thought of you coming this evening.'

He was more masterful tonight, more practised as a lover. He felt in the darkness for her chin, lifted her face to his, and kissed her again.

'Where's Grainger?' he demanded.

'Ted? Oh, he's out. He always goes out on Saturday nights.'

George's arms were very strong and very firm about her.

'Has he been all right to you?'

'Oh, George, he's been horrid. Beastly.'

She felt George's arms go rigid and there was sharp anxiety in his next question.

'What has he been doing?'

'Oh, he's made the house all dirty and he didn't do anything to help me and he complained. If Mother hadn't come round I don't know how I'd have got my shopping done.'

Marjorie felt George's arms relax again. The troubles which loomed so large in her mind did not appear so important in his, sympathetic though he was.

'Nothing else?' he asked.

'No. Oh – no, nothing like that. Of course not. I wouldn't let him.'

'You're sure?'

All sorts of doubts and fears had grown up to plague Ely during the afternoon of solitude and reaction.

'Yes, quite sure, darling.'

Her lips sought his in the darkness – she did not want this questioning to go on.

'Let's go in,' he said, later.

'Oh!'

She had not thought of that; perhaps it would never have occurred to her if he had not suggested it. At the seaside was one thing. Here in the house where she lived with Ted was quite another. Momentarily it seemed wrong. It seemed dangerous. Yet it would be safe – Ted never came home on Saturday nights until after closing time, and that was at least an hour and a half off.

'Don't ask me, darling,' she said, weakly. 'Don't. Don't.'

Ely did not ask her again, not in words, nor was he subtle enough to plan or foresee the fact that there would be no need to ask. He was drunk with desire again, with her yielding sweetness, and she pressed to him, offering herself to him – Ted had taught her that way of kissing, years ago, and it was all natural to her now. These breasts of hers at which she had suckled Derrick and Anne were strangely sensitive tonight under George's touch. Her knees were weak as she caught fire from his passion. She drooped in his arms. George was half carrying her as they crept down the garden path. The French window was open for their reception when they felt their way into the greater darkness of the sitting room. Yet in the silence there some stray eddy of Marjorie's attention caught the ticking of the mantelpiece clock, and she told herself that Mother must have wound it again when she turned out the room. The ticking faded abruptly out of Marjorie's consciousness again, along with the smell of furniture polish, along with the fear of an early return by Ted, as George's hands found her again in the darkness.

The striking of the clock roused her again, long after.

'Darling,' she whispered. 'You must go now. Ted'll be back soon.'

George was a sweet lover, not like Ted, who had no use or attention for her after he had had his fill. George still had a kiss for her, and loving words.

'I love you so much, dear. Tell me you love me.'

'Oh, I love you, darling. But you must go now. Really you must.'

'I don't want to leave you.'

'And I don't want you to go. But it's getting late. Kiss me goodnight, darling.'

She led him, unwilling, to the French window, and almost pushed him out, frightened, now that it was all over, lest at any moment she should hear Ted's key in the front door. George could sense her fear, and resentment against Grainger surged up within him. He stopped just outside the French window, and turned back to her.

'Darling,' he whispered, hoarsely. 'Promise me – '

'Oh go, please go, dear,' she whispered back. 'Somebody might hear.'

Fear spurred her caution. She whispered additional instructions to him.

'Shut the gate after you, quietly. And see that no one sees you come out of the garden. Goodnight, darling.'

Ely tiptoed back up the garden path. His head was swimming. Twice he stumbled and had much trouble in avoiding making a noise. Out in the lane he felt a little cool breeze blow past his ears, but it did nothing to cool the dull rage he felt against Grainger, who was coming home soon, and would spend all night in bed at Marjorie's side.

14

Marjorie was so weary when the reaction came after George left that she hardly knew what she was doing. She compelled herself to switch on the sitting-room light, and gradually accustomed her eyes to its brilliance. She tidied her hair with the aid of the glass hanging on the wall – Dot had given them that as a wedding present – and twitched the furniture into tidiness. She passed weakly through into the kitchen and set out the bread and butter and cheese in case Ted should want supper on his return – sometimes he did. Then she sat down in Ted's armchair to await his return. Her eyelids drooped, and she fell fast asleep.

The slam of the street door in the hall woke her suddenly. Mazed and stupid, she did not at first realize where she was or what she was doing, because not in a dozen years had she fallen asleep in a chair. She saw Ted standing looking down at her and she struggled to get to her feet in a panic. In her stupid condition she felt as if something had happened to reveal her unfaithfulness. She felt frightened and unready.

'The Sleeping Beauty!' said Ted, genially, and then, marking how her colour came and went, he added with positive concern 'Here, what's up, old girl?'

'Your supper's in the kitchen,' said Marjorie, ready at last with something to say.

'Don't want any, thanks. Lang and I had biscuits and cheese at the Crown. Tell you what I do want, though.'

He slipped one arm behind her before she was ready to evade him, and held her before him while he went on speaking.

'D'you know you haven't kissed me yet? You've been away for three weeks and still you haven't got a kiss for your poor old husband.'

Marjorie could smell the beer on his breath. Her rallying senses noted his expression. She could see that tonight he was in one of his unusual moods, but one with which she had already had acquaintance. He was going to be sentimental, maudlin.

'Well, you weren't very nice to me when I got home,' answered Marjorie, lightly, holding back from him. 'You were horrid.'

'I was fed up,' protested Ted. 'I've had the hell of a time, what with the auditors and housework and shopping and everything else. I hoped you'd be home when I got back from the office, with dinner ready and everything. When you weren't of course I got fed up with waiting for you. And when you turned up it got my goat to see that young pup Ely with his car and all calling you "Marjorie". That's how it was. Give us a kiss, old girl.'

He tried to draw her to him, but she twirled herself out of his hold, playing desperately for time.

'I don't think you deserve one,' she said.

'Oh, I do, ducky. Honest I do. I've been as good as gold all the time you were away.'

The armchair behind her barred her retreat, and he was able to take hold of her again. As his arms enfolded her she thought momentarily of George's arms round her, and she shuddered a little in her husband's grasp. Another thought of appalling clarity came to her. These were the arms that had dragged Dot's senseless body over to the gas oven, and the hairy hand that was patting her cheek had turned on the gas taps and killed her. That cleared her brain like a cold bath.

'Ducky!' said Ted. 'My precious baby! I've been lonely without you.'

He kissed her before she had time to prevent it, but on her averted cheek, not on the lips, which were sacred to George Ely. With Ted in this mood she could handle him more easily than in any other, fortunately. The hairy hands began to pat her, here and there. She braced herself to look up at him, appealingly.

'I'm so *tired*,' she said pitifully. 'There's been such a lot to do today.'

She did not have to act to obtain the effect she desired, she was mortally tired. The drawn look in her face would have melted a heart of stone.

'Tired, darling?' repeated Ted.

'Ever so tired.'

She made herself reach up and stroke his face; in the early days of her married life she had similarly made herself unwillingly hold the raw meat when she had to cut it up for stewing. She stroked his face, appealing with every fibre of her to this indulgent, sentimental side of him.

'You go straight to bed, dear,' she said. 'I'll be better tomorrow.'

Ted released her, to her inexpressible relief.

'Right you are, dear,' he said, forbearing and magnanimous. 'Are you coming now?'

'I'll be up in a minute. I've got one or two things to do first.'

Ted was just like Derrick in that he went to sleep as soon as he was in bed – provided he was expecting nothing of her. Marjorie wasted a little time downstairs, laying the breakfast, and found when she crept upstairs that her expectation was correct. Ted was fast asleep; she was able to undress and creep in beside him without rousing him. As she settled herself stealthily on her pillow it occurred to her that the events of the morning – tidying up The Guardhouse, driving up to London– seemed already to be weeks old. She wondered at it, before she, too, fell asleep, utterly worn out.

Sunday morning brought rain, the first heavy downpour for

three and a half weeks. It was welcome to London after the stifling days which preceded it. The pleasant smell of the dust in the streets being washed away came in through the bedroom windows as Marjorie dressed. She could hear Derrick and Anne chattering in Anne's bedroom when she went downstairs to light the gas under the kettle. To Marjorie, for some unknown reason of temperament, or because of some odd coincidence of circumstances – perhaps merely because of her nine hours of deep dreamless sleep – the morning seemed to be full of the promise of happiness, the grey skies and the steady pouring of the rain somehow contributing to it. She had no cares for the future as she went about her morning's work. Things were going to come right, she was sure; she did not even have to tell herself so – the knowledge was an intrinsic part of her.

She carried a nice trayful of breakfast up to Ted, and he lay late, as his pleasure was on Sunday mornings. The rain was heavy enough, indeed, to keep him at home all the rest of the morning, occupying himself with the newspaper and the Luxembourg wireless programme. On Sunday mornings he frequently went down to the Crown to meet his cronies of Saturday night, but to Ted this was not a desperately important engagement like Saturday evenings. He really did not mind missing it; especially as for some reason or other it was his custom, if he went to the Crown on Sunday morning, to drink gin-and-bitters – three or four gins-and-bitters – instead of his usual beer. And gin-and-bitters was bad for him, and he knew it even while he drank it. He was touchy and irritable after dinner if he had drunk gin-and-bitters before it. So that when the rain kept him at home he felt all the virtue of one who had valiantly resisted temptation.

Money was short after the last three weeks of bachelorhood, and it was good to think that he was three or four shillings richer as a result of intelligent self-denial. That little blonde girl whom he had met in Riddell's company last week had looked all right.

The next time he saw her he would try and get a word in with her when Riddell was busy and make a date with her for the pictures. Girls with a high-pitched laugh like that were generally pretty good if you could get them alone.

Ted had an expression by which he described the ideal existence. He called it 'the life of a lord'. This particular Sunday seemed to be approximating closely to it. The first essential was a complete absence of anything to do, no work to do, no odd jobs. There must also be absent the urge to do anything, which at rare intervals sometimes afflicted him and spoilt an otherwise promising day. Nothing to do, and all day to do it in, up to the evening. Breakfast in bed, and a long lie in, just as he had had this morning. Idleness so complete that he was not to be lured into breaking it by going out for a drink. A good dinner – that was another essential ingredient in the life of a lord. Then further idleness, lasting just so long that it was on the very point of beginning to pall. Not so that it really did pall, but so that one had the additional pleasure of knowing that it might and forestalling it, the desire for a drink coming at the exact identical moment when further doing nothing might become tedious.

Beer was good then. It blended perfectly with the other factors which play their part in the life of a lord, as though some master of music were building up some superb chord, adding note to note, each one giving further richness and harmony, not strange or unknown, but each in its way anticipated and expected and satisfying. Riddell was not there with his blonde, but Ted had not expected to see them – early closing day was when Riddell was about. That did not matter. The blonde would keep for a bit, sure enough. Madge was at home waiting for him.

Only sometimes was a new woman necessary to the life of a lord. In Ted's experience a woman was re-established high in his estimation by a few weeks of absence from or deprivation of her. She regained a large part of the charm of novelty and did not

need any tedious breaking-in. He was looking forward with positive eagerness to tonight. He did not dwell on the fiasco of last
night. That was past and done with. He had experienced yesterday an unnerving attack of fright, the first for a long time, which
had upset his temper very badly. It was quite groundless fright,
he knew, but fright was incompatible with the life of a lord. It
had led him both to await with eagerness the return of his family
and to behave like a bear when they arrived a little later than he
expected.

Today he had thrust away all memory of yesterday. His very
third tankard of beer satisfied the thirst and sense of something
lacking within him. He drank a fourth partly because of the
importunity of Lang at his side and partly because as an unnecessary luxury it accorded well with his mood, and then he walked
home through the gathering dusk and the Sunday evening crowds
– larger than usual tonight because a fine evening had succeeded
to a day of rain.

Marjorie was in the sitting-room sewing; with nearly every
garment owned by the family in need of washing (a task that
must be tackled tomorrow) she was mending reserve garments
hurriedly so as to maintain the supply until ironing and airing
should bring back into use all the pile of stuff which had accumulated today in the scullery. Ted stroked the back of her neck
as he crossed the room behind her, and then sank with a satisfied
sign into the other armchair.

'Well,' he said, in friendly fashion. 'I haven't heard much about
this holiday of yours yet. Have a good time?'

'Lovely,' said Marjorie, inspecting the darn she was completing
in a pair of Derrick's breeches.

'You had good enough weather, anyway. God it was hot up
here in London! And those dam' auditors raised merry hell I can
tell you.'

'Did they?'

'How did young Ely get on with you and Mother? All right?'

'Yes.'

'Once or twice I wanted him home again. The auditors were asking questions about his books. I could answer 'em all right, but it meant the hell of a sweat for me. But I thought if I called him back it would mean you'd have to pay train fares yesterday, so I put up with it.'

Ted waited for a word of thanks after that, but no word came. Marjorie was stitching feverishly. Ted tried a direct question.

'Did his car go alright?'

'Yes. No. We had a puncture once.'

Ted could see that Marjorie was so preoccupied with her sewing that she could hardly pay him any attention at all.

'Only one? I don't think that's so bad.'

'Just a minute,' said Marjorie, putting down her sewing. 'I left something on the oven. I'll be back in a minute.'

Ted heard her cross the hall into the kitchen after shutting the sitting-room door. He was quite philosophic about her preoccupation. He could remember the time during their early married life when she would have put down her needlework the moment he came in, and would have listened with sympathy and attention to what he had to say about the auditors. But they had been married so long now. What with the house and the kids she had plenty on her mind. He looked at the clock. He would give her half an hour more for her needlework and her other jobs. Then she would have to put it away and attend to him.

Meanwhile Marjorie had left ajar the door from the kitchen into the garden, beside the dustbin, and was creeping as silently as she could down the path to the end gate. Half way down the whistle that she had heard already five or six times since Ted's return rang out again, more loudly and imperiously than ever. Frightened, she exerted herself to quicken her pace and yet remain silent. Just inside the gate, in the shadow of the elderberry tree, she found herself in George's arms.

'Darling,' she whispered. 'You mustn't whistle so loud. I heard you the first time.'

'Why didn't you come, then?'

It was hard for George to keep his voice down to a whisper, he was beside himself with anxiety and impatience.

'I couldn't. Ted had just come in. It would have looked funny if I'd come out the minute he walked into the room.'

'Ted? Is he home?'

'Yes. He's just come in, I said.'

'What did he want?'

'Nothing. We were just talking about the holiday. Kiss me, darling.'

She wanted George's kisses. Besides, she knew that if he were to kiss her he would lose some of this painful anxiety he was displaying. She sensed his tension dwindling as she fondled him. But something else had to be said as well, and immediately. A train rattled along the cutting, reminding her of the passage of time.

'I can't stop a minute,' she whispered, mouth to his mouth. 'Ted'll think it's funny if I'm away too long.'

'Ted this and Ted that,' said George fiercely in the darkness. 'What's all this fuss about Ted?'

'Nothing, darling, except that he mustn't guess.'

'Nothing? You're sure of that?'

'Of course, darling.'

'You slept with him last night!'

'Yes dear. But I only slept with him. Nothing else, dear. You know I was going to.'

'Yes.'

That was part of George's anguish, the thought of that bed, and Marjorie in her nightdress, and Grainger lusting for her.

'Has he tried to make love to you since you came back?' he demanded. He wanted to know the very worst.

'Only a little, dear. Last night, when he came in. But he left off when I asked him to. Honest truth, sweetheart.'

'Today?'

'No. Nothing at all. Nothing.'

It was after she had said that, in all honesty, that Marjorie remembered, quailing, the touch on the back of her neck which Ted has bestowed on her on his entry. She knew Ted well enough to know what this portended.

'You won't let him?'

'No I won't. Of course I won't. I couldn't, darling.'

To reassure him she would gladly have told him now about Dot, but with Ted waiting impatiently in the sitting room there was no time for that now.

'Kiss me!' he said, fiercely.

She kissed him, her heart going out to him as it always did. It was intoxicating to be loved like this, and frightening, too.

'Oh, I must go back now, darling,' she said. She tore herself from his grasp with the same effort of will with which she mastered the passion within her.

'Promise me!' he said. 'Swear it!'

'Oh, I promise, darling. Really I do. Goodbye, darling.'

She ran, a-tiptoe, up the path again. She crept into the kitchen, and with infinite precaution she closed the kitchen door without a sound. She had to stand still for a space, her hand to her breast, waiting for her breathing to grow more easy and the tumultuous beating of her heart to slow down. There was a mirror in the scullery before which she could tidy her hair. Then she made herself walk with her usual firm step back into the sitting room. She tried to slip unobtrusively into her chair and take up her sewing again, but it was hard to be unob-trusive with Ted sitting there with nothing to do except watch her. When Ted looked at her continuously like that she knew what it meant.

'You're busy this evening,' said Ted.

'There's a lot to get done to get straight again,' she answered.

She tried to speak mildly, indifferently. She wanted no edge of complaint to creep into her voice, because that would make Ted angry, and she was frightened of him when he was angry. At the same time she knew she had been longer in the garden than she should have been. Ted might have come out and found her absent from the kitchen, found nothing on the stove; he might have guessed about George. The groundless fear made her tremble. She stabbed her left forefinger through the stuff with her needle, cruelly, under the nail, and she had to bear the pain motionless for fear of drawing attention to her own clumsiness. She was terrified. As she kept her eyes on her work she had a curious feeling that Ted, two yards away, was swelling and increasing his size until he was nearly filling the room, suffocating her. It was the same feeling as during a bilious nightmare. She experienced revulsion and a sensation of sickness. Hatred and fear and loathing were overcoming her. Had she been alone she would have broken down into a storm of sobs, but with Ted watching her she had to remain calm and indifferent, bent over her sewing, fighting with all her power to regain her strength and her wits.

'Well,' said Ted, 'you'd better buck up and finish what you're doing, because I shall want all your attention in half a minute.'

There was only the one excuse she could make. She had thought out the pros and cons of that excuse earlier in the day. She had not wanted to use it; she would have preferred to have settled the matter more definitely and satisfactorily, in accordance with the high resolves she had made in George's arms three days ago – the excuse would merely bring a postponement with no sort of permanence, and she was sensible enough to know that there is always danger in excuses and postponement; more danger still – much more – when the excuse is not only false but its falsity is certain to be revealed in course of time.

But her shaken nerves compelled her to use it; she could not bear to contemplate any more heroic course. She told her lie as bravely as she could.

'It's a curse, isn't it?' she added, lightly.

'Yes,' snapped Ted, cross and disappointed. He felt that this served him right for his sentimental moderation of yesterday.

15

Mrs Clair never seemed to sleep nowadays. There can be no doubt that she did sleep, but it was for short periods of which she later had no recollection, alternated with long wakeful intervals through the night during which she lay in bed, watching the faintly lit squares of the windows grow at first darker and then, as dawn approached, steadily brighter and brighter. Those wakeful intervals never seemed too long to her. She did not fret over her insomnia, but rather welcomed it. She felt she was employing her time to good profit, thinking out her plans and hating Ted – she had a lingering suspicion that merely by lying in bed and pouring out her venom in thought she was doing him some harm, not nearly as much as he deserved, but enough to constitute some sort of payment on account until the final settlement.

On Monday morning she was not content to lie in bed until her usual time for getting up; she had plenty to do today. She rose early, and crept downstairs quietly so as not to disturb Mr Ely – by listening at his door intently she could hear his regular breathing. He was asleep at last; she knew that he too, had spent much of the night sleepless, for she had heard his light switch on and off and had heard him turning restlessly in his bed. She knew what was troubling him, she had seen his face when he came home last night. It was satisfactory to her to know that before very long everything would come right and he would be happy as the day was long, with dear little Marjorie, and with

Derrick and Anne saved for ever from the clutches of that beast Ted, that devil Ted.

Her early rising enabled her to do two full hours' work on the pile of accumulated washing that had to be done; she was glad to get it out of the way to leave her free for the activities she saw ahead of her. She scrubbed and she rinsed. She made her way out into the little garden and put up her clothes line. It was mid August now, and that early hour of the morning bore with it the faint hint of approaching Autumn, only just noticable and yet sweepingly comprehensive, calling up to the memory all Autumn in a single breath – morning fog, and changing colours, and falling leaves, and the bonfires of Saturday afternoon gardeners; laying the first fires ready for the first chilly evening, roly-poly pudding instead of tapioca for dinner; and she must look out her winter coat to see that it really would last another winter.

This winter, thought Mrs Clair, busily pegging out the washing on the line, would be a really happy one. Although dear little Dot was gone, Marjorie and the children would be free and happy. Mrs Clair, with the pale morning sky shining into her eyes as she reached up to the clothes line, thought that when that was all settled, when that beast Ted had met with the fate he deserved, she could allow herself to fall away into old age and contemplate her end with equanimity. Meanwhile it was time to leave off washing and go in to call Mr Ely and to see he started for the office in time. It would be the first morning for three weeks; she had better see that everything was ready.

Mr Ely's face at breakfast was drawn and pale despite the tan his holiday had given him. She knew what the poor boy was suffering. Never mind, it would not be long now. She coaxed him into eating his scrambled egg – she knew already what were his favourite dishes – and saw him out of the door at twenty minutes to nine, in plenty of time for the office. Then she diligently applied herself to the routine tasks of the day, the sweeping and cleaning, washing up the breakfast things, peeling the potatoes ready for dinner. Now it was time to inspect the things on the line. The woollens could stay, but the whites and colours were ready for ironing and the sheets for mangling.

At eleven o'clock she was free for a space; she looked at the clock as she had done a dozen times already and made a fresh calculation. Ely's lunch time was one-thirty – he went out to lunch when Ted came back – and she had an hour in hand. She put on her hat and gloves and with her handbag and her leather carrying bag, she set off towards the High Street shops. She was determined upon wasting no time at all before making everything ready in anticipation of her plans.

Fortune favoured her immediately – a clear example of the reward in store for those who put themselves in the way of good fortune.

Mrs Taylor was just approaching Mountain's Café when Mrs Clair met her.

'Good morning,' said Mrs Clair.

'Good morning,' said Mrs Taylor, 'You *do* look brown. Did you have a nice holiday?'

'Yes, thank you. We all enjoyed it, although of course we missed my son-in-law very much.'

'Of course,' said Mrs Taylor.

There was a halt in the conversation, as if the two women were wondering what to say next.

'Where's Mrs Posket?' asked Mrs Clair. So inseparable were Mrs Taylor and Mrs Posket that it was an inevitable question to ask, in the unlikely event of Mrs Taylor being encountered alone.

'She's away,' said Mrs Taylor. 'She went on her holiday yesterday, the day after you got back.'

'I expect you miss her,' said Mrs Clair.

'I do a bit,' replied Mrs Taylor a little ruefully.

'Have you seen anything of Marjorie today?'

'She was just putting her washing out when I came back,' answered Mrs Taylor. 'It did look a lot.'

'I expect so, after three weeks' holiday. I'll try and go in some time today and help. Well, I suppose we've both our shopping to do. Goodbye, Mrs Taylor.'

Mrs Clair, walking purposefully along the High Street pavement, was rejoiced with the information she had received. She had been a little worried about Mrs Posket – there was no knowing what harm a nosy and interfering woman of that sort might do. Especially with that lane along the railway at the back of the house, and George Ely going out in the evenings and coming back worried and preoccupied. It was good to hear that Mrs Posket was out of harm's way for ten days or so. And it was only natural that Marjorie should have a lot of washing to do today. Mrs Clair would have liked to go round and help her with the ironing; perhaps, if all went well, she would have an opportunity later in the day. Otherwise, Marjorie would have to struggle along as best she might – Mrs Clair was not to be deflected from her present designs by a consideration as minor as Marjorie's comfort during one single day. Soon Marjorie would be free and happy.

The bank in the High Street was crowded, as always on a Monday morning, with the local shopkeepers paying in their weekend takings. Normally Mrs Clair was thoughtful enough not to dream of bothering the hard-pressed cashiers at such a time, but today it was different. She wanted to have everything ready.

She waited her turn patiently until a cashier was free.

'Good morning, Mrs Clair.'

'Good morning. Would you mind telling me how much my balance is?'

She knew, of course, the amount within a pound or two, but she wanted to be quite sure. The cashier dived back into the office part of the bank, and then returned with a folded piece of paper which he passed across the counter. Mrs Clair read it – £52.10. 11. Carefully she wrote out a cheque for fifty pounds payable to cash, cancelled the crossing, and passed the cheque to the cashier.

'One pound notes please,' she said quietly.

The cashier's eyebrows rose a little as he read the cheque. It was with some slight reluctance that he handed over to her an envelope full of money.

'That's a lot of money, Mrs Clair,' he said. 'I should be careful with it, if I were you.'

'Oh, I shall be very careful. Very careful,' said Mrs Clair, quite calmly.

She shut the money away in her handbag and made her way out of the bank. That was the first step taken. Whatever happened now she had fifty pounds in notes that could not be traced. It was only a precautionary measure. She thought it most unlikely that she would ever have to use them, more likely in a week or two's time, when everything was settled, she would be paying the money back into her account, submitting meekly to the cashier's amused smile, obviously a woman who did not know how to manage her money affairs. It was worthwhile suffering that in exchange for being on the safe side.

In her walk along the High Street she had now reached Carter's Ironmongery Stores, and she went inside. Mr Carter himself came forward to serve her.

'Good morning,' said Mrs Clair. 'I want a hatchet. Something to chop up wood and things.'

'A hatchet, Madam? Certainly. There's this little one at six-and-nine. And a larger size at eight-and-nine. And here's another make, which I should recommend on the whole. The edge is chromium steel, warranted not to rust or stain. Marvellous value at eight-and-six, madam.'

Mrs Clair looked at the deadly things lying on the counter

where Mr Carter laid them, at their glittering edges, and cunningly curved handles. It was strange how easy they were to buy. They repelled her so that she did not want to touch them, but she forced herself to put up her hand and pick one of them off the counter. She balanced it carefully in her hand – in later years it was to be one of Mr Carter's most vivid memories, the sight of that nice old lady standing in his shop thoughtfully testing the balance of the hatchet.

'Thank you,' she said. 'I'll have this one.'

'Eight-and-six, madam? Certainly, madam. Shall I send it for you, madam?'

'No thank you. I can take it with me.'

The hatchet, tied up in brown paper with all the old-fashioned care Mr Carter habitually employed, weighed heavy in the carrying bag on her wrist as she emerged once more into the High Street. Tomlin's clock told her that she still had twenty minutes to spare before returning to prepare Mr Ely's dinner. She spent those twenty minutes in walking quickly through the suburban streets completing her purchases. She turned down Marvel Lane so as to pass the police station. She walked up Simon Street, her quick, kindly eyes darting from side to side as she looked for Sergeant Hale. She did not see him.

It was, of course, as she realized, being far too optimistic to hope to encounter him in a mere twenty minutes' walk. It might be days before she would met him apparently by chance in the street. Never mind, she would go on trying. Probably, she told herself, she had days to spare, and if she had not, if matters moved to a crisis before she met him, it was not of great importance. Her plans were complete without a meeting with Sergeant Hale. The meeting was only one more precaution, one additional embellishment, like drawing out her money from the bank – not like the purchase of the hatchet, which was an integral and essential part of her plan.

When George Ely came home he found a pleasant dinner waiting for him, of cold meat and potatoes and salad and a milk pudding, and a nice piece of cheese. On the side table in the dining room lay Mrs Clair's leather carrying bag and two or three parcels.

'Goodness me!' said Mrs Clair, as his eye rested on them. 'I shouldn't have left these things here. I must have put them down and forgotten to take them out into the kitchen. Of course, there's been plenty to do today, just back from the holidays.'

'Of course,' said Ely.

Mrs Clair began to bundle the packages together. Out of the carrying bag she took the hatchet, uncovered – she had removed the paper in which Mr Carter had so carefully tied it.

'That's a fierce-looking thing,' said Ely.

'Isn't it?' agreed Mrs Clair. 'I've been wanting one for a long time, with all that chopping to do outside. I think it's a good one, don't you?'

She passed the thing over, and Ely stood weighing it in his hand, just as Mrs Clair had done in the shop.

'It seems all right,' said Ely, carelessly, returning it.

Consciously, he thought no more about it after Mrs Clair had achieved her aim. In future Ely would always be aware of the existence of that hatchet; its sudden appearance would not surprise him, or cause him to stop and think for a moment. Mrs Clair, in the exaltation of spirit resulting from the hatred which consumed her, was a cunning and farsighted psychologist.

When she had washed up the dinner things, and seen Ely off to the office again, and finally disposed of the washing, she put on her hat and jacket again. She would have liked to have gone to help Marjorie, but at present there was something else more urgent to be done to forward her plans – only a precautionary measure, like the withdrawal of the money from the bank, but one which she judged it preferable to carry out, rather than smooth Marjorie's path for her. Only a few days now, and Marjorie's path would be quite smooth; surely she could endure till then.

Neatly gloved and shod, wearing her unobtrusive little hat and coat and skirt, Mrs Clair set out to walk the suburban streets again. Up one steep street and down another; along the High Street; down Marvel Lane and past the police station; back again to the High Street; up Simon Street nearly to the corner of Harrison Way; she spent the afternoon walking demurely in constant wide sweeps through the district. She might have been engaged upon any innocent errand in the eyes of the casual passers-by – shopping or going to visit friends or to confirm a maid's reference. By five o'clock she was woefully tired, and committed the extravagance of going into Mountain's Café for a cup of tea, but she was out again at five-fifteen, walking swiftly along, her bright eyes searching every by-road at each corner that she passed.

At last she saw him, when she had only ten minutes left to her before she was due to go home in readiness for Ely's return from the office. It was Sergeant Hale; walking in all his imposing burliness down Cameron Road. She saw him just in time to be able to turn naturally in that direction, as if that had been her intention before seeing him. She crossed the road diagonally on a course which brought her into his path.

Sergeant Hale saw her approaching – it was a month or more since he saw her last, but thanks to his policeman's memory he recognized her again. He could tell as he looked at her walking towards him that she was ready and willing to talk to him – some subtle indication about her carriage showed it. She had been ready to talk to him the last time they met, too. Sergeant Hale shifted Mrs Clair from one pigeonhole to another in his mind. He put her now along with the bores and the useless time-wasters low down in their order, it is true, but one of them, nevertheless. Not so high up as to be rigorously avoided, either. Just one of the people with whom he would always have to exchange a few words, to no profit whatever, and merely consuming time amounting in the aggregate to a considerable total which might well be otherwise employed.

'Good afternoon, madam,' he said, with resigned politeness.

'Good afternoon, sergeant. I hope you are quite well?'

'Quite well, thank you, madam. And you?'

'Very well, thank you. I've just had a nice holiday by the sea.'

'That's good,' said Sergeant Hale.

He would have passed on with that, but Mrs Clair stood in such a position that he could only pass her with an appearance of rudeness.

'My daughter was with me,' said Mrs Clair, in gossipy fashion. 'The one who had to give evidence at the inquest.'

'I remember her, madam.'

'I was glad she had a holiday,' went on Mrs Clair. 'That dreadful business pulled her down so.'

'I'm not surprised to hear it, madam.'

'But I do wish,' said Mrs Clair with finality, 'that my son-in-law had come too. He couldn't get away, because he's working terribly hard at the office. I'm very worried about him.'

'Indeed, madam?'

'Yes, his manner is quite strange sometimes. I'm afraid all this work is getting on his nerves, especially coming so soon after the inquest. But I don't know why I'm telling you all this. I ought to be telling a doctor if I talk about it to anyone. Goodbye, sergeant.'

'Good afternoon, madam.'

Sergeant Hale walked on in burly dignity. Mentally he shifted Mrs Clair several places lower down in his list of bores and time-wasters. She could stop talking of her own volition, which of itself was nearly enough to disqualify her from the classification altogether. And what she had said had at least a little interest for a police officer. It was always as well to hear about people who were 'strange in their manner' and whose work was 'getting on their nerves', even though he had to listen to irrelevant matter about holidays at the same time, and even though (as years of experience had proved) not once in a thousand times was there any sequel of interest to the police. The thousandth time a bit of gossip of that sort might well be useful.

16

On Monday evening Mrs Clair sat in her daughter's sitting-room. Marjorie's face was pinched with fatigue and worry, and Mrs Clair's heart bled for her.

'Ted's out, I suppose,' she said.

'Yes,' answered Marjorie listlessly.

'Did you get your washing finished all right?'

'I had to leave the ironing until tomorrow,' replied Marjorie.

That was a postponement which was just excusable in the eyes of the good housewife if the washing had been heavy or conditions unfavourable. Today had been good washing weather, though. Marjorie must have had a busy day.

'Were the children quite good?'

'Oh yes.'

'You'll notice a big difference when young Derrick is old enough to go to school, too,' said Mrs Clair, consolatory.

'I suppose so,' said Marjorie.

'I remember how it was with me when little Dot was old enough for school,' went on Mrs Clair. 'That was just when the war started and your dear father joined his regiment.'

Marjorie did not answer for a moment. Her head was lifted as though she was listening for something.

'Yes, of course,' she said hastily, at length.

Someone was whistling in the lane along the railway. Mrs Clair heard it, and yet, sharp as she was, she thought nothing of it.

'Did you think you could hear the children, dear,' she asked, solicitously.

'No. Yes. No,' said Marjorie.

'I didn't hear anything,' said Mrs Clair.

The whistling came again, and Marjorie moved restlessly in her chair. She could not think how to deal with this new situation. It was only then that her mother realized the connection between her daughter's present abstraction and the whistling in the lane. She made a little gesture of settling herself more comfortably in her chair, as a little hint to Marjorie that she had not the least intention of leaving for a space. Marjorie eyed her uncomfortably.

'The evenings are drawing in now,' said Mrs Clair, in conversational tone. 'It's getting dark quite early this week.'

'Yes,' said Marjorie.

'I suppose they're just beginning to feel the autumn rush at the office,' went on Mrs Clair. 'Has Ted noticed it yet? Mr Ely hasn't said anything to me about it.'

'I – I think so,' said Marjorie, desperately.

'It's the sensible people,' said Mrs Clair, 'who order their gas fires early. I've got no patience with the ones who leave everything to the last minute, have you?'

'No,' said Marjorie.

The whistling in the lane was growing more imperative and more impatient. She was positively writhing in her chair. Conversation languished in the face of her obvious distaste for it.

'I'm feeling dreadfully tired,' said Marjorie, at last, in sheer desperation. 'I think I'll go to bed.'

'Yes, I certainly should if I were you, dear,' said Mrs Clair, solicitously. 'Are you going to have a bath first? Shall I come up with you and see you into bed?'

'Oh no, I shall be all right,' said Marjorie. She rose to her feet so as to drive her mother to rising too; the whistling outside seemed to be growing angry.

'You're certainly looking tired, dear,' said Mrs Clair, making ready with maddening slowness to take her departure. 'You must look after yourself.'

'Yes, I will, Mother,' said Marjorie, bustling to the door.

'Poor lamb!' said Mrs Clair, kissing her cheek.

Outside in the street she murmured 'poor lamb!' to herself again as she set off towards Dewsbury Road. Her heart was filled with sorrow for her daughter. It had hurt her to linger there so maddeningly when Marjorie's nerves were at full stretch, but she had done it deliberately, and for her daughter's ultimate good. She realized acutely that she must drive the two lovers into exasperation, heat them up to boiling point, cost them what it might. It was a shame to treat her daughter so, and poor Mr Ely, but it was all for the best.

Meanwhile in the darkness of the garden by the elderberry tree there were explanations, almost recriminations.

'Dear, what a long time you've been! Why didn't you come, dear? You heard me whistling.'

'I couldn't, darling. Mother was there.'

'You could have said you'd got something to do in the kitchen.'

'She'd have come out with me if I'd said that. Besides, she'd know that I didn't have anything to do in the kitchen at this time of night. I couldn't come, dear. In the end I had to say I was going to bed before she'd go. I'm terribly sorry, dear.'

'Where's Grainger?'

'He's out. But I don't know when he'll be back. I can't stop a minute, dear. Oh my dear – '

It was all very well to kiss and cling together there in the darkness. The feeling of frustration and exasperation persisted, was intensified, if anything. Marjorie could feel her lover's irritation, and fear was added to her bitterness.

'Tell me you love me, dear,' she whispered. 'Tell me you'll always love me.'

'Oh – I love you, dear,' he said, for perhaps the hundredth time since he had rescued her, but this time there was something in his voice – almost as if he had added a 'but' after his declaration.

'This is beastly,' he said, a moment or two later, in expansion of that implied 'but.' And then he voiced the question which Marjorie had first asked.

'What are we going to *do*?'

Marjorie did her best to soothe him.

'Don't worry, dear,' she whispered, urgently. 'It'll come right. I swear it'll come right.'

Unconsciously she was echoing the words her lover had said to her. Exactly as he had just echoed the question she had asked of him. If she lost him she would be without a friend in the world, she felt. There would be misery and doubt, danger and difficulty, and a vast emptiness in her life, the thought of which absolutely appalled her. She could foresee no sort of future even with George as her lover, but if George were to forsake her, if George's patience were to come to an end, it would be the end of everything. She felt she would die in that case.

She strained him to her breast, and his passivity, almost resistance, warned her afresh of his discontent.

'I love you, dear,' she whispered.

She wanted to comfort him, to make him more reconciled to his circumstances. All that she knew of men, nearly, all that she knew of how to please and gratify them, was what Ted had taught her – Ted, the possessive, Ted, the avid of gratification, Ted the selfish, the lustful, the dirty minded.

'I love you, dear,' she said again. 'All of you. And I'm all yours too, darling. You could do what you like to me. Beat me if you liked. Kill me if you wanted to. I belong to you, darling, absolutely, every bit of me.'

Her whisperings were maddening, like drink, to a boy (for temperamentally that was all he was) in the throes of first love. And they played on his possessiveness, too, as they were bound to do.

'I hate Grainger!' he whispered, fiercely.

'He's nothing to me. He never has been anything, never will be anything, darling, I swear it,' she whispered back; nor was she being intentionally untruthful. 'I don't know why I married him. He's hateful. I suppose I wanted to have children or something. Or I suppose I never thought I'd ever meet anyone like you, darling. It's you that I love. He'll never lay a finger on me, never again, darling, Never.'

She had three days at least still in hand before that problem would arise again with Ted. She could make promises freely when the crisis was as far off as that; and she had every intention of fulfilling them, too. It was not just to pacify George that she made those promises. She was making them to herself as well, stiffening herself ready for the struggle to come. She would never be weak again – she felt nauseated when she remembered how she had prostituted herself to Ted in the past merely for fear of trouble. Never again would she do that. In mad exaltation she promised, whispering feverishly.

And as she did so there came a sudden change in the lighting of the garden – the sitting-room light had been switched on and was shining through the French window.

'Ted's come back!' said Marjorie, in a panic.

She tore herself from George's arms, consumed with a mad fear of discovery.

'Goodbye, dear,' she whispered – she just allowed herself time for that – and then ran tiptoe up the garden path. She opened the door into the kitchen cautiously, but as she was in the act of doing so she heard the switch of the electric light being turned on. She faced Ted across the kitchen; he had entered by one door as she had entered by the other.

'Where the devil have you been?' demanded Ted crossly. 'I thought the house was empty.'

Marjorie's wavering mind grasped at an earlier recollection of the only occasion when she had had to go out into the garden at night.

'Cats,' she said, and once again she had begun the lie she found that the rest came more easily. 'They were yowling dreadfully – I was afraid in case they woke Derrick up. So I went out to shoo them away.'

'Oh,' said Ted, and then, grudgingly, 'All right.'

Marjorie's heart was beating painfully as she made herself walk quietly back into the sitting room. She wanted just to drop into her chair, but with an effort of self-control she compelled herself to lower herself down quietly and normally. She was terribly afraid in case the fluttering of her heart betrayed itself in the pallor of her cheeks. She wanted to look away from Ted for concealment, but she dare not. She had to meet his eyes.

'Had your mother here tonight?' asked Ted.

'Yes,' answered Marjorie. That was truth, anyway.

'Thought so. She always shuts the front gate after her.'

That was a proof of how sharp Ted was, how narrow her escape had been. Marjorie knew that tonight she had used up all her margin of safety. One discovery of suspicious circumstances Ted might pass, but two, never. And her mind flinched from analysing in cold blood the possibilities of what might happen if Ted discovered her intrigue. Ted would be mad with rage, she knew – and not mad in the ordinary sense of being uncontrollably angry, either. He would be cruel, heartless, brutal. Of all the affronts that could be put upon him the unfaithfulness of his wife would be the most unbearable, the one he would avenge most savagely. For her, divorce and separation from the children; for George, dismissal and starvation – those would be the least penalties he would exact. He might beat her. She had an instant vision of herself screaming with pain under his hands – twice already in their married life he had struck her with intent to hurt, but this would be worse a hundred times.

As another thought came into her head she sat up rigid in her chair. He might kill her. He had killed before, with neither pity nor mercy. He was cunning enough, and desperate enough, and savage enough. If ever she tried to defend herself from him by disclosing to him her knowledge of his crime, and by the threat of invoking the law, he would undoubtedly kill her when he saw himself endangered. She was in deadly peril, peril which might become imminent at any moment.

'What the devil's the matter with you?' asked Ted suddenly.

Marjorie extricated herself from the bad dreams which were encompassing her and looked round at him, as mildly and as enquiringly as she could.

'You're sitting there puffing and blowing like that,' said Ted. 'You've gone as white as a sheet, too.'

There was still the same old woman's lie that she could fall back on, thank God.

'I've got a bit of a pain,' she said. 'This business of mine – I've been doing too much washing today.'

'I suppose that's my fault,' snapped Ted. 'Anyone would think you hadn't had a holiday all this last three weeks. I wish I'd never let you go, if this is how you come back. I suppose you won't get straight again in the house for months now. Of course, it doesn't matter about me at all.'

Ted felt aggrieved, possibly even with justification, although he himself was not sure why. With the passing years their attitude towards each other had altered so slowly that the change had been imperceptible. But seven years ago, say, if Marjorie had been compelled to be absent from him for three weeks, she would on her return have been overflowing with affection and tenderness for him. She would have chattered to him, sought his attention, followed him with her eyes. Without actually drawing the comparison Ted was acutely sensitive to the slow change in her tonight. He wanted the flattery of her glance, of her moral dependence upon him. It irritated him unconsciously that she should be able to get along without him.

He was not acute enough, or Marjorie had been too guarded, or the occasion had not been opportune enough, for him to notice any decided change since Dot's death, or since Marjorie's holiday. At present, all very indefinitely, he was looking forward to the time close at hand when he would subject her to himself again – he knew by experience that that was a good way of reducing her afresh to dependence on him – and alternatively he was resolving, unconsciously and vaguely, to administer to her if necessary some sort of lesson which would teach her the duty that a wife owes a husband who earns her bread for her. She was beginning to need one, he thought. He would make sure about it next Thursday. That was his final decision, arrived at after counting up the days on his fingers.

17

'Are you playing tennis this evening?' asked Mrs Clair conversationally, while George Ely ate his tea on his return from the office on Tuesday.

'No,' said George. He looked out of the window as he spoke; the question had set his mind to work at once debating how soon it would be dark enough for him to go round to the lane beside the railway.

To go there each evening had become a habit with him already, although it was a habit against which he chafed. Other men could meet their girls in the light of day, could flaunt the friendship of which they were so proud, but he could not. He could not even receive telephone calls at this office, for fear lest Grainger should answer. By the time each evening came he was full of the desire to see Marjorie, full of anxiety lest any accident should have befallen her. For an hour before darkness came he was looking forward with eagerness to the moment when she should come to him.

And yet he was experienced enough by now to anticipate bitterly the disillusionments which the evening would bring. He could foresee the minutes of nervous waiting, consumed with anxiety lest Ted should be detaining her. Then there might be five minutes in the shadow of the elderberry tree – five minutes of whispering so that Mrs Taylor should not hear, five minutes of worry lest Grainger should come stealing out upon them, five minutes with the rain dripping on them if it should happen to be raining. Then Marjorie would have to go back to Ted, and he would have to return to his lodgings, jangled and irritable and upset, with another night and another day to face and then the same ordeal to be repeated. He was already showing signs of the strain, as Mrs Clair, reading his face, was quick to observe.

He showed them, too, when Marjorie came down to him at the end of the garden.

'Where's Grainger?' he asked.

'He's listening to the wireless. It's all right for the present – there's variety tonight and he likes that.'

'So I can't come in?'

'No, dear, and – and – I won't be able to stop long.'

'When do you think you will be able to?'

'I don't know, dear, I can't ever tell beforehand what Ted's going to be doing.'

She kissed him, she did her best to cram gratification into those fleeting seconds. Another idea came to him at that moment.

'Can't we go out together one evening?' he asked. 'Go up West somewhere? Pictures or something?'

'Ooh, wouldn't that be nice,' said Marjorie. It was years since she had been 'up West' with a man. The thought of doing so again was entrancing.

'Well can't we?' persisted George.

'Yes, I suppose we could,' said Marjorie, doubtfully. She had thought of it before. 'I could get Mother to come in for the evening. Then it wouldn't matter what Ted wanted to do.'

She stopped then, abruptly. The last time she had gone up to town was when she had been to visit Millicent Dunne. Dot had come in to mind the children then, and Dot had been dead when she returned.

'Well, let's do it then. Let's go – let's go tomorrow,' said George.

That was how it came about that Marjorie went up to town on Wednesday night in the 7.5 train. She only just caught it, running wildly down the stairs as the train came in, with George fuming on the platform. She was so breathless that she had neither words nor kisses for George until they had passed two stations on the way up – she could only smile at him faintly while recovering her breath. She had had to tell Ted that she was going up to see Millicent Dunne and win his reluctant consent, and she had had to tell her mother the same story. During the morning she had telephoned to Millicent at the factory where she was the welfare supervisor.

'Hullo, Mill,' she said. 'This is Marjorie speaking, Marjorie Grainger.'

'Hullo, Marjorie. Did you have a good holiday?'

'Yes thanks.' Marjorie with so much on her mind actually had to stop and think to what holiday Millicent was referring. 'What I wanted to say was I'm going out this evening and I wanted to tell Mother and Ted that I'm coming to see you. Is that all right, Mill?'

'M'm, I suppose so,' said Millicent, after a moment's pause. 'What are you up to, young woman?'

'Nothing, Mill, Nothing special. I just want to go out this once. That's all.'

'Well, take a spinster's advice and don't do it too often.'

This evening Marjorie had to give Ted his tea and put the children to bed, and Ted had been surly and obstructive as he always was on those rare occasions when Marjorie was going out to enjoy herself, and Derrick had been naughty as he always was, too, on the same occasion. Mother had come while Marjorie was frantically dressing herself in her blue coat and skirt and her one special pair of silk stockings – and Mother's arrival meant that she had given George his tea and that George would be waiting already at the station.

'I can't stop a minute if I'm going to catch the train,' said Marjorie, struggling with her suspenders. She had not stopped to put her gloves on, but she had run all the way up Harrison Way to the station. No wonder she was breathless when she sunk into the empty carriage whose door George held open for her as she came flying down the stairs.

Yet despite such an inauspicious start the middle part of the evening had been a decided success. Marjorie suggested that they should dine at the little Italian restaurant to which Millicent had taken her, and George (who hardly knew one restaurant from another) agreed. She smiled at him delightedly across the table as the waiter, romantically speaking broken English, made suggestions as to what they should eat. It was much more thrilling to dine in the West End with a handsome young man than with Millicent Dunne, who had been at school with her. At Marjorie's suggestion they drank Chianti; Marjorie could not have named any wines other than Chianti, port, and champagne, and she knew that the last named was expensive while port was something teetotallers drank in public houses; both logic and experience told her that Chianti was the thing to drink at dinner in the West End, and was what everyone drank.

It was marvellously romantic to drink red wine, and to eat hors d'oeuvres – to have a selection from a dozen different dishes all on her plate at once. The peculiar thrill of that would have been hard to analyse even if Marjorie had tried, which she naturally did not. Then a fillet of plaice, and a piece of chicken, and an ice; a cup of coffee and one of George's cigarettes – for the first time in her life Marjorie found herself really enjoying a cigarette – she had not smoked more than a couple of dozen in her life before. She took George's arm in ecstasy as they walked out along the crowded pavement. This was romance, life as it ought to be lived, and George was a marvellously clever man to have thought of doing it. They had three-and-sixpenny seats at a cinema, and saw a film which Marjorie wanted to see; it was a special joy to think that the benighted people in the suburbs would have to wait two or three months before it would be shown in the local cinemas.

Everything seemed to be going right. Even in the train coming home they were left alone in their compartment before they had travelled half way, and Marjorie could throw herself into George's arms and tell him once more how much she had enjoyed herself, and how much she loved him, and they could kiss, madly and passionately. It was while they clung to each other, lip to lip, that the joy of the evening began to fade; it was those kisses, maddening, delirious which started the trouble over again. Twice they had to draw apart when the train stopped at stations, and each time Marjorie came back to him, her slender body limp with surrender in his arms and her knee against his.

They were dizzy with passion when they got out of the train and walked up the steps to Simon Street. George drew her into the darkness of the lane beside the railway.

'Somebody might see!' protested Marjorie feebly, but next moment she was in his arms again.

'Oh, I don't want to leave you, darling,' she whispered. 'I don't want to have to go home.'

She added fuel to his flames by what she said to him. Ted had taught her, on their honeymoon years ago, how to rouse a man's passion. She did it instinctively now, the eloquence of her lips aided by her unresisting body as it hinted as what could not be told in words.

'Wouldn't it be lovely, dear,' she said 'if I didn't have to leave you? If we were going to spend the night together. Would you like that, dear? Would you like to sleep with me?'

'Yes – oh yes,' said George.

'We haven't ever spent a whole night together,' said Marjorie.

'Oh, I'd love to wake up in the morning and see your face beside me on the pillow. You look nice with your hair ruffled, darling.'

'Oh, I wish we could,' said George. 'I wish to God – '

He wished for so many things that he could not begin to list them. Nor was he helped by the up train, which passed ten minutes after the down train, rattling along the cutting below them.

'I'll have to go in when the next train comes,' said Marjorie. 'Ted's so sharp. Only ten minutes more, darling. Oh darling – '

'I've *got* to see you soon,' said George, a moment later, holding back from her kisses, his head swimming. 'I've *got* to. What's Grainger doing tomorrow?'

'Tomorrow? What day's that? Oh, Thursday.' A sudden recollection altered her tone as she repeated – 'Thursday.'

She had made calculations just as Ted had done. She knew that on Thursday would come the crisis.

'What's the matter with Thursday?' demanded George. His jealous fear had caught that alteration of tone.

'Nothing,' said Marjorie. 'Nothing, really, darling. But I don't expect Ted'll be out tomorrow. He never has anything special on Thursday evenings.'

Her tone was not absolutely convincing as she prevaricated. But she could not tell her lover that the break between herself and her husband was yet to come, when she had given him to understand that it had long been in existence.

'What's bothering you, dear?' asked George. 'There's something worrying you.'

'No, there isn't. There isn't, really. It's only that I don't want to leave you, darling. I don't want to go in, and yet I've got to. Listen! There's the train.'

The next train down stopped with a squealing of brakes at the station two hundred yards away. Reluctantly he released his hold of her; she was not sorry to leave him now. She was frightened in case he should press her on the subject of what was alarming in the prospect of Thursday night.

'Let's go back to Simon Street, darling,' she said. 'When I come from the station at night I always walk along the road if I'm alone, never along the lane.'

At the corner of the lane she held up her face to him again.

'Better not come any further, dear,' she said. 'Goodnight, darling. Sleep well.'

She turned and ran, then, down the slope of Simon Street and round the corner to Harrison Way. The light in the first floor window of No. 77 showed that Ted was not yet asleep. He was not even in bed, but was half undressed when Marjorie came into the room.

'You're pretty late,' he said. That was comforting. It meant that chance had not revealed to him how she had been spending her evening.

'I'm always late when I go to see Mill,' said Marjorie.

'Funny old cow she is,' said Ted. 'I can't think what you two find to say to each other. You always seem to have a lot.'

He put on his pyjama coat over his hairy chest and got into bed while Marjorie hung her best navy blue coat and skirt over hangars.

'Buck up with that light,' he said. 'I'm sleepy.'

George had followed her at a distance down Harrison Way. He too had seen that light in the first floor front window, and he had guessed that Grainger was waiting there for his wife. It had been in his mind that it might be as well to remain on the spot in case Grainger had discovered anything and Marjorie should need his help. But the sight of that light upstairs drove that notion away. He saw the hall light switch off as Marjorie went upstairs, and he knew then that she was in the bedroom with Grainger. The imagination that she had stimulated tormented him with vivid pictures as he stood there staring up at the light. Grainger was looking at the slim beautiful body which was denied to him. Ely was crazed with jealousy, standing there in the silent street. The light went out and she was in bed beside Grainger now. Perhaps he was resting his coarse hands upon her.

Ely almost moaned aloud as the thought came to him. He turned away at last, walking madly through the deserted streets on his way back to Dewsbury Road. And at the corner of Cameron Road a fresh thought, breaking through his crazy self-torments, caused him to hesitate in his rhythmical stride. There had been something queer in Marjorie's voice as she spoke about Thursday night. What was there in the prospect of Thursday night to worry her? In bed George Ely could find no peace. No sooner had he mastered his jealous imaginings that he was suddenly wide awake again, wondering about Thursday night.

18

Thursday night was one of darkness and small rain. The little wind that blew was cold and cheerless. There was nothing about the weather which would help George Ely to be patient while he waited beside the elderberry tree. He whistled again, impatiently, and stared through the darkness at the house where Marjorie was concealed from him. There was a light in the sitting-room, shining through the curtains of the French window. Behind those curtains was Marjorie, and because she did not come to his call immediately it was to be presumed that Grainger was there too, enjoying the light and the warmth and Marjorie's presence. God only knew what might be going on in that sitting-room behind the veil of the curtains. Ely was bitterly, madly jealous. He clenched his fists in the darkness. He could not distrust Marjorie, nor disbelieve her vows and protestations. Marjorie was on his side against Grainger – he was their common enemy. He felt desperately in need of Marjorie's assurance that all was well with her. He whistled yet once more, boiling with impatience and anxiety.

Now she came to him, gliding down the path like a ghost.

'No, don't kiss me, dear. I mustn't stop a minute. Ted'll wonder what I'm up to.'

He strove to pull her to him, and she resisted him.

'No, darling, really I mustn't. I just came to ask you to go away tonight. It's no use waiting for me. It isn't, really. Ted's being beastly.'

She had not meant to say those last words. They slipped out during her hurried explanations as she strove to prevail upon George to let her go quickly.

'What d'you mean? What's he doing?' It was a growl rather than a whisper.

'Oh nothing, dear, I didn't mean that. I only meant that I must go in again now. I can't stop.'

Ted was being beastly, sure enough, but she did not want to tell George about it – she would not even if there had been time tonight. Marjorie had resolved to fight this particular battle by herself. It was the moment of crisis for which she had been steeling herself all day. She could not tell George that she had been fobbing off Ted with excuses ever since last Saturday, for that would disclose the necessary corollary that along with the excuses had gone an implied promise for tonight. And Ted was in the sitting-room awaiting her return – it would only be a matter of seconds before he started to look for her to discover what she was doing.

'What is it, darling? What's the matter?' There was agony in Ely's voice as he sensed her agitation.

'It's just that I'm afraid Ted'll come out. Oh, let me go, dear. Goodbye, darling. Goodbye. See you tomorrow.'

She was gone, leaving Ely in the darkness staring after her. His hands were clenched until they hurt; his collar was too tight for him, but these discomforts were unnoticed items in the wave of misery which was engulfing him. His helplessness shocked him.

'What can we *do*?' he said to himself. 'What can we *do*?'

He stood chafing at his impotence in the garden for a space before he stamped off, up the lane along the railway. An electric train rattled by before he reached the corner in Simon Street. Then he walked in misery along the wet roads in the lamplight back to Dewsbury Road.

In the sitting-room in Harrison Way Ted was trying to put his arms round Marjorie, as every detail of his behaviour that evening had predicted that he would.

'Have you got time to kiss me now, old girl?,' he said.

Marjorie gazed round the room like a hunted wild animal. There was no refuge, no succour there. Not in the faded wallpaper, nor in the threadbare carpet, nor in the battered chairs nor in the cheap loud speaker. There was the usual heap of clothes to be mended lying in the basket by her chair. To be sitting quietly mending clothes at this moment would be paradise, but there was no chance of it. Ted was looming up over her. She had a nightmare feeling, as if he were twenty feet tall and six feet broad, as if the whole room were filling with Ted's body.

His hands were stroking her throat.

'No!' she said. 'No!'

She struck out feebly with her arms, blindly. One weak fist hit Ted on the nose and mouth.

'What the hell?' he demanded. 'What the devil d'you mean?'

He drew back from her a pace. His earlier suspicions that she was going through a phase of coolness towards him were confirmed, but he had not anticipated as hostile a reception as this. He was angry, and the sight of Marjorie's face, white and lopsided with loathing, made him angrier than ever.

'I – I can't' said Marjorie. 'I don't want to.'

'You'd better get over that quick,' said Ted. 'You've had time enough.'

Marjorie gulped. This was the moment, visualized in a hundred different forms, when she would have to tell Ted that she no longer cared for him in that way, when she was to persuade him to agree to leave her alone for the rest of their lives. She was to promise him in return all the freedom he desired – once or twice this week in hopeful moments she had pictured his falling in with the suggestion, grudgingly, perhaps. But it was infinitely more difficult even than she had imagined. She plunged desperately into speech, holding out her hands to fend off Ted's overpowering bulk the while.

'No,' she gabbled. 'I can't sleep with you any more, Ted. I – I've finished with all that. Please don't ask me any more. You can do what you like, Ted. You can have who you like. I shan't mind. But leave me alone. That's – that's what I wanted to say, Ted.'

She was blind even though her eyes were open, as though a solid fog were round her. She stood, seeing nothing, in the brief silence that followed. Ted's voice when he spoke seemed to come from a long way away.

'I see,' he said, and there was an edge to his voice. 'That's the idea, is it?'

'Yes.'

Vision had returned to her. Now that she had said it all she could see him plainly again, shrunk to his natural size, but not the less menacing because of that. The tempest of rage, insane and uncontrolled, which she had anticipated, showed no sign of appearing. His eyes narrowed and his thick lip compressed. Ted had not been unprepared for this outburst, and he knew how he was going to deal with it.

'You think you're going to get away with that, do you?' he said, with a cold intensity far more frightening than any anger. 'I keep you and pay for your clothes and give you slap-up holidays, and that's how you behave. What's at the bottom of all this?'

'Nothing,' said Marjorie. 'Nothing, except that I don't want to.'

'Who's the other man?' Ted shot the question at her as though from a catapult. 'Who is it?'

'No one,' said Marjorie steadily. She had anticipated that question, and the fact of being asked it helped her to gather herself together.

'Who is it?'

'No one,' repeated Marjorie. Nothing on earth would make her say otherwise. 'No one, really and truly.'

Ted believed her – not so much because she lied so steadily, as because that was what he wanted to believe. It would have been a terrible blow to his self-esteem if he had learned that Marjorie preferred another man to him. He looked at her with his narrowed eyes again, and she shrank away before him, and as he moved towards her she shrank back further still. That in itself was gratifying to him. It pleased him to see her so frightened of him. Somewhere in the back of his mind was the thought that it would be a delicious and new experience to subject her to himself while she was in this mood, shrinking and reluctant. He could compel her, he knew. He had thought of the ideal method – the germs of the inspiration had lain ready to sprout in his mind for years back. The notion was intoxicating and exhilarating to him. He only hoped that she was very set and determined in this new course of hers. The more set she was, and the more chaste and virginal she aspired to be – for that matter the more distasteful he had become to her – the more enchanting would be the reluctant surrender he knew he could command from her. He knew that there was a way (and he knew she had not thought of it, so that it would be a surprise to her) to reduce her to instant, abject subjection. He was thrilled at the thought; the anticipation was delicious. He explored farther to test how determined she was.

'You'll bloody well do what I tell you,' he growled at her, head and chin coming forward.

'No!' she said.

'You *will*!'

'No I won't. I won't!'

He was satisfied now that she was absolutely determined. So much the better. Soon she would be his yielding slave, obedient to any command he cared to give.

'Now listen,' he said. 'You're a fool. I could beat you – make you do what I said.'

'You couldn't! You can't make me!'

'Oh, so I can't, can't I? You're sure of it, are you? I haven't got to beat you at all. There's young Anne upstairs. What about her? A dam' good hiding tonight wouldn't be one too many for her. And I wouldn't mind giving her one, either. Shall I go up and fetch her down? Eh?'

'Ted!'

It was the climax of horror. Marjorie was on the point of fainting – she leaned back against the wall, her face dead white. She knew that Ted would do it – would drag Anne from her bed and strip her and beat her.

'Eh?' said Ted again, looking at her. 'Come here to me.'

She opened her mouth to scream, but from her dry throat there only escaped a little pitiable sound, no louder than the bleating of a new-born kid.

'Come here to me,' said Ted. This was the hour of his triumph. He would not move forward an inch to bring her to him. She must come, on her own legs, submissive.

'It's your last chance' snapped Ted. 'Anne's last chance.'

'A – a – ah!' screamed Marjorie.

The door was beside her, still ajar. There was still flight. At her first step hysterical fear took charge of her. She leaped out into the hall before she knew she was going to do so. She heard Ted's step behind her, and flung herself towards the front door. She reached it in time, and ran and ran and ran through the streets where the small rain was falling. She was hatless and coatless. Her eyes were streaming with tears, her upper lip was beslobbered with slime, as she ran, down the steep slope of Simon Street, across the side turnings to Dewsbury Road. She ran swiftly and blindly. Nor did she consciously guide her steps. Perhaps she would have run like this had there been no hope of finding help. As it was, habit and instinct drove her to where Mother was, where George was, where her childhood's home had been.

She ran silently, without her slipper heels touching the pavement, gasping and sobbing as she ran, as swiftly as some Olympic runner. One or two pedestrians saw her pass, and turned to stare after her, but she went past them so quickly, and there was so little to be gained by attempting to overtake her or by calling to her, that, wondering, they let her run on and did nothing.

The latch of the gate had been familiar to her since childhood. Her hand found the knocker of the door without seeking for it. She hammered at the door, hammered madly, until her mother came with quick steps to open it. There was George in the hall, too, drawn by this thundering on the door.

'Mother!' sobbed Marjorie. 'It's Ted!'

'Come in, dear. Come in, and let's shut the door,' said Mother soothingly.

She gave no sign of her triumph. She had known that something like this was bound to happen soon – exactly what, she had not been able to foretell, but some crisis of this sort which would deliver Ted into her hand.

Marjorie stumbled into the hall. They could see her face wet with tears. She was almost inhuman with fear and nausea.

'What's the matter, darling?' said George. 'What is it, dear?'

'It's Ted!' she repeated, her voice going up to a scream. 'He's a devil! He's wicked! He's beastly!'

'What's he done,' demanded George.

'Oh, he's – no, I can't stop here! I mustn't stop here! I must go back! Quick!'

She turned distractedly back to the door, fumbling for the latch.

'We'll come back with you,' said Mother with instant decision. 'George, you go with her. I'll catch you up in a minute.'

They went out into the street, George silent and hot with rage, Marjorie stumbling weakly now, with dreadful sobs tearing her at every step. A few seconds later Mother came running up to join them. In her hand swung the leather carrying bag, and in the bag was something heavy, but neither George nor Marjorie noticed it. No one spoke for fifty yards, and it was Marjorie who broke the silence. Her voice was weak now. It was as if she were sighing what she said.

'Hurry!' she said, and she tried to set an example, her weak legs nearly giving way beneath her. 'He's going to hit Anne! Perhaps he's hitting her now.'

'Why was he going to do that?' asked George.

'To make me sleep with him. He's cruel. He's dreadful. George, you don't know what he is. He's – he's – oh, hurry, hurry!'

She urged herself forward; it was a minute before she had breath enough to speak again.

'What are we going to say to him, Mother?' asked Marjorie.

'We're not going to say anything to him,' said Mother, grimly. 'We're going to kill him.'

George at her side gave a quick, sharp breath. He had heard what she had said, and it had chimed exactly with what he himself felt. He was insane, berserk with rage. He gave no thought to weapons as he clenched his hands at his sides; he did not know what it was that swung heavily in the leather bag Mrs Clair carried. Marjorie heard, too. She was mazed and stupid with misery, but she heard and understood. If Ted were to die Anne would be safe for always. That was her predominating thought. Very vaguely and mistily she went on to think that Ted's death would solve all the other problems, too, but she was hurrying too fast and was too consumed with anxiety to follow up that line of anticipation.

'I've thought how we can do it,' said Mother, ready to combat any irresolution, but it was unnecessary. No one had any comments to make. Neither George nor Marjorie was thinking clearly enough to be deterred by any thought of consequences, or even to realize the possibility of any consequence. They walked fast through the streets, the three of them. The steepness of

Simon Street did not hold them back. They hastened down the slope of Harrison Way.

'This way,' said Mother, mindful as ever of practical details.

They walked in through the side entrance, into the kitchen, and stood there for a second, Mother listening, and the other two for the moment irresolute.

'Come along,' said Mother; her leather carrying bag was still in her hand. They were following her into the hall when she thrust Marjorie back.

'Wait there,' she said to her, and then drew George with her across to the sitting-room door.

Marjorie, standing on the threshold between kitchen and hall, where her mother had halted her, heard the sitting-room door open.

'What the hell?' she heard Ted say, loudly and angrily. 'What the devil d'you think you're doing in my house? Clear out, both of you.'

Ted was naturally angry. He had been baulked of his triumph over his wife, and though he knew that is was only a postpone-ment, that soon she would have to come crawling back to him, tamed and submissive, even a postponement was irritating, espe-cially a postponement after the pubs were shut.

'Did you hear what I said?' Ted's voice came plainly to Marjo-rie's ears. 'Clear out. As for you, young Ely – '

'Take this, George,' said her mother's voice, calmly and quietly.

Marjorie could not guess what it was she was giving him. Then she heard Ted say 'Christ!' in astonishment and fear, and imme-diately after the muffled sound of a blow and then a fall. Somebody – it seemed to her as if it was a voice she had never heard before – began to wail.

'Oo – oo!' said the voice, pitifully.

'Hit him again, George,' said Mother.

Marjorie heard a crunching sound, and then heard it again, but the wailing stopped short at first.

Mother came back into the hall. Her face was dead white, but she looked very calm and unruffled.

'It's all right now, dear,' she said. 'You can come in.'

Something was lying on the floor; it wore Ted's office clothes, and a black – no, a red – pool was round it. George was standing there, his face flushed and his nostrils spread open wide. He was breathing as hard as a dog in summer, and swinging idly from his right hand was a little axe, covered with red, too. His eyes were fixed in his head, and he stared motionless at the opposite wall – motionless save for the idle swinging of the axe. Some of the red on the axe formed itself into a long sluggish drop, like treacle, and then fell with a 'plop' on the linoleum.

'We've got plenty of time,' said Mother, looking at the clock still ticking on the mantelpiece. 'But we mustn't waste it. Here, give me that, George.'

She took the axe from his unresisting hand, stood for a moment as though considering what to do with it, and then carried it out into the kitchen. Marjorie heard the iron top of the boiler stove being lifted and replaced; Mother had evidently dropped it in there. Mother came briskly back again.

'I've lighted the gas under the kettles,' she said. 'We'll want a lot of hot water to clear up this mess. You can start on that, Marjorie, while George and I are gone. There mustn't be a mark, not a trace left. We'll have to wash that rug through.'

'What are you going to do?' asked Marjorie – the first words she had spoken since she had entered the house.

Mrs Clair leaned forward towards them so as to impress them more deeply with what she had to say. With her opening words she reached up to George's lapel and shook him to rouse him to consciousness.

'We're going to carry him out down to the railway,' she said. 'We'll put him on the lines. Before they have enough light to see him tomorrow there'll have been a dozen trains go by. They won't ever be able to tell that it was – this – and not suicide.'

'Mother!' said Marjorie. She was not so much shocked as surprised at her mother's duplicity and readiness of resource.

'Oh,' said Mrs. Clair. 'I've made all the arrangements. I told the police days ago that he was getting funny in his manner.'

She met George's eyes and Marjorie's unflinching. They could guess if they like how much of this was her doing; she did not care now that it had been successful. She had never foreseen that it would happen on this particular evening and in this particular way – all she had done was to make a quarrel inevitable, a crime of violence inevitable, and had stood ready to supply the weapon and the means of extricating them from the consequences. Probably they would never guess how much was planned and how much was an inevitable chance.

'Oh, come along,' said Mrs Clair, testily. 'We mustn't waste any more time. George, you take his shoulders. George, pull yourself together now. That's right. Take his shoulders and I'll take his legs. Put the light out, Marjorie, and then open the French window. That's the way. Come along, George.'

Mrs Clair was whispering now, with the opening of the window.

'There's a chair here, George. Mind how you go round it. Remember the step. You're just coming to it. That's right. Step quietly.'

Their slow soft footsteps died away down the path. Marjorie stood for a moment on the step by the French window. Her head was clearing fast. She pulled the window to, leaving it ajar. Then she drew the curtain across it once more, and stole across the dark sitting-room to the lighted hall. There was a clear picture in her mind's eye of the dark pool at the further end of the room, its shape and its size. Even in the darkness she was able to avoid stepping in it, but she shuddered as she crept by it.

19

Sergeant Hale was walking down Simon Street. Later that night he had an appointment with a 'copper's nark' – a man who in exchange for a few shillings was willing to give information regarding the criminal activities of his associates. Hale expected no information this evening; the purpose of the meeting was merely to hand over to the copper's nark money he had lately earned. It would take less than a second. But the hour chosen was sufficiently late, after the closing of the public houses, to make it very unlikely that anyone would see it done, and the rendezvous was sufficiently out of the way to be safe.

As he walked heavily yet silently in his rubber-soled shoes down Simon Street Hale knew that he was ten minutes early. It was a regrettable weakness of his, of which he had been conscious from childhood, to be ten minutes early for any appointment. At the corner of the lane beside the railway, at the back of the odd numbered houses in Harrison Way, he paused for a moment. If he made a detour, walking down this lane to the farther end, and so to his appointment via Trecastle Road, he would be late for his appointment by at least five minutes, or perhaps even more. It was a prospect which mildly irritated him, and his impulse was to discard the thought. After all, Constable Clough, No. 79, who had this beat at present, was reliable, and the lane had therefore been properly patrolled.

Next Sergeant Hale, about to walk down Simon Street, remembered how that woman – what was her name? Mrs Clair, that was it – had spoken to him about her son-in-law who lived in one of the houses backing on to the lane – 77, where that girl gassed herself – saying that he was going queer in the head. It was that which turned the scale. The sergeant decided that he might as well walk down the lane, just to see if there was anything deserving his attention.

In No. 77 there was a light in the back living room, shining through the curtained French window. That was all, when the sergeant arrived at the garden gate. Then, as he was about to move on, he heard a door – it sounded like the door from the kitchen into the scullery – open and close, and another light in the back of the house was switched on, not shining directly into the garden, but onto the side of the house next door. Someone must have just come home and entered by the side door. The sergeant lingered on idly against the hedge; this sign of activity in the house was just enough, combined with what Mrs Clair had said to him, to keep him waiting a second or two longer, almost against his wishes.

And then he heard, distinctly, a man's voice raised in anger or surprise, and then the voice was cut short. Even this was all comparatively insignificant – just enough to keep the sergeant from continuing his walk. The sitting-room light went out. They were probably going to bed – but no, the French windows were being cautiously opened; the sergeant heard the unmistakable gentle noise of it, a little muffled. This was more interesting. Someone was whispering, someone was creeping slowly down the path. The sergeant withdrew along the hedge away from the gate; he found a little gap in it which would help to conceal him in the darkness. Whoever it was – and it sounded like two people – came creeping down the path. The gate squeaked a little, and someone came out and looked both ways as though to make sure no one was about. Sergeant Hale stood very still in his niche in the hedge. This time he heard a fresh whisper – a woman's voice.

'Come on,' it said 'it's all right.'

From the deliberation of their steps it seemed as if they were carrying something heavy. So they were; with sharp nervous gasps they lifted their burden onto the top of the railings which fenced off the railway. One of them began to climb over, and Sergeant Hale thought it was time to interfere.

'What's all this?' he demanded, emerging from the hedge.

The woman squeaked with fright and surprise; the man jumped down again from the railings with guilt clearly visible in every movement despite the darkness. Neither of them said a word.

'What's that you've got there?' asked Sergeant Hale. He had no suspicion at all as to what it was, but he brought his electric torch out of his pocket and flashed it on the bundle against the railings.

'My God!' he said, and his hand went like a flash to his whistle.

Then it was that Mrs Clair recovered her quickness of wit. She leapt for his hand and clung to it.

'Come on, George,' she said. 'Hit him! Go for him!' George came rushing in and locked his arms around the sergeant's broad figure at the very moment that the sergeant threw off Mrs Clair's grip. The two men swayed and tottered in a tense struggle, grunting with the efforts they were exerting. George was still dull of brain, as he had been ever since he had struck that blow in the sitting-room. He fought hard against a practised fighter. And even as they closed Mrs Clair turned and ran wildly up the garden path again. One single thought streaked through her brain as she ran – she thanked God that she had had the foresight to take that fifty pounds out of the bank, that she had brought it with her tonight, in her handbag.

She snatched open the French window. Marjorie was just enter-ing into the sitting-room, pail of steaming water in one hand and a scrubbing brush in the other. At her mother's sudden entrance she started and screamed; the pail fell with a clatter, sending a torrent of water across the floor.

'Come along!' said Mrs Clair. 'Come along! It doesn't matter about that.'

She took her handbag hurriedly out of the leather carrying bag on the side table. She seized Marjorie's arm and dragged her out of the room.

'Is your hat upstairs?' she asked, in the hall.

'Yes,' said Marjorie.

'Then we'll have to do without it.'

She snatched open the front door and hurried Marjorie into the street. They were almost running as they went on down towards the High Street. They had hardly covered a hundred yards when they heard behind them the sound of a police whis-tle, clear and penetrating in the silent night.

'We mustn't hurry now,' said Mrs Clair. She moderated her pace, and they walked almost slowly now, two apparently respect-able and harmless women, who might well be expected to ignore the pealing of the police whistle behind them.

Only one or two people came to their doors at the sound, and Mrs Clair and Marjorie walked sedately past them, every step taking them nearer to safety. They turned a corner at last, and then another. Now they were in the High Street, and Mrs Clair wasted half a second as she stood uncertain as to which way to turn. The approach of a motorbus decided her. She hailed it and they got in.

'Two, to the terminus,' said Mrs Clair, giving the conductor a shilling from her handbag.

It was a long ride, all the way to Croydon. Passengers got in and out, and at every fresh entry the women peered round for fear it was a policeman. Mrs Clair was shaking with fear; not with the fear of any consequences which would follow what they had done but with the blind panic fear of the pursued, now that the decisive moment had passed. She felt weak and cold. She was conscious that her face was pale and her hands trembling. Then she realized that Marjorie beside her was convulsed with sobs. It would draw attention to them. People would easily remember a young woman, hatless and coatless on a rainy evening, who sat sobbing in an omnibus. That would help the pursuers, later. Mrs Clair forced herself to appreciate the fact that they were in no immediate danger, that no one could arrest them in the next few minutes.

Mrs Clair rallied her ebbing strength. For herself she would be content to abide by what she had done, but poor little Marjorie must be guarded and protected. She sat upright in her seat, forcing herself to appear serene and unruffled, and she nudged Marjorie to call her attention to herself. Marjorie started and looked round at her, and met her mother's severe frown and shake of the head. It reminded Marjorie insanely of the wordless reproofs she had received in church, nearly thirty years ago, when the sermon had grown wearisome to her. The warning conveyed by her mother's gestures, but to a far greater degree the example of her mother's apparent calmness, steadied Marjorie too. She made herself check her sobbing, and to settle herself in a natural position on her seat. They could not talk, could not exchange meaningless conversation, as might have been best if they wished to be inconspicuous. But they sat rigid, side by side, restraining themselves from looking round over their shoulders whenever anybody new climbed into the bus, all the way to Croydon.

Mrs Clair, for this matter, had no time or attention to spare for refinements of acting. Her mind now was busy with plans of escape. Save the elementary precaution of drawing that fifty pounds from the bank she had taken no thought about it before, so confident had she been that there would be no need for flight. Now the long journey to Croydon seemed all too short for her to consider the details of what they were to do next – and the details, as Mrs Clair acutely realized, were as important as the main plan.

Croydon was a great traffic centre, she was aware, and from there trains and buses left in all directions, back to London, to other suburbs, down to the sea coast. They must gain the coast, she decided instantly. The holiday season was still at his height. August had not yet run its course. They were two homeless women, now, and where would it be more natural for two women to seek temporary lodgings than in a holiday town? There was the question of tonight, too. Without luggage, and with Marjorie without hat or coat, every hotel and lodging house would look askance at them, would remember them afterwards. Tomorrow they would be able to remedy that, but tonight they would not dare to find a room for them. Mrs Clair conjured up her memories of south-coast towns, wondering whether they could shelter there all night or not.

'East Croydon Station,' chanted the conductor, as the bus came to a stop.

Mrs Clair nudged her daughter again, and they followed the large contingent of passengers who were leaving the bus. In the brilliantly lighted booking hall Mrs Clair studied the indicator board. There was one more train due to leave for Brighton that night, in a quarter of an hour's time. She opened her handbag and peeled a note from her precious roll, and approached the booking office window.

'Three singles, Brighton, please,' she said, firmly. As they went down the steps to the platform Marjorie whispered urgently to her – she had revived sufficiently now, thanks to her mother's example, to take an interest in their plans.

'What did you buy three tickets for?' she asked.

'Never you mind,' said Mrs Clair.

One ticket went into her handbag, and she only tendered two to be punched at the gate. The idea which had guided her had been that the police would be inquiring after two women; the purchase of three tickets would help to throw them off the scent if they followed it as far as the Croydon booking office here. But she could not bring herself to explain this to Marjorie. It seemed to her an indelicate subject to discuss with her. So she said 'Never you mind,' just as she had said it when the child Marjorie had begun asking questions about how she was born. And Marjorie was reminded of that when her mother answered her. In this new helplessness of hers and dependence on her mother she seemed to be returning to her childhood.

There was a belated boy selling evening newspapers; Mrs Clair bought two. Then the train came in and half emptied itself of passengers. There were only three other people in the compartment Mrs Clair chose, and she was able to seat Marjorie in a corner and sit beside her. She passed her a newspaper and set her an example by opening the other one and holding it up in front of her. Mrs Clair was thinking quickly and clearly of everything again now. It would not be her fault if those other passengers were able to recognize their descriptions later. The train ran on through the darkness, its steady rhythm being constantly broken by stops at intermediate stations – this was the last stopping train between London and Brighton. All the other three passengers, the man with the spats and the gold watch chain, the woman who had been shopping at Peter Robinson's, and the youngish man with the pale face, got out before Brighton was reached, but a young married couple with a tendency to giggle got in, and they were never alone throughout the tedious journey. Marjorie read the same paragraph of print – something involved and to do with stocks and shares – over and over again as it swayed before her eyes while she held the newspaper in front of her. It meant no more to her at the end of the journey that at the beginning.

When the train stopped at Brighton Mrs Clair lingered so as to enable the young couple to be clear of the carriage before she started to descend. Marjorie had put down her newspaper on the seat with the intention of leaving it behind, but her mother took it up again.

'I expect we shall want these,' she said, cryptically.

At the barrier their tickets were taken from them without question and without a glance directed at them, and they came out into the streets. There was only the tiniest rain falling now, an almost negligible amount, and here in this town of holiday makers Marjorie's hatlessness would pass without remark.

'What are we going to *do*?' asked Marjorie, and then she shuddered, clinging to her mother's arm. She remembered so well the other occasions when that question had been asked.

'Oh, we'll be all right, dear,' said her mother placidly.

Downhill, of course, led to the sea, to the illuminations and the promenade – Mrs Clair knew this not from any topographical deductions but from experience of many seaside towns. The illuminations had mostly faded out by now, but the promenade was well lighted with street lamps, and as they emerged into it they were greeted by the sound of gentle fine-weather waves breaking upon the beach. The breath of air from the sea was a tonic after the stuffiness of the railway carriage. It called up a wave of memory in Marjorie's mind. The last time she had breathed sea air George had been with her. Then, inconsequently, a fresh memory arose, blotting out its predecessor – the memory of something huddled in a red pool on the sitting-room linoleum.

'Oh, Mother, Mother,' said Marjorie.

Mrs Clair's thin arm pained her where her daughter's fingers gripped it.

'There, there,' she said soothingly. 'Just a little way further.'

They were on the promenade now, close to the pier. Mrs Clair walked steadily along towards Kemp Town. In one shelter there were two people still sitting – lovers, presumably. They passed several more shelters before Mrs Clair stopped.

'Let's sit here,' she said.

As she lowered herself to the bench she suddenly realized that she was very, very tired. Marjorie sat beside her.

'Here,' said Mrs Clair. 'I've brought these to keep you warm.'

In the train she had remembered that newspaper helped when one was exposed to cold. Away back in the war she had put sheets of newspapers between the blankets.

'Tuck this up round you,' said Mrs Clair. 'Under your skirt.'

Marjorie stood obediently while her mother lifted up her clothes and provided her with an additional petticoat of news-paper.

'There,' said Mrs Clair. 'That'll be better. Just a minute. I'll fold this one to go under your – under you when you sit down. Comfy? Now try and go to sleep, dear. Put your feet up. That's right. Goodnight, dear.'

With the cessation of traffic the sound of the sea came more clearly to them still. They could hear the little waves breaking, the rattle of the shingle as the water ran back. For a space Marjorie almost believed she would sleep. She was so tired, and her mother had been so comforting. Then as she sat there with eyes closed she head a measured tread approaching. Her limbs stiffened. She was tense with anxiety. Murder! Was this the police come to arrest them? She stared through the darkness at her mother's profile seen dimly in the opposite corner.

'Mother!' she said in terror.

'Sh!' said Mrs Clair.

The tread came nearer. It was level with them now. Then it passed by – it was only some belated pedestrian making his way home along the promenade.

'Go to sleep, darling,' said Mrs Clair. 'Mother's here.'

That was an old formula, too, thirty years old.

It took some time for the rapid beating of Marjorie's heart to quiet down again. Then, more than once, she dozed, lightly and fitfully. Each time she awoke with a start, sweating with terror. Some new frightening thoughts had come to her. She had not noticed Ted's eye at the time – the one eye there was to be seen – but she remembered it clearly now. Half open and dull, so that you could see just a bit of lifeless white and some of the pupil. The vision of it came to her, twenty times magnified as she slept.

'Sh! dear,' said Mrs Clair. 'Mother's looking after you.'

Then something else, if possible more terrible, occurred to her.

'Mother!' she said, starting out of her doze. 'What about the children?'

'Somebody will be looking after them all right. Don't be afraid about that,' said Mrs Clair soothingly.

That must have been telepathy, for Marjorie's question had come just when Mrs Clair was in an agony of anxiety about the children herself. But she allowed herself to show no sign of her anxiety when she reassured her daughter.

'I don't mean now, Mother,' said Marjorie, wildly – it had not occurred to her until then that there was a chance that her sleeping children were at this moment alone in the house – 'I mean what'll happen to them? What'll they do when – when – '

Words failed Marjorie to describe the vague future of whether or not they should evade the police.

'Oh, don't worry about them now, dear. They'll be all right. We'll see about it, afterwards.'

Mrs Clair had no notion in her head about what would happen to the children – there was pain in her head as she thought about them – but she spoke as firmly and as reassuringly as she could.

'And there's George, Mother! What happened to him?'

'I don't know, dear. But don't worry. Go to sleep, dear.'

'Did – did they get him?'

'Perhaps they did, dear. Perhaps not. We'll know tomorrow. Go to sleep now, there's a good girl.'

Later the chill of the night struck through the newspapers with which Mrs Clair had tried to keep her daughter warm.

'I'm so cold, Mother. I'm shivering.'

Marjorie was more like a little child Mrs Clair had once held to her bosom than ever.

'Poor lamb!' she said. 'There! Never mind.'

Mrs Clair took off her jacket and wrapped it round her daughter's feet and legs.

'What about you, Mother?'

'Me? I'm all right. Shut your eyes now, and you'll be asleep before you can say Jack Robinson.'

The gentle surf continued to beat upon the beach. There was a time when Marjorie actually slept, despite her shivering limbs and chatting teeth, her mother sat upright watching over her, grimly refusing to allow herself to shiver or her teeth to chatter.

Slowly the dawn came into the sky, and the landscape turned from black to grey before Marjorie awoke again.

'It's daytime now, Mother. Can't we go yet?'

'No, not yet, dear.'

They were less conspicuous, in Mrs Clair's opinion, sitting still in the shelter than walking through the town where there would be nothing for them to do as yet and where there would by now be a few people in the street. The hardy before-breakfast bathers began to descend, crossing the promenade on the way to the beach. The women watched them with dull eyes as they entered the water, some timid and some bold. It was past eight o'clock before Mrs Clair decided that it was safe to move.

'I think we can go now, dear. We can find some breakfast, I

daresay. Put your hair straight first, my lamb. Here – use my comb and mirror.'

She looked Marjorie over anxiously to make sure that she showed as few traces as possible of the night she had been through.

'It's a pity,' said Mrs Clair, 'that I haven't got any make-up stuff for you to use. That'll be one of the first things we'll buy. Now let's come and find a cup of tea somewhere.'

The posters were already up outside the newspaper shops. A batch of them stared them in the face as they turned a corner. Suddenly while they were ascending into the town again Marjorie stopped and clutched at her mother's arm.

'SUBURBAN DEATH MYSTERY. MAN DETAINED.' They read, and on another – 'LONDON RAILWAYSIDE CRIME.'

'You mustn't jump like that,' said Mrs Clair. 'You mustn't, really, dear.'

She nerved herself to walk on without faltering in her step, certainly without looking round to see if anyone had noticed them; she forced herself grimly to read the last poster in this line –

'SUSPECTED MURDER IN LONDON SUBURB.'

'Come along, dear. Walk properly,' said Mrs Clair, as if she were still bringing a restive five-year-old Marjorie home from church.

There were a few people breakfasting in the multiple-branch restaurant which they found – Mrs Clair peeped through the door to make sure of that before going in. In the women's lavatory Marjorie asked the question she had had on her lips for some minutes now.

'Mother, is George the man they've detained?'

Mrs Clair looked quickly round the empty washroom, saw with relief that the two doors beside her were both marked 'Vacant,' and then turned upon her daughter.

'You *mustn't* ask questions like that *at all*,' she said, with surprising vehemence considering that she was speaking low. 'Don't say anything about it to me *ever* unless I've said something first. Or first thing you know *you*'ll be detained next.'

Marjorie's lower lip began to tremble.

'Stop that!' snapped Mrs Clair.

Cup after cup of hot strong tea in the restaurant helped to revive both of them. They could neither of them eat anything.

'Well,' said Mrs Clair with a glance at the clock. 'We can start our shopping now.'

A macintosh and a hat for Marjorie, lipstick and powder, those were the first things they brought. Marjorie felt as if she were in a dream, a nightmare, so much of a nightmare that even buying a hat was a distasteful business, and the more distasteful because her mother was looking on with the eyes of a hawk to make sure that the hat she bought was inconspicuous, quiet, commonplace.

'We must have a change of clothes,' said Mrs Clair, considering. 'And nightdresses for where we stop tonight. And a brush and a comb.'

She was growing frightened at the inroads these purchases were making upon her money – and fifty pounds had seemed such a fortune to her frugal mind! – and yet she steeled herself to go on with it. Every one of these purchases were necessary if they were to sustain the pose of holiday makers – and that they must do, to evade capture. She left Marjorie standing on the kerb, her arms full of parcels, while she went alone into a shop and bought a shabby suitcase second hand. Otherwise the shop keeper might remember them; in a side street they were able to pack the parcels into the suitcase, which they lugged with them along the street. Fortunately it was not unusual to see women dragging suitcases through the streets of holiday towns.

They sat down exhausted on a public bench beside a bit of green.

'Now listen carefully to what I'm going to say,' said Mrs Clair; she had looked all round her to make sure that no one could hear. 'We've got to change our names. That's something we must do. I think I'd better be Mrs James. After all, I was Mrs James Clair until your dear father died. Mrs James. Remember that. What are you going to be?'

'I – I don't know,' said Marjorie.

'Pull yourself together,' said Mrs Clair briskly. 'What'll it be? Mrs Smith? Mrs Jones? No, those are too common. Mrs Robinson. That's it. Mrs – Mrs Henry Robinson, Christian name – Adelaide. Mrs Adelaide Robinson, née James. And I'm your mother, Mrs Frances James. I think I'd better still be your mother, dear.'

Mrs Clair forbore to explain that she could not trust her daughter to keep from calling her 'Mother,' unawares when they were in the hearing of others.

'Yes,' said Marjorie.

'It's no use just saying "yes". You must fix it in your mind for good,' said Mrs Clair.

'Yes.'

They sat still and watched the traffic flowing by on the far side of the green square.

'Adelaide,' said Mrs Clair, suddenly, and received no reply. 'There! You see? You're forgetting already. Don't forget, your name's Adelaide, and that's what I shall call you, always.'

'Oh yes, Mother.'

Marjorie felt sick with exhaustion. She was not in the least sleepy. She had no desire to close her eyes. All she wanted to do was just to sit here indefinitely, thinking about nothing.

20

'We shall be comfortable here, Adelaide,' said Mrs Clair, looking complacently round the little room, with the texts on the walls and ugly brass bedstead nearly filling it.

She spoke slowly and clearly, for she suspected that the grim landlady was pausing outside the door to listen to their opening conversation; and she wanted to maintain the pose she had taken up when they had asked here for lodgings, of a widow who had seen much better days and was still self-consciously genteel. She took off her hat and jacket, allowed plenty of time for the landlady to move away, and then walked quietly round to the door again and assured herself that there was no one behind it.

'We're all right now,' she said, coming back to her daughter. 'Lie down now, and have a little rest.'

They turned down the coverlet, and Marjorie lay down under the top blanket, her skirt and her shoes removed. Mrs Clair sat under the window on the single bentwood chair and opened the evening paper she had brought in with her – the evening paper posters had haunted them since noon; as she lifted the paper to read it she still had their words before her eyes –

'SUBURB MURDER MAN CHARGED'
'SUBURB MURDER TWO WOMEN MISSING'
'POLICE HUNT FOR TWO WOMEN'

It was there on the front page – 'This morning at the South Suburban Police Court George Frederick Ely aged 24 of 16

Dewsbury Road was charged this morning with the wilful murder of Edward Grainger, of 77 Harrison Way. On the advice of His Honour Judge Mason the prisoner reserved his defence until he could be legally represented. Mr Southwell, representing the police, said, in asking for a remand, that he proposed today only to offer formal evidence. There were very strong grounds for the belief that other persons besides Ely were implicated, and until these persons were apprehended (and he had no doubt that this would be only a matter of a few days) it was in the prisoner's interests as well as in those of justice that a remand should be granted. Prisoner, a strikingly handsome youth, was accordingly remanded for a week.

'Later the police issued a statement as follows – "The police consider it desirable in the interests of justice that Mrs Marjorie Grainger of 77 Harrison Way and Mrs Martha Clair of 16 Dewsbury Road should come forward to assist by their evidence in the investigation of the murder of Edward Grainger, husband of the former. Any information regarding the whereabouts of these two persons should be given to any police station, or by telephone to Whitehall 1212."

'Our representatives on the spot understand that the police have been making enquiries regarding the purchase of a hatchet in the shops near the scene of the arrest, the hatchet in question having been discovered in the vicinity of the crime.'

That was all. Mrs Clair read it twice, and then a third time. She had no regard for the journalistic side of it – for that typical touch which described George Ely as 'strikingly handsome,' nor the subtle allusion to the hatchet which would whet the interest of the public into interesting themselves in the whereabouts of Martha Clair and Marjorie Grainger. It was sufficient for her purpose that there had not yet been issued publicly any description of them. The police would have one, she supposed, but that was not so important. Tonight at least they were safe from prying landladies. She folded up the newspaper and looked across at her daughter on the bed.

'I don't think we'll go out tonight, Adelaide,' she said in the clear yet fussy voice she had adopted. 'We've had a tiring day, haven't we?'

'Yes,' said Marjorie. She moaned a little, and turned her head from side to side on the pillow.

'I'll get the things unpacked,' fussed Mrs Clair.

Later there came a thump on the door.

'Your supper's ready,' said the landlady's voice outside.

Bread and cheese and tomatoes and tea – they had neither of them eaten more than a mouthful all day, and Marjorie, listlessly, had no appetite still.

'Really, Adelaide dear,' said Mrs Clair. 'You must try to eat a little to keep your strength up.'

Marjorie shook her head.

'This bread's nice and new. Please,' said Mrs Clair.

She herself ate some, although she had no more appetite than Marjorie. With difficulty she coaxed her daughter into forcing some down.

'We shall be going to bed early,' explained Mrs Clair to the landlady. 'We are tired after our journey.'

The landlady nodded indifferently – Mrs Clair had told her they lived in Reading.

'"Alf past eight breakfast?' was all she said. 'And what'll you 'ave?'

Upstairs, as Mrs Clair shut the door, Marjorie stood looking at her with an expression of bewilderment.

'I – I don't feel very well,' said Marjorie. Her knees were sagging under her, and Mrs Clair was just in time to catch her as she dropped. She lowered her onto the bed, undid the band of her skirt, took off her shoes, bathed her face with a flannel dipped in the jug on the washstand.

'There, there, my lamb,' said Mrs Clair soothingly. 'You'll be better soon. I think you're better already. Let Mother help you into bed, darling.'

She stripped off her daughter's clothes. There was no false modesty between them at this juncture, no careful donning of one garment before taking off another. Marjorie's waist was marked with the dull red corrugations left by the suspender belt she had worn continuously for thirty-six hours, but otherwise her naked body was flawless – her splendid arms and shoulders and legs still retained the tan of the recent holiday. As Mrs Clair slipped the new nightdress over her daughter's head she thought to herself that Marjorie showed no sign of having borne two children. That was more than she could say for herself, and Mrs Clair was liberal-minded enough to attribute it to the better methods and management of the new generation. She brushed out Marjorie's hair, and tied it back in a pigtail.

'Go to sleep now, darling,' she murmured, opening the bed and sliding Marjorie's legs into it. 'Sleep well, my lamb.'

She smoothed the short hairs back from Marjorie's forehead, before turning away to make her own preparations for bed.

It was strange to her how she felt neither tired nor sleepy. She just felt old, as she put it to herself. Stiff and feeble and weak, as though the clock of her life were running down, but not a bit tired, and certainly not sleepy. It was quite an effort to climb into bed, and once there it was pleasant to lie placid and still, gazing out into the darkened room. There was no hatred now to disturb her peace. That devil Ted had met with what he deserved. She was surprised to find that she felt no regret at not having poured into his dying ear (as once she had planned) the information that his wife had been unfaithful to him – had slept joyously with the pretty boy who had killed him. That was all past and done with. Hatred was ended now. What was left was a rich, warm overmastering love for her daughter beside her. Mrs Clair could feel the welling tenderness in her bosom as she listened to Marjorie's breathing and felt the warmth of her body. It was only for that Mrs Clair wanted to go on living. She was full of this overmastering love. In its comforting warmth she drifted imperceptibly into the light but refreshing sleep of old age.

It was some time in the early morning that Marjorie woke her – Marjorie had slept long enough to recover from mere animal fatigue, and in that hour when vitality is at its lowest dreadful visions had awakened her. She could not face them alone in the dark.

'Mother, oh Mother,' she moaned; her writhing fingers gripped painfully at her mother's lean thigh.

'What is it, darling?' whispered Mrs Clair, instantly awake. She took Marjorie's hand between her own two, stroking and fondling it.

'Mother, I want to know,' said Marjorie, her mind's eye tortured with hardly seen memories. 'Mother – *what happened to his other eye?*'

'Sh, dear,' whispered Mrs Clair. 'Sh, darling. There's nothing to worry about. That's all over now. We're forgetting about that now.'

Mrs Clair knew well what was troubling Marjorie. She had the same memory, of that dull half-opened eye with the lifeless white exposed, and she had seen, as her daughter had not, what had happened to the other eye under the edge of the hatchet wielded by Ely's maddened strength.

'Mother,' said Marjorie feverishly, tossing herself over on to her side and reverting to another worry. 'Mother, will they hang us, you and me?'

'No, my dear, of course not. They never will. Mother is looking after you, dear. Don't worry, my lamb. There's nothing to worry about.'

She prevailed over those nightmare worries in the end. She

coaxed and soothed her into some kind of tranquillity, until fatigue reasserted itself and Marjorie slept again – not too well; she started and muttered even during her sleep. Dot had done just the same when she was a little girl.

Next morning was Saturday; the streets and the promenade and the pier were more crowded than yesterday, because the visitors were reinforced by the long-weekenders. And everywhere there seemed to be posters, outside the shops, and displayed by newsvendors on the promenade –

WANTED WOMEN FULL DESCRIPTION

It stared at them at every turn; Mrs Clair bought a newspaper.

'We can hear the band from this seat, Adelaide,' she said. 'Let's sit down.'

She had no thought of paying threepence apiece for seats nearer to the band – not while the money in her handbag was dwindling at such an alarming pace. They sat, just as Marjorie had sat with George on so many promenades during that holiday that seemed so long ago, and Mrs Clair opened the newspaper with as great an appearance of casual interest as she could muster. Here were their descriptions, sure enough –

'Marjorie Grainger. Aged 32. Height five feet five. Dark hair and eyes, and small hands and feet. Of athletic build, was very sunburned when last seen. Probably wearing a brown woollen jumper and skirt.

'Martha Clair. Aged 59. Height five feet one or two. Grey hair nearly white, eyes hazel. Is of neat appearance and is very active for her age. Probably wearing a black coat and skirt and black hat with black bone buckle at side.'

Mrs Clair drew a breath of relief when she read these descriptions. They were wrong in several essential details. Marjorie was wearing her red-and-grey jumper with her brown skirt. And she herself – some people might perhaps say her eyes were hazel but she would describe them as grey. The black coat and skirt and hat meant nothing. Half the women of England over fifty wore black coats and skirts; and hats answering to the description given could be seen in any street. Altogether they were not very good descriptions; Mrs Clair wondered who had provided them. The heights were probably suggested by that police sergeant, but Mrs Clair fancied that Mrs Taylor who lived next door to Marjorie must have told about the clothes. It would be like Mrs Taylor to get them wrong.

Marjorie stirred restlessly beside her.

'What do they say, Mother?' she asked.

Mrs Clair silenced her with a look; there were two other people sitting on the crowded bench, and she could say nothing for fear of being overheard. She went on reading the front page, and her new feeling of reassurance died away, and was almost replaced by dismay, as she did so. There were two short paragraphs dealing with the probable whereabouts of Mrs Grainger and Mrs Clair. There did not seem to be least doubt of their being caught soon. A watch on the ports was being maintained, but it was known that the two women had no passports. It was believed that their resources were very scanty – that meant (Mrs Clair told herself) that the police had discovered about her fifty pounds and could guess how short a time it would last. Lastly, it would be obvious to anyone that it would be easy enough to identify two women, a mother and a daughter, travelling together. There was a broad hint in conclusion for the public to keep its eyes open for them.

Mrs Clair experienced a period of penetrating clairvoyance as she sat thinking about all this. Never before had she stopped to consider the relationships between press and police and public but now she was aware of their intricacies in a flash. Those posters over there –

HUNT FOR TWO WOMEN

would be enough to sell newspapers in hundreds, in thousands, and it was that which the press wanted. A manhunt was a good selling item; a woman-hunt was still better. She knew, too – it had been the same with her in the old days – that a good juicy murder helped to sell newspapers. People who read on Tuesday of a young wife suspected of murdering her husband – especially a young wife with a 'strikingly handsome' lover – would buy another paper on Wednesday in the hope of reading more. And a bloody affair with an axe was better reading than any cold dealings with rat poison or weed killer – Mrs Clair appreciated now how clever the police were to let out that detail to stimulate the interest of the public and to ensure the cooperation of the press.

The hunt was in full swing now; perhaps the police could just sit back and wait for the public to do their work for them. Everyone, every hotel keeper, every lodging house keeper, would be on the lookout for a mother of fifty-nine with a daughter of thirty-two, and if they found them would deliver them up to the police with no more thought for the feelings of the two women than a huntsman has for the fox or the shooter has for the pheasant. Partly it would be to gratify their own sense of self-importance; partly because it was all part of the game the hunted women might as well be tennis balls. Mrs Clair boiled with indignation against the public for enjoying Marjorie's troubles as though they were a free show; and then she was cold with fear again. It was all very well to assure herself that there must be thousands of pairs of mothers and daughters staying in lodgings all over England. Some of those pairs might even be suspected or arrested, for that matter – unjustly. That would hardly matter to them, for an hour's investigation would result in their being set free again, nor did Mrs Clair care about other people's troubles anyway. But the chance of Marjorie and her being arrested through the nosiness and self-importance of the public was what was worrying her. Until she read this newspaper she had not been specially concerned with that danger – most of her activity had been directed towards leaving no trail that the police could follow. It was maddening to think that she had been to all that trouble ineffectively; that the hounds could sit down and go to sleep until a halloo from a worker in the fields should tell them where the fox was.

Mrs Clair's exalted clarity of vision persisted. She saw the world as a vast expanse of menacing black water, with powerless ships floating on its surface. Here and there were whirlpools, and sometimes ships were caught in them and were whirled round and round and then dragged down for ever. She and those she knew had drifted near one of these whirlpools. Dot had gone first – Mrs Clair sighed to think of the agonies in Dot's mind when first she had been seized and whirled round. Ted had followed her into the gaping hole. Now George Ely was caught, and was hurtling round on the very lip of the hole – it would only be a short time before he, too, should disappear, poor boy. She herself and Marjorie were just beginning to feel the drag and the suction. Perhaps they would follow George soon. And outside them, perhaps to be drawn in too, there might be others – Derrick and Anne, perhaps.

As she formed this mental picture Mrs Clair's mind was innocent of any thought that perhaps it was partly her fault, that perhaps she had contributed of her own volition to this disaster. To Mrs Clair it all seemed entirely inevitable, fated, predestined and it is possible that she was right.

It was a filthy business, a tale of lust and murder and revenge, unredeemed by any of the nobler qualities of mankind, devotion, self-sacrifice, love. That was Ted's fault. His filthiness had started it, and his filthiness had slimed everyone whom it touched. He had had to be fought on his own ground, lust for lust and passion for passion, adultery for adultery, and murder for murder. It might be best to carry the tale to its conclusion as speedily as possible, get it over and finished and forgotten.

Mrs Clair shook herself out of that train of thought with a start. That just showed the folly of daydreaming. She had actually started to think about giving up, about handing Marjorie over to the police and the hangman. That was madness, and wicked madness at that. Never, never, never would she do that. She did not care about herself. It was the thought of Marjorie which was troubling her. She must do everything she could for Marjorie. Mrs Clair set her little white teeth – not a false one among them – and vowed to herself that she would die in the last ditch to save Marjorie. Sweet, dear, loved little Marjorie. She must start again to think about what they were to do next.

Marjorie had her hand on her knee and was shaking her.

'Mother, Mother, why don't you listen to me!'

'What is it?' answered Mrs Clair, and added, with an effort, 'Adelaide.'

'I think I've just seen Mrs Posket go by along the front,' said Marjorie.

Mrs Clair would have started had she not controlled herself. At it was she sat rigid and silent for two or three seconds. There were people close beside them on either side; she must not display any fear of Mrs Posket.

'Oh really?' she said at length, and she hoped that her voice did not sound as stiltedly unnatural to other people as it did to herself. 'Of course, Mrs Posket was going to Worthing for her holiday. Very likely you were right, dear, and it was her. You can get into Brighton very easily from Worthing. What – what a lovely sunny day it is, my dear.'

The urgency of her glance made Marjorie stammer an agreement. They sat there silent, then, for two long minutes, minutes which seemed like hours, while Mrs Clair raked the promenade as far as she could see with eagle eyes. Then at last –

'Well, I think we've sat here long enough, my dear,' said Mrs Clair casually. 'Let's go on now.'

They crossed the promenade quickly and found shelter up a steep side street.

'Are you *certain* it was Mrs Posket?' demanded Mrs Clair.

'Yes, Mother. Quite certain. She didn't see us.'

'No, I'm sure of that,' said Mrs Clair, bitterly. She had no illusions about what Mrs Posket would do if she saw those two friends of hers whom the police were after.

'What are we going to *do*, Mother?' wailed Marjorie, hurrying along at her mother's side.

'We're going back to our lodgings. We can't afford to be in the streets with Mrs Posket about.'

In the hall of the lodging house they saw the landlady. She was standing, resting her back against the wall, reading a newspaper – obviously one found in the room of one of her lodgers.

'You're back early,' said the landlady. 'Your dinner isn't ready yet, not by a long way.'

'No,' said Mrs Clair, and even while she uttered the monosyllable her questing mind thought of a lie to tell quickly. 'We've just come back for a book I left behind. We'll be going out again until dinner time.'

'I see,' said the landlady.

She was a tallish woman, dark, with a bony and angular face. She looked a little strangely at them, closely, running her eye up and down them with what might just be bad manners.

'You run up and fetch it, Adelaide,' said Mrs Clair. 'Your legs are younger than mine. I'll stay here and talk to Mrs – do you know, it's very rude of me, but I've quite forgotten your name again. My memory is dreadful.'

'Hudson's my name,' said the landlady.

She was still staring at Mrs Clair, who felt sure now that she was noting the black hat and costume, and wondering whether her age was fifty-nine and that of her daughter was thirty-two.

'Wonderful how well the summer is lasting, isn't it?' said Mrs Clair bravely.

'Yes, it is indeed,' said Mrs Hudson, and then, suddenly. 'What was it like at Reading?'

'Oh dreadful,' said Mrs Clair. 'The – the biscuit factories are so noisy.'

'H'm yes. I suppose so,' said Mrs Hudson.

Marjorie came down the stairs again. Mrs Clair shot her a quick glance. Perhaps she could be relied upon to lie effectively. Anyway, the chance must be taken.

'Have you got it, dear?' she asked, maternally.

'Yes, in my handbag,' said Marjorie boldly. She had thought of that lie while up in the solitude of the bedroom, and had been nerving herself to say it all the way downstairs.

'That's good,' said Mrs Clair. 'Well, we'll get along now. We'll be back at half past twelve, Mrs Hudson.'

'Right you are,' said Mrs Hudson, and they emerged again into the freedom of the street – a freedom poisoned by the possibility of their encountering Mrs Posket.

'We're not going back there at all,' said Mrs Clair decisively. 'It's a pity that we'll have to leave behind all the things we've just bought.'

'But what are we going to *do*, Mother?'

'We can't go back there,' said Mrs Clair, ignoring the question. 'She suspects.'

'Oh, Mother.'

'Yes, she does. I could see that. She'll be telling the police the first minute she has to spare, and they'll be waiting for us at half past twelve. It's eleven now,' said Mrs Clair, looking up at a street clock. 'Let's walk along this way, where the streets are quieter.'

And where there was less chance of meeting Mrs Posket, was the unspoken addition. Mrs Clair walked briskly along. She apparently felt no trace of the fatigue of yesterday and the day before.

Marjorie at her side was stiff and weary already. She was quite unprepared too, for the decision which her mother was about to announce.

'You're going back to London, my dear,' said Mrs Clair. 'And I'm not coming with you, either. We've got to separate.'

'Mother! Whatever do you mean?'

'I mean just what I say, my dear.'

Mrs Clair had formed her decision rapidly enough. It was obviously unsafe for them to remain together; and just before leaving the lodging house Marjorie had told a good lie in a good way, which proved that left to herself she would be safe – Mrs Clair had never believed in mollycoddling children, either. Marjorie, as soon as she found herself compelled to think and act for herself, would probably recover at once from this complete childlike dependence on her mother which she had been displaying.

'But why, Mother?' Why must we separate?'

'Because everyone's looking for two women together. They can recognize us easily. Look at that Mrs Hudson. If we're separate it'll be much harder for them. They'll never catch us. It's the best thing we can do – the only thing for us to do.'

'I suppose so,' agreed Marjorie, doubtfully; the truth of what her mother was saying was obvious to her tired mind. 'But why should I go back to London?'

'London's the safest place for you, dear. Anywhere else you can meet people you know. But not if you go to the other side of London. Ealing, say, or Acton, or out on the other side, Hornsey, isn't it?'

There was a profound truth in what Mrs Clair was saying. The opposite corners of the County of London are farther removed from each other for all practical purposes than are places fifty miles apart. The chances against any one of the few score people, all dwellers in South East London, who knew Marjorie by sight, encountering her in the side streets of Acton or Hornsey were incredibly slight. It was a self-evident truth to any suburb dweller like Marjorie.

'Yes,' she said. 'But – but – I don't want to leave you, Mother.'

'Stuff and nonsense!' said Mrs Clair, brisk and kindly. 'You managed without me quite well all the years you were married. You'll be able to look after yourself all right.'

'I shall be lonely, Mother.'

'I expect you will, dear. But no one's ever died of loneliness yet. You'll have plenty of money. I've got plenty for the two of us. We'll go the station now. I hope there's a train soon. Now listen carefully, dear. This is important. Here's your money. Open your handbag. That's right. Now you're going to London, and as soon as you get to Victoria you must get on the Tube and go as far as you can. I think Acton would be best. You'll have to buy yourself another suitcase and things. That's a pity, but you'll manage it all right. Find yourself some quiet lodgings, dear. Cheap ones. You'll be able to live for weeks and weeks on that money if you do. Tell them you've got a job in the City, and go out every day as if you had. You can go to libraries and places to pass the time. And the pictures are cheap if you go before one. After about a month you can start looking for a job. You'll get one all right, dear. You'll find something. You'll settle down and be happy again, and forget all about this. I'm sure you will, dear.'

It was a long speech that Mrs Clair had poured out, tumbling the words one over the other in her anxiety to get it all said. It was a good example of her quickness of decision; she had thought it all out in the few minutes since leaving the lodging house. She had thought just as quickly as in that brief moment when Sergeant Hale had emerged from the hedge, when she had launched George Ely upon him to give her time to escape with Marjorie.

'And what about you, Mother?' asked Marjorie, unwilling and doubtful.

'Oh, I shall be all right,' said Mrs Clair. 'I can always look after myself. I've got all the money I need. I'm going to get lodgings, too. Later on I'll find a job as housekeeper. I often thought that's what I'd do if Dot got married.'

'But I don't want to leave you, Mother,' said Marjorie again as they turned the corner and approached the station.

'Nonsense, girl. We can't pick and choose what we want to do and don't want to do. Here we are. Let's go and see if there's a train.'

There are always plenty of trains running between London and Brighton; as it happened there was only a quarter of an hour before the next.

'I'm going to say goodbye now, dear. Don't kiss me. I shall sit over there and wait till your train goes, but we'd better not speak again. Run and buy your ticket and then get in your train. Goodbye, darling. Goodbye. Goodbye, darling.'

Mrs Clair sat, a rather forlorn and lonely little figure, on one of the benches in the station, bravely combating the tears that made her eyes wet. She saw Marjorie emerge from the booking office with her ticket, and saw her pass the barrier safely and enter the train. She sat until the train had left, and she would have liked to have sat much longer, because now she felt desperately tired, but she feared to do that. Someone might notice her, and later that might direct the hunt after Marjorie again. With a little sigh she got up from the bench and walked out of the station, briskly and upright as was always her way, even though her eyes were still dazzled with the tears that foolishly kept welling up in them.

Mrs Clair had no intention whatever of carrying out the programme she had sketched out to Marjorie. To begin with, she had no money. Everything she had, with the exception of two coppers to chink together, she had emptied into Marjorie's handbag. She had no desire to live if she were separated from Marjorie, and she had no desire to prolong her life at the cost of increasing Marjorie's danger – the money which was plenty for one would have been far too small if divided by two. As long as Marjorie were safe she did not care what happened to herself. She had made up her mind what she was going to do.

She walked through the quiet side street, walking, eternally walking, trying to disregard her growing fatigue, struggling with her tears. She was quite surprised at herself when she found sobs rising in her throat. She fought them down – people would begin to notice her soon, and that would never do. Not yet, at least; a street clock showed her that it was not yet time for Marjorie's train to have reached Victoria. She walked on and on. She knew where the police station was, because she had noticed it earlier that morning. She walked back there, when at last the clocks showed her that Marjorie was safe in London again. Outside it she paused for a moment, making sure that her clothes were tidy and her hat straight. Then she walked quietly in, up the steps. A big police sergeant was perched high up writing at a desk, and did not at first condescend to notice the little old lady who stood patiently waiting for his attention. At last he looked down at her and she told him who she was.

21

The carriage in which Marjorie sat, crouching in a corner, was fortunately empty. She was not quite free from observation, because it was a corridor train, and there was a steady passing to and fro of people along the passage way down the middle of the carriages. Every time anyone came along Marjorie shrank down into herself. She turned herself so that she looked out of the window and presented only the back of her head to the passers by, and she tried to screen her face, too, with her hand on her cheek. The landscape swirled by before her eyes, and the sound of the wheels beat steadily but quietly upon her ears. Everything – even the precautions she was taking to remain unobserved – seemed unreal to her except the fear that was in her heart. That was like a great pain of such overwhelming intensity that everything else became unnaturally insignificant like the circumstances of a nightmare. Fear gnawed at her heart, and coursed like white flame along her veins. The unreasoning pleasure which the human face finds in hunting has its natural counterpart in the senseless agony of the hunted. It was not possible for Marjorie to await stoically the next turn of the wheel, not to find any grim satisfaction in the mathematical calculation of the chances for or against her. She could only suffer, unthinkingly. The hour that the train took to travel from Brighton to Victoria ate away her little strength.

And as the wounded solider on the battlefield, or the man

dying from cancer, seems to be suffering all the pain that can be inflicted, and yet at intervals shrieks under new and still more savage stabs, so with Marjorie; the steady current of her pain quickened at intervals, when she thought of Derrick and Anne in some workhouse now, presumably, and of her mother – bitter agony it was. And once, to the steady drumming of the wheels, she thought of George Ely. It seemed to her as if her palms could actually feel the harsh braids of the rope which awaited his neck. She bit her lip and writhed in her seat under the torment. When the train ran into Victoria Station she could hardly stand, could hardly totter to the carriage door. And at the sight of the platform, massed with the midday Saturday crowd, she drew back for a second in fear. That mass of people, her unreasoning instinct suggested, might be waiting for her.

Victoria Station was full of people, as was to be expected at just after noon on a summer Saturday, a bustling, noisy mob. Marjorie, standing on the platform, waiting for the strength to carry her to the ticket barrier, made an effort to collect herself. She knew quite well what she had to do – or rather she felt she would know if only she could think about it. She tried to tell herself that in those bustling hurrying crowds lay her best change of evading observation. She tried to hearten herself as her mother would have done.

But the din of the station drained her of her last strength. She knew that she would be fainting soon, and fainting would mean detection and arrest. The effort necessary to do what she ought, to buy a suitcase, to travel to the suburbs, to find lodgings, was as far beyond her as it would have been for her unaided strength to drag along the train in which she had just travelled. Her will and her wits were as wanting as her strength. She was a feeble little animal moved only by her instincts the moment that effort to rally herself had faded out. Victoria Station meant only one thing to her now – Millicent Dunne and Millicent Dunne's flat.

It was the old association of ideas which guided her, nothing else. Without knowing where she was going she crept through the crowd to the Wilton Road exit from the station. Here was the house, with the front door open. Up the stairs to the second floor. This was the door; she knocked on it, and it was instantly opened by Millicent, still in her coat and hat, just home from the office.

To Millicent it might have been the landlady knocking, or some neighbour to borrow milk or an egg. She never dreamed that it might be Marjorie. But she stood aside, and Marjorie came in, blind eyed, with slow short steps, to stand stock still in the middle of the room, while Millicent shut the door and, as an after-thought, locked it as well. Then she came to Marjorie.

'Well, Marjorie?' she said, quietly. 'Well, my dear?'

There was nothing else she could say. The tears were rolling down Marjorie's cheeks, and falling upon her bosom, as she stood with her blind eyes turned to the windows.

'You poor darling!' said Millicent, moved to intense pity, and she took her into her arms.

Later Marjorie was sitting in the armchair. There was no doubt that this was Millicent's bed sitting room – her 'flat', as Millicent would say to people who did not know it. The divan with the brown cover against the wall was the bed at night. The window was hung with the curtains which Marjorie had helped to choose, and which had been hemmed on Marjorie's sewing machine. There was a photograph of Anne as a baby on the mantelpiece. And Millicent was bending over the gas ring which was an adjunct to the gas fire, and chattering as usual.

'It'll have to be eggs,' Millicent said. 'It always has to be eggs. Do you know, when I get my promotion, and have a real flat, I'm never going to eat an egg again. And I shall always cook the things that *smell*. Onions. Fresh herrings. But if you even *think* about fresh herrings here Mrs Hardy's up in two shakes of a lamb's tail and knocking at the door and saying that the whole house is complaining about the stink. Anyway, it's eggs this time. Three, altogether, Fried, boiled, poached or scrambled?'

Marjorie shook her head. She could even smile, now.

'I don't mind,' she said.

'It's an awful choice to make,' said Millicent. 'Especially when you've hesitated before those four possibilities about five times a week for six years. Come on, give it a name. Choose and save me the trouble.'

'Boiled, then,' said Marjorie. That meant the easiest washing up afterwards – it was the choice she always made at home when it was left to her.

'Right,' said Millicent, filling the egg saucepan at the tap.

Millicent could always talk, and years of experience in her present employment had taught her how to fill up any awkward gap with bright chatter. She talked industriously, while laying the table, cutting bread and butter, opening a tin of fruit in a whirl of extravagance. Later, looking back on this time, she could not imagine how she was able to talk brightly all about nothing during that first hour – she did not make sufficient allowance for her own professional ability. But to such good purpose did she chatter that Marjorie actually ate an egg and bread and butter and a mouthful of tinned fruit salad, actually smiled at her sallies, actually forgot for forty minutes why she was hiding here in Millicent's room.

Millicent put the last of the crockery back in its cupboard. Thoughtfully, she took her cigarette case and holder out of her handbag, and lit a cigarette.

'Bed or chair?' she asked. 'I expect you're tired.'

That was the first, the most insignificant hint that had been let fall between them that Marjorie was not paying an ordinary call.

'Oh, I'm tired, Mill. Tired out. They're after me. Mill, can I stop here?'

'Of course you can,' said Millicent.

The ice had been broken now. They would have to talk this out, and the sooner the better. Millicent paced up and down the room, her cigarette holder between her fingers. A long time back, actually while she was cracking her egg, the phrase 'Accessory after the fact' had come up into her mind, and to her credit she had not allowed it to interrupt her flow of small talk, nor was she allowing it now to influence her actions. She was risking prison, the loss of her beloved job, her whole future. That was of no importance now with Marjorie needing help. She paced up and down the room while Marjorie watched her. Discomposed by the scrutiny, self-conscious, she fidgeted with the ornaments. She parted the curtains, and looked out, down to the noisy street two storeys below.

That was when her self-control wavered. The slight wincing of her expression as she drew back from the window called Marjorie from the bed in a panic again.

'What is it?' asked Marjorie. 'What did you see?'

'Nothing, dear,' said Millicent.

'You did! What was it?'

Marjorie opened the curtains too, and looked out. She could not have said what it was she expected to see – a cordon of policemen, perhaps, or a mob approaching to lynch her. As it was, the wide street was empty of all danger. There were some children playing, some taxicabs crawling along, a few people walking peacefully along the pavements. Nothing dangerous at all. But right opposite was a newspaper shop, with its row of placards, and the middle one bore red letters, letters of blood, which she could read as clearly as if they were close before her, even though in her present tenseness they shrank and dwindled until they appeared microscopically small.

MRS CLAIR ARRESTED

*

The wires had borne the urgent message from Brighton. Men with telephone receivers at their ears had bawled it out in Fleet Street offices. Printing machines had stopped while typesetters' fingers raced over keys. Then the vans had dashed out under the reckless guidance of the drivers, with great bundles of newspapers and posters, careering through the streets so as to try and catch the last of the great tide ebbing out of London, to secure as many as possible of the coppers which would eagerly be taken from pockets when those red words were read.

It seemed as if now there was no added pain for Marjorie, as if her cup was so full that nothing could make it fuller. Her face bore no alteration of expression now, as Millicent looked at her. She met Millicent's gaze with an answering stare, immobile, stupid.

'Didn't – didn't you know?' whispered Millicent.

'No,' said Marjorie.

She stood stock-still, numb and unfeeling.

'Lie down again, dear,' said Millicent.

It was only later that Marjorie was able to think, to weep again.

'Mother did it for me!' she said, suddenly. 'She meant to, all along. I never guessed. What are they doing to her now, Mill? Are they being cruel to her?'

'No, of course not,' said Millicent, soothingly.

The tone that she used, her manner, her words, reminded Marjorie of how her mother had spoken to her during this two days' nightmare, and by an odd freak of her character helped her to regain her stability. Mother had guarded her and protected her. She realized with sudden clarity how utterly dependent she had been upon her mother, and that the moment she found herself left to her own resources she had immediately fled to Millicent in search of some new support. It would not happen again. Millicent, watching, saw with surprise how Marjorie's expression hardened. The childishness, the stupidity, vanished. By a sudden transformation she became, in a few minutes, the old Marjorie Millicent had always know. For the first time since Thursday Marjorie was thinking clearly, was in complete control of herself.

'I oughtn't to be in here,' said Marjorie. 'It isn't fair to you. You oughtn't to have let me in.'

Millicent shrugged her shoulders.

'I should stay here as long as you can if I were you,' she said. 'Make the most of it.'

'You're kind to me, Mill,' said Marjorie. 'You might have told them where I was.'

'It's not for me to do that. You're my friend.'

Millicent could not help but look inquiringly at Marjorie as she spoke now. She knew no more of what had happened than any other member of the public; the brief paragraphs in the newspapers had told little enough. She had never even heard of George Ely before – so much had happened since that tragic evening, only a few weeks before, when she had seen Marjorie last. The newspaper paragraphs had called up to her mind a picture of two angry women and a young lover, a bloody drama in which an axe played a part. How it had come about she could not imagine; but she had suspected for years that Ted had used Marjorie brutally. But whether Ted had got what he deserved or not, it was natural for Millicent to offer Marjorie unhesitatingly all the help within her power; that inquiring look implied no more than excusable curiosity. Marjorie noticed it, all the same.

'You think I did it!' she said, sharply. Her voice rose a semitone again.

'No, I don't think so. I couldn't believe that,' answered Millicent, and then, watching Marjorie's tired face, 'Tell me how it happened, if you like.'

It was a relief for Marjorie to talk. She poured out all the story, all the misery and horror of it. Millicent kept herself from wincing as she listened. Faster sometimes, and slower sometimes,

Marjorie told her it all. The discoveries regarding Dot's death she poured out in a few breathless sentences. She stumbled and hesitated when she told of George Ely, but that was not so much because of shame as because now it seemed to her as if it had never happened. It seemed impossible to her that she had ever put her arms round his neck or felt his kisses. Her memory told her that she had, but she found herself distrusting her memory. It was if it she were trying to recover the details of some novel she had read long ago, and which on reconsideration did not ring as true as she had first thought. She slurred that part of the story over with no thought of excusing herself.

The details of the last evening of Ted's life were much more vivid in her memory. She recounted each in its turn, the bald sentences reconstructing the whole picture in life-like fashion in Millicent's mind. And then she went on to the flight, to the incidents of the last two days. Here her words began to fail her again. It was only by inference, by the play of horror over Marjorie's tortured face, that Millicent was able to guess at what she had been through during the last forty-eight hours.

'That's how I came here,' said Marjorie, vaguely, her gestures trying to convey the fear and weakness which had overcome her at Victoria Station.

'I understand,' said Millicent.

Marjorie looked beseechingly at Millicent's compassionate face.

'Will they hang me if they catch me?' she asked.

'No!' said Millicent, hotly. 'Never! You aren't – guilty of anything.'

She stumbled in the middle of that speech, all the same. She had begun the asseveration in all good faith. It was only after she had begun it that doubt came to her. Marjorie had been told before they reached the house what was going to happen there – 'We're going to kill him!' her mother had said. All the same,

Marjorie had admitted George and Mrs Clair to her house, had stood by without interfering while the crime was committed. Legally, she was equally guilty of it in consequence, whatever her moral justification, whatever excuses she could put forward regarding her state of mind at the time. Bad luck, or bad management of her defence, could hang her, could reduce this beautiful woman into a mass of dead flesh. Millicent felt within her that strange prick of curiosity regarding someone whose life was in danger from the law which crams the court at a murder trial, and she hated herself for it in the same instant.

'Is that true?' asked Marjorie.

'Yes,' said Millicent, stubbornly. She could not bring herself to say otherwise at first, whatever she felt. She met Marjorie's searching look as openly as she could. Then she forced herself to mention the source of her doubts.

'But look here, old thing,' she said, trying to speak convincingly and yet casually at the same time. 'You must be careful what you say, if – if ever you have to say anything. Never tell *anyone* else about what your mother said as you walked up Simon Street. Except your solicitor. Tell him, of course. But *nobody else.*'

'What do you mean?' asked Marjorie, honestly at sea. Ignorance and fear between them had prevented her from ever trying to estimate the strength and weakness of her position with regard to the law.

'I can't explain, somehow,' said Millicent, still trying desperately to be casual. 'But I'm sure I'm right. I mean it, dear. Always remember what I'm telling you, *always.*'

Millicent was trying to warn Marjorie against making damaging admissions in one of those 'voluntary statements' so dexterously drawn from prisoners by the police, but try as she would she could not be more explicit. That would have called for a cold-blooded mention of the words 'police' and 'arrest', and savoured of an indecency she could not tolerate.

22

For Millicent it had been hot and uncomfortable in the little single bed with Marjorie at her side. Most of the night she had lain grimly motionless, suffering cramp and discomfort rather than run the risk of disturbing Marjorie, deeply asleep beside her, and whose heavy breathing testified to her exhaustion. She heard the milkman come clinking along the corridor with his tray of bottles – by special arrangement he was admitted to the building early each morning to leave the customary half pint (it was invariably half a pint) outside each door, behind which slept some single professional woman. Apart from that, the building remained silent until much later on this Sunday morning than on weekdays.

Later she heard a few doors open and shut, and a few hurried footsteps along the corridors. That would be the Catholics, going off to early Mass. The Low Churchwomen and the infidels always stayed in bed much later than that. It was only by slow degrees that the house awoke fully, and the opening and shutting of doors as the professional women took in their milk became more frequent, as a certain subdued murmur of life, like a somnolent beehive slowly awakening, began to reach her ear. Not until then did Marjorie beside her stir and wake. Fear was still with her – Millicent saw her clutch the bedclothes and stare round her until she remembered where she was – but it was not nearly as acute as on her arrival yesterday. Indeed, she smiled, like a child, when she saw Millicent beside her.

'Did you sleep well, dear?' asked Millicent.

'Ooh yes, thank you,' answered Marjorie.

'Well, you can just go on resting until I get some breakfast ready,' said Millicent.

She climbed out of bed and pottered about the room in her nightdress. There was no chance of her getting a bath, she knew – on Sunday mornings the few bathrooms were all appropriated by a clique with a series of secret signals, who let each other in, and who lay and soaked to the exclusion of every one else all the morning. Millicent always took her bath in the afternoon on Sundays. She washed at the handbasin and dressed, put on the kettle and brought in the milk, laid the breakfast tray and brought the table to the bedside. Marjorie lay and watched her dreamily as she moved busily about. She was bathed in a feeling of comfort and security. She had a friend; she had a home. The misery of the last two days – which seemed to her memory to have endured more like two months – had come to an end. The contrast was delightful, as long as she was drugged with sleep and could only be conscious of what was outstanding in her situation. Then suddenly she stiffened as she lay in bed. Unhappiness was renewed in that moment. She felt again all the old sick weakness. Now she was ashamed of herself as well. Until now panic had hardly allowed her to think of anyone except herself.

As an undercurrent to her thoughts there was the knowledge that she had not troubled her head about Mother and George – Mother had spent last night in prison, in a cell, with the shadow of the gallows hanging over her as for two and a half days it had hung over George. But this was only the undercurrent. It was Derrick and Anne that she was thinking about. Her misery was intensified by the fact that she could not imagine at all what had happened to them, could not visualize for a moment in what circumstances they were awakening this morning. The dread word 'Institution' came up into her mind. The word bore with it associations of bad food, harsh treatment, cold and draughty rooms. Little Anne would shrink within herself in such a place, enduring it in uncomplaining distress, but Derrick would protest, would struggle, would refuse to put on the harsh Institution clothes, would voice his dislike of the Institution food, until some hateful wardresses, tight lipped and dry eyed, would punish him, suppress him, crush him into dazed submission from which he would never emerge again, not even in manhood.

'Oh God!' she said. She would have blasphemed more wildly if the words had come to her lips; she was full of an unvenomed rage at a world which would allow such things to happen. 'Oh God!'

And she was full, too, of a bitter contempt for herself that she had left her children to suffer this, and had not given them a minute's thought in all these hours. There was no self-pity in her now. She could see herself as she was, weak, easily dominated, and yet selfish. In her black misery she blamed herself for everything that had happened, with no thought for Ted's responsibility.

'Time to wake up, now, young woman,' said Millicent, bringing the table to the bedside, the china clinking cheerfully.

'I don't want any breakfast – I can't eat any,' said Marjorie. She sat up in the bed, her hair wild, with no thought for the shoulder of her nightdress which had slipped down.

'Nonsense, of course you can. Start with a cup of tea,' said Millicent with determined cheerfulness. She had been aware of the new misery that was afflicting Marjorie; she even had come near to guessing its cause, and she had known that no more mere words on her part could combat against such realities. All she could do was to offer a cup of tea.

'It's the children!' said Marjorie.

'I'm not going to talk about anything like that until you've had your breakfast,' replied Millicent firmly. 'Toast or bread and butter?'

Millicent held on firmly to trivialities. Her welfare work at the factory had accustomed her to doing this. Confronted with a crushed finger or a broken heart the first remedies she brought forward were always a cup of tea and an interval of small talk. They gave a breathing space in which to recover sanity. She did the same instinctively now, fighting down the dread feeling that this time she was in an impasse from which there was no escape at all. She was playing bravely for time, for she could see no solution of Marjorie's difficulties save one, and that she dreaded.

'I don't think,' she said, holding up the milk bottle to the light 'the milk's nearly as good now as when they first began putting it in bottles. There's not half the thickness of cream on top now. Have you noticed it?'

It was a subtle lure. Ten years of domestic preoccupations asserted themselves. Marjorie could be inveigled into discussing domestic economy. They talked sanely for a few minutes, the clatter of the teacups accentuating the homeliness of it all.

And then an abrupt knocking at the door burst the fragile bubble.

'What's that?' gasped Marjorie. She was a white as death on the instant.

'Oh, nothing,' said Millicent. She was frightened, too, but she brought herself to face the inevitable. Calming herself with an effort, she made herself walk stoically to the door and open it.

'Oh, good morning, Mrs Hardy,' she said. The manageress stepped quickly into the room, while Marjorie cowered in the bed. Mrs Hardy included her in an all-embracing glance round the disorder of the room.

'I have to draw your attention,' she said, icily, 'to the terms of your agreement, Miss Dunne. One condition of tenancy here is that only the tenant is allowed to sleep in a single flat. If you expect to have friends staying with you you must take a double one.'

'Oh, I forgot that,' said Millicent. 'I'm sorry, Mrs Hardy.'

'You must see that it doesn't occur again, Miss Dunne.'

Mrs Hardy made a dignified exit, and Millicent hastily locked the door again behind her.

'Do you think she saw me?' asked Marjorie. 'Has she gone for – for –'

Millicent's frantic appeal in dumb show for silence checked her before she could say more. Millicent knew that someone listening at the door had reported to Mrs Hardy that she was violating her agreement by having someone spend the night with her, and Mrs Hardy herself might be listening now. They were both of them trembling.

Marjorie saw how shaken Millicent was, saw her white cheeks and trembling lips and the sight cleared her brain like a fog rolling off a landscape. The card-castle of the illusion of ordinary security which had been built up during the five minutes before Mrs Hardy's knock had fallen, but to Marjorie now it was no more than the fall of a card-castle. She had no tears to shed over the ruins. Nothing worse could ever happen to her now than had happened so far. She flung back the bedclothes and stepped out of bed.

'I'm sorry,' she said. 'I shouldn't have come here. It wasn't fair to you. You don't want to be mixed up with a woman like me.'

Marjorie had looked upon herself in various lights before, as Marjorie Grainger, Mrs Edward Grainger, as Anne's and Derrick's mother, as Mrs Clair's daughter. To herself she had been one or other of those during the days of flight. Now she saw herself with clarity as 'a woman like me', as a suspected murderess, an adulteress. She was fantastically unafraid of what they might do to her. The calm of resignation descended upon her, the same which often enough in history has supported martyrs on their way to the stake. Mrs Hardy's knock, Millicent's distress, had proved the last straws in the load of misery which she had so far borne. She could bear it no more. She looked round the room for her clothes. This newfound clarity of mind did not extend to mundane details. She fumbled as she sorted out her underclothes; she turned distractedly to the washbasin, and confronted by the mirror over it she put up her hands instinctively to her hair.

'What are you going to do?' whispered Millicent, staring at her wild-eyed. Her professional calm was gone now.

'I don't know,' said Marjorie. She laughed, a little high pitched. Perhaps she was hysterical; perhaps at that moment she was mad. 'That woman's settled it for me. I can't bear any more of this.'

She rinsed her face with cold water and dried it with a towel. Nearly naked, she found herself reaching for her hat and handbag, and laughed again. Millicent stared at her fascinated as she pulled her vest over her head, and slipped into her dress.

'Marjorie,' she said 'you're not going to – to –'

Millicent feared lest she was going to kill herself, but the thought was so far from Marjorie's mind that even Millicent's unfinished question suggested nothing to her.

'I'm going out of all this,' said Marjorie. 'They can do what they like to me. I don't care.'

She was pulling on her stockings now, sitting on the edge of the disordered bed.

'The children,' said Marjorie meditatively as she did so. 'I'm sorry for the children.'

There was deep pity in her voice as she spoke, heartfelt and sincere, and yet unmaternal. Marjorie did not belong to this world any longer.

'I can look after the children,' said Millicent, eagerly. 'If – if they need looking after. I'll see they're all right. I'll be good to them.'

'Yes,' said Marjorie. 'You always were fond of Anne. You liked her better than Derrick even. You'd be a good mother to them. You know about children although you've never had one yourself.'

She stood up with her hat in her hands.

'Marjorie!' said Millicent again. 'What are you going to do?'

The only answer she had was the same laugh. Perhaps it was the cessation of tension consequent upon the new state of mind which set Marjorie laughing, shrill and soulless though her laugh was.

'I'll come with you,' said Millicent desperately, and that did something to make Marjorie a little more human.

'No!' she said. 'I won't let you. You've had enough trouble from me as it is.'

Millicent caught at her hand, but Marjorie shook herself free, twirled herself out of reach, twirled herself past Millicent towards the door, and laughed again triumphantly.

'Goodbye, dear,' she said. That inhuman tenderness flooded her voice again. 'Goodbye, darling. You're a dear love, Mill, dear. Goodbye.'

She unlocked the door and passed out into the corridor while Millicent gazed at her helplessly, with dropped jaw. It was five seconds before she ran out after her, and in that five seconds Marjorie was gone.

Out in the street, at this late Sunday morning hour, Marjorie breathed deep and freely, turning up her face to the sky. There was a light rain falling; she hardly noticed it. She was free now, free of all apprehension or doubt. It was good to be in the street, to breathe fresh air after the stuffiness of Millicent's room, to be able to look all down the length of the road instead of having her view confined by four narrow walls. That was all she wanted at the moment. She was conscious of nothing save the pleasant sensation of walking briskly and breathing deeply.

There was nothing of consciousness to guide her now. She was an automaton in charge of her instincts, and her instincts drew her homewards, inevitably. For nearly ten years she had lived in the house in Harrison Way, and it was to that house that she directed herself. Old associations of ideas, reasserting themselves, may have quickened her step with the anticipation of seeing her children again, her husband, the old familiar furniture, so dead was her conscious memory. She found herself amid a group at a bus stop, and automatically boarded the bus. She found silver in her handbag to pay her fare. Not even the twisted bundle of one pound notes which her mother had thrust in there – only yesterday! – could rouse her from this new, strange indifference. The rain was heavier when she alighted at the High Street corner, and the streets were empty in the wet Sunday noontide. She walked briskly up the steep slope of Simon Street, revelling in the feel of the raindrops on her face. She turned down into Harrison Way.

Sergeant Hale emerged from No. 77; he was going to have his dinner, and he was leaving a constable in charge of the house. There were newspaper reporters who would pull the whole place to pieces if he did not, so great was the thirst for news regarding this business. His morning's search had failed to throw any new light on the death of Edward Grainger – though in a case as clear as this nothing much in that way was to be expected – nor had it given any further indication as to where Mrs Grainger was likely to be found. Sergeant Hale had no doubt that she would be found speedily, all the same. He was glad when his duty kept him at No. 77, because, as he said to himself 'They often come back.' He would not have been in the least surprised if she had walked in that morning.

At the gate, still considering this point, he looked up and down the road before setting out towards his home. He saw her walking down towards him, and hurried to meet her. She looked up at him and smiled, amazingly, at being thus welcomed. Before that smile Hale blushed and stammered like a boy as he loomed over her. Like a schoolboy struggling x stage fright in some school play he uttered, disconnectedly and in an artificial tone, the words that placed her under arrest and cautioned her as to what she might say. The caution was justified. It awakened one tiny fragment of Marjorie's sleeping memory. Millicent had said 'Never tell *anyone* else about what your mother said as you walked up Simon Street.' That was the only thought which moved at all amid the stagnation of Marjorie's mind as she submitted to Sergeant Hale, and it was that which saved her, later.

Mrs Posket, at her bedroom window, was looking gloomily out into the rain. She had come back from her holiday yesterday when everything was over and done with. It was infuriating to think what she had missed. Murders and arrests and escapes had happened within fifty yards of her home without her being there to witness them. Silly little Mrs Taylor had been there, had tales to tell of police whistles heard in the night, had been interviewed by reporters, had been right in the thick of it, while she was absent. Mrs Posket was beside herself with annoyance. But determinedly she had tried to make the best of things. Yesterday, at the moment of her arrival home, she had managed to get hold of Sergeant Hale and make the obvious corrections in the absurd description of Mrs Grainger that Mrs Taylor had supplied. Now she was sitting at her window hoping to retrieve some new fragment of the wreck. Her optimism was well-founded, for from her bedroom window, almost outside her front gate, she saw something which would supply her with funds for conversation for the rest of her life. She was the only eyewitness to the arrest of the notorious Mrs Grainger. To accentuate the importance of this, in her subsequent descriptions of it, she always maintained that of course Mrs Grainger was certainly guilty, and that the jury's verdict was utterly incorrect. Not many people agreed with her.

A Note on the Text

Hollywood, 1935: The young C. S. Forester is offered a contract to write a film script. He had previously come across some late eighteenth-century volumes of the *Naval Chronicle* and after the Hollywood contract, these accompanied him on his sea-journey back to England via Central America. The result: the first Hornblower novel.

Forester missed England during his stay in California. Not foreseeing the pressure that would grow on him to write more Hornblowers, he now wrote a classic London thriller about murder, sex and revenge, *The Pursued*. In his personal notes, Forester refers to it as 'the lost novel… It was written, sent to London and Boston, accepted and made the subject of signed agreements'.

But the Spanish Civil War intervened. Forester now went to Spain and the Peninsular War of 140 years previously stirred his interest. With a new sense of excitement he realized that this could be a second Hornblower novel.

Forester wrote 'It would not be fitting for *The Pursued* to be published between these two [Hornblower] books'. After 'a long and solemn telegram from Boston', publication was delayed. 'The lost novel was really lost. It is just possible that a typescript still exists, forgotten and gathering dust in a rarely used storeroom in Boston or Bloomsbury'.

Oxford, 1999: I assist Dr Colin Blogg in founding the C. S. Forester Society, in appreciation of the author's narrative skill, his flawless English prose and his studies of 'the Man Alone', set against well-depicted contemporary backgrounds. I had been reading Forester since schoolboy days, went on to read English at Oxford and was confirmed in my estimation of this great writer. So when an unpublished Forester novel appeared in a small auction in London we were determined to acquire it. Colin and I are now owners of the script bearing the typist's name.

London, 2011: Penguin Books (which now owns Forester's old publishers, Michael Joseph) arrange publication of this little master-piece of London life between the wars: *The Pursued* – so very nearly, the One that Got Away. An extraordinary find and a rare first view of one of the great English twentieth-century novelists at the peak of his powers.

Lawrence Brewer, Peopleton, 2011